SECRET AGENT
6th GRADER

3 BOOK COLLECTION

BY MARCUS EMERSON

EMERSON PUBLISHING HOUSE

This one's for all you secret agents…

Emerson Publishing House

Book design by Marcus Emerson.

SECRET AGENT
6th GRADER

My head was spinning, and I had no idea where I was. All I knew for sure was that I was sitting on a chair in a dark room. It was cold, and I could hear water dripping from somewhere behind me. Plus my socks were wet.

Wonderful... I *hate* wet socks.

"Hello?" I tried saying out loud, but my mouth was as dry as uncooked pasta so it only came out as, "*Bleh-bloh?*"

From the shadows across the room, I heard a wooden chair plunk on the floor. "Welcome back, Mr. Brody Valentine," said a boy's voice. "Funny last name you have, isn't it?"

1

I took a breath and blinked. "There are some things in life we can't choose. Last names… would be one of those things."

"You're right," he replied, stepping forward, but staying hidden in the shadows. "Some of us are just born unlucky, aren't we?"

I remained silent, studying the room while the kid kept talking. From the look of it, I figured I was in a larger storage closet, probably near the school's cafeteria. The smell of steamed broccoli lingered in the air. You'd think that would be proof enough that I was around the lunchroom, but the boy's locker room *also* smelled like steamed broccoli. I *know*, right? *So* nasty.

The boy continued. "When you woke up this morning, you had no idea of the little adventure that awaited you at school, did you?"

I cracked a smile and chuckled softly.

"Unless," the boy whispered, "you *did* know of this adventure, which would mean you're just as guilty as the *rest* of them. Tell me, Brody, *where's* the journal?"

"Someplace safe," I replied as I sat up in my chair. My head was swelling with pain. "Someplace far away from here."

The boy paused. "You know this is over, right? This little game you and your friends are playing... they've already ratted you out. You're *done*."

I wasn't sure if the boy was bluffing or not so I didn't respond. I don't think anyone would've tattled on me, but after the day I've had, I couldn't really be sure. I knew that sixth grade was going to be tough, but not *this* tough. Secret agent stuff, spy gear, special codes, and conspiracies – that was a lot for *anyone* to carry on their shoulders, especially someone like me!

I'm literally a nobody at Buchanan School, or at least, I *used* to be before today. Now it's almost like I'm the most wanted kid in the entire school, and trust me when I say it *wasn't* on purpose.

My name is Brody Valentine and this is the story of how I accidentally became a secret agent. Don't make fun of my last name either. Like I said earlier... there are some things in life we *can't* choose.

I remember it like it was just this morning… probably because it *was* just this morning…

ME
(BRODY VALENTINE)

Check it out – that's my school picture. Scrawny little dweeb, right? Hardly secret agent material. I bet spy agencies have this photo hanging in their offices to show them what kind of person *not* to hire. My parents tell me I have a big heart and that's all that matters, but telling that to a sixth grade boy is the same thing as beating a video game on easy – it's something that takes almost no effort, but at least you can move on to the next game.

I know. I get it. I'm not destined to be a great football player or ultimate fighter, but I accept that. Instead, I'll be the super billionaire computer nerd that controls half of the world and—wait, that makes me sound like an evil villain, but I'm not *that* either.

I'm just an ordinary dude, at a *not* ordinary school called Buchanan. It's important to note that my school is trying this new thing where the sixth graders have the freedom to choose their own classes like they would in middle school. It's a neat idea, but it doesn't make middle school *less* of an adjustment. It just makes sixth grade that much *more* of an adjustment.

I got to Buchanan a few minutes before homeroom. The bus driver always cuts it way too close. Apparently the last stop on his route is a gas station where he gets coffee and donuts for himself. The rest of the students wait in the bus as he sips hot coffee and flirts with the cashier for several minutes. She's *cute*, but seriously? How he still has a job is a mystery to me.

I'm the kid that rushes through the hallways, trying my best not to bump into anyone. You'd only see me if I bonked into you. I usually mumble an apology and keep on going, hoping you don't say anything. Kids would shrug me off as antisocial, but the truth is that I'm just *really* shy.

I was at my locker, placing some books into my backpack. The bell was going to ring in just a few minutes so everyone was rushing through the hallways, doing what they could to be on time.

As I lifted one of my textbooks, I felt a dull ache in my side. Groaning, I dropped the book and stretched my arms back. There was a bruise around my ribcage from gym class the day before. There's a game a few of us play called "Chicken." We're a little too old for the playground at recess, but that doesn't stop us from going over to the monkey bars during gym for this game.

Have you ever played it?

Two people hang from the bars and only use their legs to knock the other person off. Kicking is against the rules, but wrapping your legs around the other person's body isn't. When one kid has a good grip on the other, they try to pull them off the bars. It's not usually dangerous because everyone lands on their feet, but the last time I played I just happened to slip and fall into one of the giant garbage barrels next to the monkey bars, which is how I got the bruise. It was entirely my fault so there weren't any hard feelings.

Over the sound of frantic students, I could hear the morning announcements playing over the speaker system. Large flat screen televisions hung at the end of each hallway and would play an animation of the announcements. Every now and then, it would play a video about keeping the school clean.

A couple weeks ago, someone pulled a prank and hijacked the system, playing a video of a tap dancing cat over and over again. I suspect the televisions are hooked up to a video player somewhere in the building. How else would it be so easy for a dancing cat to get on TV?

As I shut my locker, I heard some students talking nearby.

"Hey," said a boy. "You got any more of that candy?"

"A little bit," a girl replied. "But go get your own! I spent *all* my lunch money on this!"

"But I can't go down there! I still owe them money for the last few candy bars they gave me!" the boy replied.

She chuckled at him. "Then I guess you're outta luck. Looks like you'll have to buy some carrots from the *vending* machines."

The boy sighed. "*Sick...*"

I stood at my locker, staring at the two kids having the conversation.

When the girl noticed me, she looked embarrassed, but it quickly turned to anger. "What are *you* lookin' at?"

I wanted to say something sarcastic like, "A new

alien life form!" but instead, I went with something safer by *actually* saying, "Nothing, sorry."

As I walked away, I hoped that she wouldn't say anything else to me. Thankfully, she didn't.

The class I had homeroom in was past the lobby of the school, where Buchanan had just installed the new vending machines that girl had mentioned. When everyone first heard about them, they were excited and hopeful for bags of hard candy or chocolate bars. You can imagine our disappointment when we found out it was going to be stocked with healthy alternatives to junk food.

They were refrigerated machines filled with bite-sized vegetables, and gluten free snacks. The sweetest thing in them were yogurt covered pecans, which I have to admit can be pretty tasty, but that's after an entire *day* of no sweets.

The girl and boy were talking about *actual* candy though. Sure, the school provided healthy alternatives and was cracking down on junk food in general, but that didn't mean it wasn't available still. You just had to know where to look. I don't know how everyone else can eat so much of it though… too much for me and my teeth start to feel gritty.

As I stepped into the front lobby, I grabbed the straps of my backpack and held tight. Keeping my eyes on the ground, I started walking forward, making myself as limp as possible just in case someone bumped shoulders with me. It was like a jungle out there – boys showcased how tough they were by having the strongest shoulder bumps – it was the sixth grade version of a pecking order.

Y'know what I'm talking about? When there's a group of birds, those birds will single out the weakest member of the bunch and then pick on that poor animal until it's basically kicked out of their circle. The bird that was kicked out doesn't often survive. That's what's called a pecking order. I know, right? Birds can be *jerks*.

I looked up and saw the faces of kids as I walked by, imagining that they had giant beaks for noses. Someone sneezed from a few feet away. I LOL'd because it sounded like a squawk from a chicken.

And then only a half second later, the universe delivered a swift body slam of life changing events right to my door.

"Gangway!" shouted a voice.

I turned around, putting my hands up in case someone was about to run into me. Turns out, my instinct was correct, and a student tackled me to the ground. My backpack gave just enough cushioning that I didn't shatter to bits. "What gives?" I shouted, rolling to my side.

My attacker glanced at me as he stood from the ground, and I recognized him immediately. It was a good friend of mine, Linus. We weren't best friends, and never did anything together outside of school, but he was one of the few geeks I could have a normal conversation with at lunch. And by "normal conversation," I mean we talk

9

about what happens to a zombie if a vampire bites them. He thinks the zombie would be cured because they'd become a vampire. But a zombie's already dead, right? So that means the vampire just sucked zombie blood, which would turn the vampire *into* a zombie!

…anyway, Linus was standing over me.

LINUS

"Sorry, man!" Linus said as he looked down the hallway.

Through some of the students, I saw two hall monitors trying to make their way toward us. Both of them were dressed in black suits and had dark sunglasses over their eyes. None of the monitors I knew ever wore fancy clothing like that, but maybe their dress code had changed.

Linus spun around and scampered down the hall. The *least* he could've done was help me to my feet! I guess he wasn't as good of a friend as I thought.

The two hall monitors flew by me, barely noticing I was there. I sat for a moment, feeling stupid that I was on the floor in the middle of the lobby while other students swarmed around me, rushing to their classes. Not *one* kid stopped to see if I was alright. It was like I was invisible!

Finally, I sighed, setting myself up one of my knees. Luckily none of my fragile bones had been broken during the scuffle. I stood, ready to continue my trek to homeroom, but something fell from my shirt. It surprised me because it sounded like a crinkle from a package.

Staring at the floor, I studied the tiny plastic packet. "What are *you?*" I whispered, half expecting it to speak to me. Shaking my head, I rolled my eyes. "I really *do* watch too much television."

The package that fell was a fortune cookie, still contained within its little plastic wrapping. I had no idea where it came from. My family hadn't eaten Chinese food for dinner in, like, a month so it couldn't have been from my home. Did Linus drop it when he smashed into me?

If I had known that cookie was going to change the course of my entire life, I never would've grabbed it from the floor.

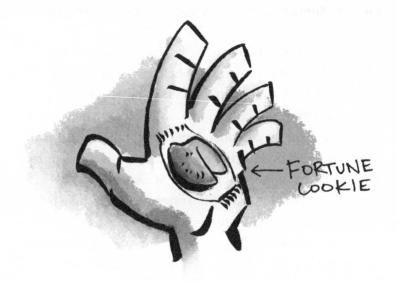

←FORTUNE
COOKIE

    I picked it up, realizing I was the only student in the lobby. Uh-oh, I thought. That was bad news because that could only mean…

    The tardy bell suddenly shrieked like a banshee.

    "Crumb!" I shouted, clutching at my backpack with one hand and the fortune cookie with my other, completely crushing it by accident.

    The bits of cookie were trapped within the plastic packaging. Bouncing it in front of my face, I tried to read the fortune on the little slip of paper inside, but it was weird. It wasn't like any fortune I'd ever seen before. It was a sheet of notebook paper with a handwritten message.

    Tearing it open, I let the crumbled pieces of cookie

fall to the floor. I don't like the taste of them anyway so I didn't mind. The slip of paper on the inside was from the corner of a notebook, and even had the light blue lines on it. The back was blank, but the front had numbers written in pencil.

"Do not lose," said the first line.

And the second line read, *"4247.019.5."*

Weird, I thought. It was more of an instruction than a prediction. Normally these things say something about having a bright and shiny day or winning a ton of money, but this one just said *not* to lose. It was more of a warning if anything. You better not lose or else! Or else… *something!*

And what was up with the lucky numbers on the second row? Actually, lucky *number*. The two points in the number meant that it all went together, but what kind of number had two points in it?

"Stop right there!" said a voice from behind me.

My heart skipped a beat. Why didn't I just walk to class? Now I'll probably get busted for skipping! I slipped the sheet of paper into my pocket, and turned around slowly. To my surprise, it wasn't a teacher, but the hall monitors that had just been chasing after Linus.

"Hey, guys," my voice cracked, intimidated.

One of the monitors stepped forward, tugging at the bottom of his suit coat. Then he adjusted his tie and turned his head until his neck cracked. "What do you know of the boy we were chasing after?" he asked coldly.

I shrugged my shoulders. "Nothing really. We sit at

lunch and talk sometimes, but that's about it."

The monitor glanced back at his partner, who curled his lip and shook his head.

"What's this about?" I asked, feeling anxious. "I'm late to class so I should be on my way." I moved forward, but the monitors stepped in front of me, blocking my escape.

"We've seen the two of you and your nerdy conversations during lunch, and sometimes in gym class," said the monitor in a cold whisper. "You'll have to come with us."

I felt confused. "What are you talking about? You watch us talk to each other? That's not the creepiest thing ever," I said sarcastically. "Besides, what's wrong with a little zombie discussion?"

The monitor's face remained expressionless, as if he were a robot. "We can do this the easy way, or the hard way. I'm sure the principal would rather have it be the easy way."

Suddenly I felt sick to my stomach. I guess it *wasn't* about zombies after all. Mentioning that the principal was involved was all I needed to hear. "Fine," I sighed, and then softly said, "To the principal's office we go."

About five minutes later, I was seated on a bench outside an empty art room. The only instruction the monitors gave was to sit on the bench until further notice. Why they hadn't taken me straight to the principal's office was beyond me. Did Principal Davis want to speak to me in the art room? And what in the world was this about anyways?

Leaning against the brick wall, I shut my eyes and tried to calm myself. My heart was racing in my chest like I had just run a seven-minute mile, which if you knew me, you'd know I can't run the mile in under twelve minutes.

Footsteps echoed on the walls of the hallway, and I straightened my posture. I didn't know what kind of trouble I was in that Principal Davis had to get involved, but it couldn't have been good. I kept my gaze lowered, the way a dog does when they know they're in trouble.

"Brody Valentine," said a boy's voice.

I looked up, surprised to see that it *wasn't* Principal Davis, but another sixth grade student that I recognized from a few classes. He was wearing the same suit as the other monitors, but he wasn't wearing glasses. Under one of his arms was a manila envelope. He held his other hand out to me, not to help me up, but to greet me with a handshake.

I grabbed it, and pulled myself off the bench.

The boy faked a smile. "My name is Colton."

When I was to my feet, I suddenly noticed a strong smell that reminded me of my grandpa. I sniffed at the air until I realized it was *Colton* that smelled. It was the way my grandpa smelled when I sat next to him at church. Not stinky, but like he was some sort of vanilla pine tree. "Dude, are you wearing *perfume?*" I asked.

COLTON

Colton furrowed his brow. "It's not perfume, it's *cologne*."

"What's the difference?" I asked.

"Cologne is what *dudes* wear," Colton replied.

"That's just what they call it so guys don't feel embarrassed buying it," I said.

"Nuh uh," Colton said defensively.

I turned my head at him. "Do you spray it on your neck and clothing?"

His eyes narrowed, but he didn't answer.

"Exactly," I sighed. "You're wearing *perfume*."

Colton shook his head and changed the subject. "Looks like you were involved in a little accident this morning, were you not?"

"What *is* this?" I immediately asked. At this point, all I wanted to do was get to homeroom. "Are you a hall monitor? Why are you guys in suits?"

Pointing his open palm to the door of the empty art room, he gestured for me to enter. "All your questions will be answered shortly. If you please, I'd like to ask you a few things about your friend, Linus."

As I walked into the room, I spoke. "Linus? What's the deal with him? Why were your goons chasing after him?"

Colton pulled one of the stools out from under a desk. He dropped the manila envelope on the surface of the table as he took a seat. After taking a deep breath, he said, "It's nothing serious, really."

"Seems pretty serious to me," I said as I sat in the chair across from him. I glanced at the entrance of the room to where the other monitors were stationed and guarding the door. It was obvious that whatever this situation was about *was* pretty serious. In my best "tough guy" voice, I spoke. "Your guys were chasing after him, and now *I'm* being questioned. Tell me who *you guys* are!"

Colton nodded as he patted at the air in front of him. "It's alright, really. I'm part of Buchanan's secret service division of hall monitors, and those 'goons' as you called them are two of my best men."

"So you *are* hall monitors," I said.

"Not really," Colton replied. "We work separate from those other guys."

"Do they even know you exist?"

"Their captain, Gavin, knows," Colton said. "But he's the only one that does."

I slouched in my seat, sighing. "And now *I* know…"

Colton chuckled, and then returned to the subject at hand. "What do you know about Linus?"

"He's a friend," I answered. "We like the same things, but he's one of those guys who I can only talk to about those same things, y'know? Most of the time there's just awkward silence until one of us breaks it with some talk of zombies or space stuff."

Colton flipped open the manila envelope and scribbled notes as I spoke.

"Like, that's literally all we talk about because we have *nothing* else in common," I said, realizing how sad it actually sounded.

Glancing up from his notes, Colton asked, "Has he ever mentioned anything that might've sounded strange to you? Odd?"

This time, *I* chuckled. "He says that vampires *might* actually be a real thing because back in the 1600's, they used to—"

Colton raised his hand to stop me. "That's not what I meant."

I put my hands in my pockets and leaned back

against the desk. "Whatever, man. Don't you think it's *odd* to think that if vampires *were* real, then they'd probably just be—"

"Holy buckets!" Colton said with a burst, obviously flustered. "Anything odd about this *school!*"

"Oh," I sighed. "Be more clear with your question next time. If you're referring to something specific then maybe it's best if you don't phrase your question in such a generic way."

Colton started rubbing his temples. He looked like he was growing impatient. "We *don't* think it was an accident that he tackled you. Did he say something or give you anything?"

I set my hand on my thigh, feeling for the small piece of paper in my pocket. "No. He said sorry, and then took off."

"Did he *give* you anything?" Colton asked, sitting forward.

I shook my head.

"Listen," Colton sighed. "To be honest, I don't know exactly what any of this is about either, okay? All I know is I've been ordered to bring Linus in because he has some sort of journal he carries around with him, but that's it – I don't even know what's *in* the journal. Usually when an order is secret to the point where even *I'm* not allowed to know the details, it means something big is happening."

A *journal?* All *this* for a *journal?*

I stared at Colton's eyes. "So you're just doing your

job?"

"Right," Colton said with a grin. "And you know what? *I don't care* to know the details. They're irrelevant to me... *meaningless*. Linus has something in his possession that's put him on someone's radar and now he's a wanted criminal."

"Wanted criminal?" I asked, confused. What was this, the wild west? Linus said some pretty outrageous things in the few conversations we've had, but never anything that might lead me to think he was a *criminal*. "Who can even issue something like that at this school? The principal?"

Colton shook his head. "My orders come from the president."

The more I heard, the more confused I became. "Sebastian? *President* Sebastian?"

PRESIDENT
SEBASTIAN

President Sebastian was the newly elected school president of Buchanan. He's an easygoing kid with a smile that'll make you trust him with your life. He's also a bit of a smooth talker, which is probably why he won the election so easily. They say he can sell ice to Eskimos. None of the other candidates even had a chance. He's awesome at sports, has a cheerleader girlfriend, is getting an A plus *plus* in social studies, has *never* needed braces, has a thick head of hair, owns two dogs, and somehow has *tons* of money. He's the *perfect* sixth grader.

"What's Linus wanted *for?*" I asked.

Colton sat up and lifted his arms as if he were surrendering. "Don't know, don't care. I just need to find him so if you have any information about where he *is* or where he was *going*, or *anything* else, it would be *appreciated.*"

"What's the principal say about all this?" I asked.

"My orders *don't* come from the principal," Colton repeated.

Everything in my body was screaming at me to hand over the fortune from the cookie, but I couldn't bring myself to do it. My leg burned in the spot where the piece of paper was in my pocket. Not literally of course, but you know how your arm will start to itch if you *imagine* there's an itch there? That's what was happening to me.

I'm not sure why I lied to Colton, but I did. Maybe it was because I was bored with being a nobody in the school. Maybe it was because I wanted some kind of action and adventure. Or maybe it's just because I'm dumb. "No. I don't know anything about Linus that might help you."

Colton folded his hands and exhaled slowly. "That's a shame, because you seemed like a kid with common sense." He stood from the desk and cracked his knuckles.

I didn't know what he was planning on doing, and luckily I didn't have to find out. The speaker by the door crackled, and a girl's voice spoke loud and clear. "Colton, to the front office please. Your bike is parked in a tow away zone. Colton, to the front office *immediately*."

"Blazes!" Colton shouted as he hopped off his seat. "My *bike* is in trouble?"

As Colton started walking to the front door of the art room, I managed to sneak a peek at the page he had written notes on. The manila folder was open on the desk next to me. The paper on top was filled with chicken scratched words and doodles that looked like blueprints. Paper clipped to that sheet was my school picture.

What the heck was my picture doing in his folder?

Stopping at the door, Colton flipped around and headed back to the desk. Slapping the folder shut, he slid it along until it fell into his hand. "Don't want to leave this thing sitting out, do we?"

I didn't answer, watching as he left the room. Before he disappeared out of view, I saw him say something to the two monitors guarding the door. They both nodded at him, and he was gone.

I clutched at my backpack and headed to the exit of the art room. One of the monitors turned around and pointed back at the desk.

"Sit tight, Brody," he said. "Colton will be back shortly to finish your questioning."

"This is insane," I said. "I'm missing class right now. Just let me get out of here! If he needs to ask more questions, he can get a hold of me later!"

Suddenly there was a loud *pop* that came from the hallway. It sounded like the slap you hear when someone belly flops into a swimming pool.

The two monitors spun around immediately. I heard the sound of footsteps running on the linoleum flooring of the hallway, and then saw the monitors sprint away from the door.

"Freeze!" I heard both of the monitors shout as they raced away from the art room.

A normal kid would've taken the opportunity to run out the door and get to class, but not *this* kid. I sat in place, frozen in fear at what might happen if I disobeyed the order to sit tight. A few different scenarios went through my head. Detention? Expulsion? Dare I say it... *community service?*

And then a soft voice came from the door. "Brody Valentine!"

I sighed. I was the only kid in the room at that moment – was it really necessary to use my *entire* name?

I looked up and saw a girl poking her head around the doorframe. She was another sixth grader that I was familiar with. Her name was Madison, and every single boy in the school had a crush on her at one time or another. She was athletic, funny, and more popular than anyone I'd ever seen in my life. She was the complete *opposite* of me. So what was she doing saying my name? How did she even *know* my name? Didn't she have better things to do? Like *brush her hair* or something?

"Valentine!" she said as she waved at me. She glanced down the hallway, and spoke in a hushed whisper. "Hurry up!"

I didn't know what to do so I just stared at her. "Huh?"

She sighed, remaining crouched as she snuck over

to me. She grabbed my arm and pulled me to my feet. "Those monitors are gonna be back any second, so we have to hurry!"

I shook my head, trying my best to understand what was happening. "What're you talking about? What's going on? How do you know my name?"

Madison stopped. "We've been watching you for awhile. Linus said you were someone to keep an eye on so… we kept our eyes on you."

A chill ran down my spine. "Is watching me from a distance some kind of *hobby* now? Like 'bird watching,' except it's called '*nerd* watching?'"

Madison didn't answer my sarcastic quip. She held tight to my arm and forced me to follow her to the door. Before stepping out, she looked around the corner to make sure the monitors were out of sight.

"Madison, was that loud popping sound you?" I asked.

She nodded her head. "So was the call from the principal's office. Colton's gonna kick himself when he remembers he doesn't even *own* a bike. And call me *Maddie*. I *hate* Madison."

When the coast was clear, she jumped into the hall and started sprinting in the opposite direction of the two monitors. I did my best to keep up, but this girl was on the track team! She ran like a cheetah!

"Wait up!" I said, clutching at the cramp in my stomach. I staggered behind her, embarrassed. This was worse than gym class!

When we reached the corner where the hallway turned, we stepped into another one of the empty rooms. She shut the door behind us, but didn't flip on the lights.

Maddie didn't waste any time. "*Where's Linus? What have they done with him?*"

My brain freaked out, and all I said was, "*Whaaaa?*"

"Linus!" she said in a harsh whisper. "We know he made contact with you just before he went off the grid – what did he say to you?"

I shook my head, more confused than I'd ever been. "He... he said...," I mumbled. "He said he was sorry for bumping into me! That's it, I swear!"

She clenched her fist and banged it against a desk. "Did you see where he went afterward? Did those monitors catch him?"

"I don't know," I said, honestly. "After he knocked me down, he got right back up and started running again. The monitors ran past me, chasing after him… they didn't even help me up."

"This doesn't make any sense," Maddie repeated under her breath as she paced back and forth. "What about the journal? Did he give you the journal?"

There it was again – the mention of a journal.

"What's the big deal about this kid's journal?" I asked. "Like, his diary or something? What boy keeps a *diary* on him?"

Maddie sneered at me. "It's not a *diary* – it's a *journal!* A place for Linus to keep his notes and illustrations so he can reflect on them later. It's filled with clues and secrets that could bring down the entire *school!*"

At this point, I felt like all this over exaggeration had started boiling over. This was some kind of cruel joke someone was playing on me because I was an easy target. I mean, really? A journal filled with secrets that would tank the school? Yeah, right.

I rolled my eyes. "Okay, I get it. Ha ha, very funny. Let's all make fun of the dweeb who talks about vampires and zombies, huh? What's the deal? Was this some kind of dare from your cheerleader girlfriends?"

Maddie grabbed my shoulder and forced me back. "This is *not* a joke!"

Shocked, I sat perfectly still. Maddie was a lot stronger than she looked, trust me.

"The agency doesn't know for sure because we lost contact with Linus," Maddie continued, "but a lot of us think he's in possession of a disc containing all the passwords to Buchanan's computer system."

"The passwords to the computer systems?" I asked. "Why's that a big deal? What can someone do with those?"

Maddie's eyes flashed with anger. "If those passwords got into the wrong hands, it could mean devastation for every kid here. You could give everyone straight A's, switch school schedules around, change the answers to every test, create fake holidays to get days off… you could even delete permanent records."

I paused. "You mean you can delete kids from existence?"

Maddie nodded. "Existence from the school, yes. It would be like they never attended here. Did Linus give you *anything?*" she asked again.

This time, I decided not to hide the fortune, probably because I was one of those boys who used to have a crush on Maddie. *Used* to? Who am I kidding? I reached into my pocket and pulled out the slip of paper with the fortune on it. "He dropped this," I said, setting the paper on the desk.

Maddie stared at it. "What's that?"

I shrugged my shoulders. "I dunno. I was hoping you could tell me."

She pulled a chair up to the desk and examined the fortune. "He just gave this to you and ran off?"

"Not exactly," I replied. "He dropped a fortune cookie that was still in a plastic wrap. And *then* he ran off. When I opened the package, I found this hand written fortune inside."

"Clever," she said with a chuckle. "It's just like Linus to do something weird like that."

Maddie and Linus must've been close enough to understand when they were being quirky. "I didn't open it on purpose," I said in my defense. "I accidentally crushed it open, and since it was already broken apart…"

"No," Maddie said, "He meant for you to open it. Who can't resist the urge to bust open a fortune cookie when they find one? I hate fortune cookies, but I still crack them apart to get at the paper inside."

"Hey, me too!" I said, excited. "I hate fortune cookies too! Looks like we have something in common, right?"

She stared at me for a moment, and cocked an eyebrow.

I looked away.

"Do not lose," she said, reading the fortune.

"Weird, right?" I asked. "It's like telling us to win at everything."

"It's probably telling us not to *lose* this *paper*," she said softly, chewing her lip.

I tightened a smile and did my best not to look as stupid as I felt. "Maybe that too," I said. "That would make more sense, I guess."

"But what about these numbers?" she asked, pointing at the bottom row. "*4247.019.5*. What a strange number to write out. What could that mean?"

"Phone number, maybe?" I suggested.

"Not enough digits," she replied. "There are four numbers before the first point. Then three before the second point, and then one at the end."

"Could he be splitting the numbers up?" I asked. "Could that be his way of listing out *three* numbers?"

"Maybe," Maddie said. "So then the first number would be four two four seven. And then second would be zero one nine, with the last number being five."

I whispered my thoughts out loud. "Four thousand two hundred and forty seven... nineteen—"

"But it's *not* nineteen," Maddie said, interrupting me. "It's *zero* nineteen. Linus intentionally put the zero in there, but *why?*"

I groaned, sliding back into my chair. "*Grrrrrr, math!* Math is my *worst* enemy!"

Maddie laughed, but continued talking. "So zero one nine, or zero nineteen. What's that mean?"

Raising my eyebrows, I joked. "Maybe it's a combination to some secret safe Linus stashed away."

Maddie's eyes opened wider as she gasped. "That's it! This is a combination!"

I paused. "Huh?"

"You were right," she explained. "It's not zero one nine, but *nineteen*. And I bet it's nineteen *point* five!"

"But you just said Linus probably meant to have the zero in there."

"Right," Maddie said, and then spoke rapidly. "It's zero nineteen point five because it's referring to the *locker* the combination goes to."

"Zero nineteen point five?" I repeated. "You know how crazy that sounds? Buchanan doesn't have lockers that end in *'point five.'*"

"The lower level does," Maddie said. "All the lockers down there are half the size as the ones on the first and second levels. They're stacked on top of each other so the 'point five' refers to the bottom row of lockers. The zero at the beginning of the number refers to which level of the school it's on. Lockers on the first floor start with the number one, and lockers on the second floor start with the number two."

I nodded, finally understanding. "So the zero means it's in the basement."

"Exactly," she said.

"So the combination is the first number?" I asked, still a little confused. "Four two four seven?"

Maddie studied the sheet again. "If we split the numbers into three, we have the answer."

"No more math!" I moaned.

She ignored me. "The first two numbers make forty two – too high for our combinations so the first number *has* to be four. The last two numbers are the same – it

31

would be number forty seven, which is also too high."

"So the combination is four, twenty four, seven?" I asked, feeling proud that I had solved the puzzle. I mean, figured it out *after* Maddie laid it all out for me.

She looked at me suspiciously, and asked, "How *much* did you tell Colton?"

I shook my head. "Nothing! I didn't tell him anything!"

"Did you show him this cookie?"

"No!"

Maddie chewed her lip again, and then spoke. "Did he say anything to you about this?"

I sat silently for a moment, trying to remember something Colton might've said. "No. He didn't say much. Only that Linus had a journal they were looking for, but nothing about what was *inside* it. And he said his orders didn't come from the principal."

Maddie shook her head, sighing. "I'm not surprised about the principal part. Hall monitors are usually controlled by the school's security team. So I guess it looks like *we* are headed to the '*dungeon*,'" she said with a smirk.

Great, I thought, the "*dungeon*," which was the name students used when talking about the lower levels of Buchanan. The only classes down there were band, woodworking, and show choir. And it was the only place in this entire building that I never wanted to see. I considered writing a note to my parents in case I disappeared forever.

"What do you mean, '*we?*'" I said sharply. "I'm *not* going down there, and I don't think you should either unless you *want* your photo to be on the back of a milk carton!"

Maddie put one hand on my shoulder, and stared into my eyes. I thought for a moment that she was going to agree with me until she pushed me back against the chair. It hurt.

"Listen up, you little pimple," she whispered. "Unless you're happy sitting quietly in the back row for the rest of your life, you're gonna come with me!"

I clenched my jaw, doing my best to ignore the pain in my shoulder. "I *am* happy as just another face in the crowd!"

Maddie's eyes slowly drew open. "I don't understand. Don't you want to be *more* than just a sixth grade student? Haven't you ever felt like there's *more* to your life?"

"Not really," I whispered.

Shaking her head, Maddie headed for the door. "That's too bad. Linus must've been *wrong* about you."

I stared down, listening to her footsteps on the floor. I know I just told her I didn't feel like there was more to my life, but I was lying. What kid *doesn't* want *more* out of life?

I sit in class and zone out thinking of what I'd do if I even discovered I had superpowers! I stare out the window of my parent's car imagining I'm driving a hover bike in the ditches! I even have a plan set up in case zombies ever invaded my town!

Of course I wanted more from life!

"Wait!" I shouted, much louder than I meant to.

Maddie stopped in the doorway and turned her head. Her smile told me I didn't need to explain myself. "I *knew* you'd change your mind."

Several minutes later we approached the staircase that led into the lower levels. We made it through the hallways of the school because homeroom had just dismissed so the corridors were filled with students going to their first period classes.

The bell rang again just as Maddie and I arrived at the staircase. As I stared into the lower level, it was already obvious that this part of the school hadn't been taken care of like the upper levels. The fluorescent lights along the tiled ceiling were flickering on and off, as if telling us to stay away in Morse code – not that I understood Morse code though.

I grabbed the railing along the wall and started walking down the steps. "So this journal that everyone is after… you say it contains all the passwords to Buchanan's computer system?"

Maddie shrugged her shoulders. "That's what the word on the playground is."

"But that doesn't make any sense," I muttered.

Rolling her eyes, Maddie spoke sarcastically. "Oh right, I guess you're the expert in all of this now, aren't you?"

My hand gripped the railing tighter. "I'd like to think all my years of playing video games have trained me for this."

She stopped, staring daggers at me. "You think this is a *game?*"

I paused again, crinkling my nose. "...yeah."

"It's *not*," Maddie said, raising her voice. "And you have no idea of what you're up against!"

"You're right!" I said, upset. "I *don't*, and nobody seems to want to give me any answers either! I've been sent on some mission to the dungeon of the school, to where kids have been known to *disappear* from time to time, just to find a locker that *might* or might *not* contain something that could flip Buchanan upside-down!"

Maddie folded her arms and looked off to her side. "Fine," she snipped. "You're right. You deserve to know a little bit about what's happening." She jumped the last few stairs and landed on the floor of the dungeon. As she continued down the hall, she said, "Ask away."

I walked quickly to catch up with her. "First of all, tell me what this is about."

"You know as much as I do about what's happening at the moment," Maddie said. "Linus has a journal that contains some passwords – passwords that others don't want revealed. He's hidden it away because he probably knew the monitors were going to come looking for it."

"Who does Linus work for?" I asked.

"Classified," Maddie answered bluntly.

"Who do you work for?"

"Same people as Linus, but that's still classified," she replied.

I felt my face grow warm. "Then who do those monitors work for?"

Maddie stopped. "The monitors work for Buchanan School. Duh."

Finally, an *actual* answer. "Who's at the top of their chain?"

"The principal," Maddie said, placing her hands on her hips. She glanced farther down the hallway.

"The principal is behind all this?" I asked, shocked. "But Colton said his orders came from the *president*."

Maddie looked back at me as she continued her

path down the dark hallway. "Sebastian? I don't know why he'd be involved in any of this. The last I heard was that the head of Colton's department was Principal Davis."

I didn't know how to respond. Colton told me one thing, and Maddie was telling me an entirely different thing. "Either way," I said, "Principal or president, both are a little unrealistic, don't you think?"

"And yet..." Maddie continued, "Here you are in the dungeon searching for some clues."

I remained quiet as we marched down the dark corridor. The lights continued to buzz overhead as they cast an annoying blue glow. Scanning ahead wasn't helpful at all because it was like the hallway disappeared in shadows the farther I looked.

Kids were sitting on the floor, clutching at their half eaten chocolate bars, sick from sugar shock. I did my best to avoid eye contact.

Suddenly, a taller boy stepped directly in our path. "Hey guys, whatcha lookin' for today?" he asked as he held his opened backpack toward us, presenting a bag filled with candy.

Just from the one second I had to look in the bag, I saw king sized candy bars, extra large suckers, all kinds of individually wrapped hard candy, and more sugar bombs than I'd seen in my life. It was like Halloween.

"Beat it, loser," Maddie said coldly as she stepped around the young boy.

"Come on, man!" pleaded the boy. "If you're down

here, it means you're lookin' for *candy*, and ya ain't gonna find better prices than me!"

CANDY!

I couldn't look away from the satchel of goodies. I wasn't a sugar addict, but even *I* felt a *little* tempted.

Maddie grabbed my arm and pulled me along. "Brody, we have to go. Don't waste your time with this kid. He isn't worth it."

The boy smiled, exposing the braces over his huge teeth. "You'll be back," he whispered. "It's only a matter of time before you start craving some chocolate covered caramels."

Weird, I thought, because the instant he said it, I actually started craving them. I shook my head, to clear my mind from thoughts of candy. Then I spoke to Maddie again. "I had no idea the candy problem was this bad down here."

"It's gotten worse over the last few weeks," Maddie replied, studying the numbers on the lockers as we passed them. "Funny 'cause this wasn't much of a situation until they installed those vending machines upstairs."

"Sebastian really pushed for those machines too," I added. "You'd think he'd try his best to curb what was happening down here."

Maddie raised an eyebrow. "I don't think he saw it coming. None of us really did."

I scanned the crusty tiles on the ceiling as I followed her, but then bumped into her back. She had stopped walking before I noticed. I stumbled a bit, trying to keep my balance, but also because I was embarrassed.

"Pay attention," she whispered as she pointed at one of the lockers on the bottom row. "Look. Nineteen point five."

I stared at the locker. Green paint chipped off and revealed a rusted sheet of metal underneath. The combination padlock had cobwebs hanging from it, probably from never being used. "Gross," I said.

Maddie rolled her eyes at me. "Grow up," she said as she put her fingers through the cobwebs. "It's just some spider webs. It's nothing to be—"

Instantly, she drew her hand back and squealed so loudly that my ears hurt. Jumping up and down and wildly flapping her hands, she yelled, "Something touched my fingers! There's a spider in there! *Sick sick sick sick sick!"*

I laughed, clutching at my stomach. "*Grow up*," I said, mocking her voice.

She slapped my shoulder and giggled, catching her breath. Then she nodded toward the locker. "Take care of it," she said with a smile.

I quickly wiped away the webs and smeared my hands across my jeans to make sure none of the demon creatures were crawling on me. I *hate* spiders.

Maddie knelt down and started twisting the lock in circles, entering the combination. After she was done, she glanced at me as she pulled up on the handle.

Click.

The door to the locker pushed out about half an inch. Maddie took a breath, and then flipped it open the rest of the way.

I didn't know what to expect, but I braced myself for anything. And by "braced myself for anything," I mean I covered my face and dove to the ground, whimpering like a puppy.

"*Would you get up?*" Maddie growled, whispering. "What's the *matter* with you?"

The cold floor was against my body as I looked up. Other kids from down the hall were staring at me like I was a crazy person. Look at what I've been reduced to... laying in the basement of Buchanan School while sugar addicts felt sorry for *me*.

"*Get up already!*" Maddie ordered. "You're

embarrassing me!"

I pushed myself off the ground, and dusted off the front of my shirt. Cracking my neck like a boss, I approached locker nineteen point five. Peering inside, I saw a very disappointing sight – at the bottom of the dusty locker was a single yellow crayon, but that was it. There was *nothing* else.

"Serious?" I sighed.

Maddie picked up the crayon and inspected it. "Look here at the bottom," she said, pointing the butt of the crayon at my face. "The number sixty two is etched into it."

"Did Linus scratch that in there?" I asked. "Some more secret code stuff?"

Maddie nodded.

"This is all so anti-climactic," I groaned. "I thought

at least there would be some kind of secret spy box filled with junk to play with."

Lowering the crayon, a smile cracked across Maddie's face. Then she set her foot into the locker and pushed down until it clicked. Instantly, the back wall of the locker unbolted and slid out of view. A small black bag rolled from the container and flopped onto the floor.

"There's your secret spy box," she said.

"Whoa," I said, unzipping the bag. The inside wasn't filled with much, but it was still the coolest treasure I'd ever seen. There was a pack of stink bombs, a pad of blank hall passes, an old school wrist watch, a pair of glasses with a fake nose and mustache, and a stack of one-dollar bills.

Maddie continued to keep an eye out. "Strap on the watch," she said. "It's also a walkie talkie."

My heart skipped a beat as I tightened the watch to my wrist. I felt like I was a secret agent suiting up for a deadly mission. "Who else has a watch like this?"

Another smile appeared on Maddie's face as she pulled her sleeve up, exposing the exact same watch that I was now wearing. "They come in handy," she said. "Trust me."

I looked at the yellow crayon in her hand. "So what's the deal with that thing?"

Maddie sighed. "It's a code. Yellow, sixty two."

"Another locker?" I asked.

"No," she said, shaking her head. "They're instructions, but there's only one person in the school that can decipher it."

I remained silent, waiting for Maddie to continue.

"Sibyl," Maddie said.

"Sibyl?" I asked. I never met anyone at Buchanan named Sibyl. "Okay. So who is she and where's she at?"

"She's a fortune teller, and on *our* team," Maddie replied as she started walking deeper into the basement of Buchanan. "And *we* don't find her. She finds *us*."

About ten minutes later and several turned corners in the basement, we were far enough away from the steps for me to know that if I lost Maddie, I'd be lost in the dungeon forever.

The farther we went, the darker it became. Sugar addicts were all over the place, mumbling nonsense as their bodies went through various stages of a sugar crash.

"I feel sorry for these kids," I said, following Maddie through the halls.

Maddie sighed. "It won't last long. As soon as lunch rolls around, these kids will get some proper food in their bellies and be fine again. But you're right. Up until lunchtime, this is a sad sight."

My legs were starting to burn from all the walking. "So where's this Sibyl kid you were talking about? If *she* has to find us, then why all the walking?"

"She has her own base, so to speak," Maddie explained. "But it's not like she's sitting behind a desk or anything. She has to be called upon."

"Like with a phone?" I asked.

"No," Maddie continued. "She can only be called in the girl's restroom down here."

"Um, what?"

"In the girl's restroom, all of the toilets have to be flushed at the same time," Maddie said. "That's the code we follow when we need her help."

"So weird," I whispered.

The lighting in this section of school came completely from the fluorescent bulbs above us. Without any windows, the lower levels were a dark and depressing place. I started to understand why others called it the "dungeon."

Finally, we reached a water fountain with swinging doors on both sides of it. The signs on the doors were hand written with the word *"boys"* on one and *"girls"* on the other. I wasn't surprised to see an *"out of order"* sign hanging from the fountain.

Maddie turned and pointed her finger at me. "Wait out here, and *don't* talk to anyone."

I nodded. "Roger that, ten four."

"*Nerd*," Maddie whispered, pushing the door to the girl's bathroom open.

When the door shut, I slipped my hands into my pockets and leaned against the cold lockers on the wall. The hallway we were in wasn't any different from the rest of the hallways in the dungeon – they were all equally terrifying. I was beginning to second-guess my decision for adventure and excitement. Maybe being left all alone in the dark had something to do with it.

"Hey, kid," came a thick whisper from the shadows.

I held my breath, staring into the dark, doing my best to see what kind of *monster* I was about to get attacked by. My brain froze, but I knew if I sounded scared, then I would appear weak. "Heeee…. Heeeeeee…. Heeeeeeeeeeeeeeeello?" Yeah, that didn't sound weak at all.

A boy dressed in a suit stepped out of the darkness, and approached me. It was Colton, but his two henchmen weren't with him. Somehow, I was relieved that it wasn't another kid trying to sell me candy, but all the relief washed away when I remembered I had just escaped from him only moments ago.

I stepped forward, afraid to say anything, so I just stared at him like a baby seeing fireworks for the first time.

Colton raised his open palms at me and shook his head. "No, it's alright. I'm not lookin' to bring you in or anything."

His big blue eyes told me he was being honest. "Then what? Did you guys follow me down here?"

"We've been following you for awhile," Colton said. "But that's not the point, and we don't have a lot of time before your girlfriend comes out of that bathroom with Sibyl."

"She's *not* my girlfriend," I said, feeling more disappointed than I'd ever admit. "If you know about all this, and you're not trying to stop it, then what *do* you want?"

45

Colton shook his finger at me. "By now you know a little more about the situation, so I wanna give you another chance to *help* me."

"Help you?"

"Mm hmm," Colton hummed. "You're gonna find that journal for us, and when you do, you're gonna hand it over along with the rest of the kids you're workin' with."

"Why would I do that?" I asked, folding my arms tightly.

"Because I'll make sure you're seen as the hero. President Sebastian has even said there's money for you if you help us," Colton said, bluntly.

I knew he wasn't lying. There were kids in the school who had rich *parents*, but Sebastian was actually rich *himself*. He had money, and wasn't afraid of flaunting it. Maybe being the school president came with perks... like a paycheck.

Colton continued. "Let's say you find that journal. And then let's say you do whatever it was Maddie and Linus were planning on doing with it. What do you think would happen to *you*? You honestly think you won't be expelled the instant that journal comes to light? Do you even know whose side you're on?"

I didn't want to believe him, but part of me did. I truly had no idea what side I had taken when I came to the dungeon with Maddie. Was it possible that I was working with the bad guys?

Behind the wooden door of the girl's restroom came the sound of all the toilets flushing at once. It was the signal Maddie used to get Sibyl's attention.

Colton's eyes shot at the door as he stepped back into the shadows. He pointed his finger at me one last time and spoke. "When you find that journal, you bring it straight to us. *Don't* listen to anything Maddie says to you, and *don't* open that journal."

I stepped forward, wanting to confess that I *wasn't* the action hero I was pretending to be. "But..."

Colton interrupted me. "*We're* the good guys, Brody. Get us that journal, and we'll make sure you're seen as the hero."

And then the hall monitor slipped away in the shadows of the dungeon. If this were a movie, I would've thought that was awesome, but this wasn't a movie, and I only felt creeped out.

The bathroom door swung open, and Maddie stepped out. A girl walked through the door after her and smiled at me. This must be Sybil, I thought.

SIBYL

She had a very clean complexion under her short blond hair. She couldn't have been any younger than us, so I figured she was in the sixth grade too. At her side hung a beat up leather satchel.

"My name is," I started to say, but Sybil interrupted

me.

"Brody, yes, I know," Sybil said.

"Wow! You *already* knew my name!" I said. "You really *are* a fortune teller!"

Sybil rolled her eyes and glanced at Maddie. "No, Maddie told me you were waiting outside the bathroom for us."

"Oh," I said, lowering my head. "So do you just hang out in the bathroom all day, waiting for someone to flush all the toilets at once?"

Sibyl sighed. "No."

"Huh," I grunted.

"Maddie tells me you're quite the agent," Sibyl said, changing the subject. "On your way to becoming a real hero, aren't you?"

"Not really," I replied. "I'm just sorta tagging along. We'll see how much of a hero I turn out to be when this is all over."

Sibyl smiled softly. "Every journey starts with a single step, right?" she asked. "And a hero is born *during* the journey – *not* at the end of it."

The tiny amount of confidence I felt from Sibyl's words was enough to create a warm feeling in my chest.

Sibyl held her hand out to Maddie. "Let me see the clue Linus left for you."

Maddie reached into her pocket and pulled out the yellow crayon. She held the bottom out toward the fortune teller and spoke. "Sixty two. That's what's scratched into the bottom of this."

Sibyl took the crayon in her hand and stuck out her lower lip, studying the piece of colored wax. She hummed a tune I didn't recognize. It must've been her way of thinking. Finally, she said, "I haven't seen one of these since the second grade. Strange that Linus would use such an old school puzzle."

"Can you decode it?" Maddie asked.

Sibyl smiled. "My name is *Sibyl*, isn't it?"

I felt confused. "What's that mean? What does your name have to do with this?"

The fortune teller turned toward me and spoke. "Everyone's name means something. Sibyl actually means *'fortune teller.'* Cool, huh?"

"Whoa," I whispered, and then turned toward Maddie. "What's *your* name mean?"

Maddie looked up at me, frowning. "Madison means nothing. It's just the city I was born in. My parents weren't too creative."

"How about me?" I asked, excited.

Sibyl shrugged her shoulders. "How am I supposed to know? I don't memorize the meaning of every single name. I have better things to do!"

"Right," Maddie said, irritated. "And right now we need to decode Linus's message."

Sibyl agreed, reaching into her satchel. After fishing around for a second, she removed a gadget that was made from a folded sheet of paper. It looked like a pyramid. "This is an origami fortune teller."

I recognized it immediately after she said it. "I

remember playing with those back in the day!"

Maddie scratched at her cheek. "If this is such an old school technique that Linus is using, how do we know that the information inside that will be helpful?"

ORIGAMI FORTUNE TELLER

"The information inside this device will last forever," Sibyl explained. "In twenty years, if someone leaves the same clue as Linus did, it'll still point in the right direction."

"If I'm *still* a sixth grader in twenty years," I said, "I'll be pretty bummed out."

The two girls just stared at me. I guess I wasn't as funny as I thought.

The origami fortune teller Sibyl was holding had writing all over it. The four corners on the outside each had a color. The inside had numbers, and other scribbling. Linus's crayon must've had the correct path to take on the device in order to get to the message he wanted to deliver.

Maddie held the yellow crayon up again. "Yellow is the first instruction."

Sibyl put her fingers in the bottom of the fortune teller and started flipping the device apart each time she said a different letter. "Yellow – Y – E – L – L – O – W." When she was finished she looked at Maddie, waiting for the next instruction.

"It's not sixty two," Maddie said.

"No," Sibyl said. "It's the number six and the number two." She flipped the origami fortune teller in and out as she counted. "1 – 2 – 3 – 4 – 5 – 6."

At last, Maddie said, "Two."

Sibyl winked at me as she opened the flap with the number two on it. She looked down and read it quietly while moving her lips.

"What's it say?" Maddie asked excitedly.

"Lower than a chicken's garbage," Sibyl whispered.

Maddie's eyes slowly panned upward. I could almost see the gears grinding in her head as she tried to understand what Sibyl had just said.

"That's it?" I asked. "Is that another riddle or something?"

Sibyl tightened her lips and looked at me. "Every answer in this is a riddle that leads to another location."

"After so many years, wouldn't you already know the answers to each riddle?" Maddie asked.

"This thing has only been used twice," Sibyl replied. "I've never landed on this flap before."

At that moment, the bell started ringing, signaling the end of first period. The hallway we were standing in soon became a flurry of students rushing to make it to their next class. Because there were so many children, a couple spots in the herd moved slower than others. It was like rush hour, but with kids instead of cars.

When I turned to ask Sybil more questions, she was gone.

Maddie placed her hands on her hips. "Lower than a chicken's garbage," she repeated patiently as she watched people walk by. "What could that mean?"

"I have no clue," I replied.

Maddie took the lead and started moving down the hallway. Hopefully she was headed for the stairs so we could leave the dungeon. Weaving in and out of other students, I stayed as close to her as possible, doing my best not to lose her.

Every few feet I saw some kids opening candy bars and taking monster bites out of them. There were even a few teachers munching on some sweet treats as they stood by their classroom doors.

"Where are we going?" I asked Maddie.

She didn't break her stride. "To the gymnasium," she said.

"The gym? Is that what you have for second period?"

"No, but we'll be able to hang out there while we

try to figure this riddle out. Mr. Cooper is pretty cool like that."

I laughed. "Cool like that? Or just doesn't give a spew about taking attendance?"

I couldn't see Maddie's face, but I could tell from her voice that she was smiling. "Both."

A few minutes later, we were out of the dreadful dungeon and on the first level of the school. We sped by the front lobby. Kids had already filtered into their second period classrooms, leaving the hallways almost empty.

"Hurry up!" Maddie ordered. "We're going to be late!"

My side started to cramp again. How in the world do athletes work through pain like this, I thought. "Late to what? A class we're not even supposed to be in?"

"You're an agent today," she snipped. "The principal will understand."

At that moment, my shoulder accidentally bumped shoulders with someone else. I stared at the ground, afraid of who it was that I unintentionally challenged.

"Sorry, man," said a boy. "Didn't see ya there."

Relieved, I looked up. It was another sixth grader that I recognized from my last period class, English. His name was Chase Cooper. "Sorry, Chase. I hope I didn't hurt you."

Chase grinned, rubbing his shoulder. "It's not a problem," he said. "I mean, my *ninja* skills might be affected, but for only a day."

I laughed at his joke. *Ninja* skills? Can you imagine that? Ninjas at Buchanan School? *That'll* be the day.

"Chase, are you coming?" a girl shouted from the other end of the lobby. It was Zoe, his cousin.

Chase leaned over and waved. "Yeah, I'll be right there," he shouted. Then he stepped past me and nodded. "See ya, dude."

"See ya," I replied.

Maddie watched as he walked away. "You know that kid?"

"Yeah," I said. "He's a pretty cool guy."

She watched Chase as he walked away, and then looked at me. "There's more to him than you might think."

"Like what?"

"It's classified," she said, turning away. "Maybe someday you'll be allowed to view his file, but not today."

I raised my eyebrows and shook my head, confused. "Whatever."

Before we could make it any farther in the lobby, the school bell rang out like a bell because well… it *was* a bell.

"Wonderful," Maddie groaned as she stopped in the middle of the lobby. She turned toward me and held her hand out. "Gimme your backpack."

I tightened my fists around my straps. "What? Why?"

"We don't have any time," she said quickly. "Just give it to me!"

I stared at her, unflinchingly. "What do you need? Just tell me and I can—"

Suddenly, a voice erupted from behind us. "Excuse me!"

I froze up instantly.

Let me explain something again real quick – I'm not the most adventurous kid in the world. I like my days predictable and boring. Boring is good – there's no *trouble* in boring. I'm not *un*popular, but I wouldn't say that I'm a loser. I'm just your average, stereotypical dude trying his best not to attract attention, y'know what I mean? I *just* want to get through sixth grade unnoticed and unharmed.

That's why getting caught outside of class caused me to freeze up.

"What're you two doing out here?" the adult's voice asked from behind us. "*Hall passes*, please."

I slowly turned to face my certain death. It was Mrs. Olsen, the science teacher. I wanted to throw the question right back at her and ask her why *she* was outside of class, but I knew that would guarantee a day's worth of detention. I started mumbling a response, "Um, we just… uhh…"

I felt Maddie yank my backpack off of me. She leaned closer and whispered. "Distract her for a second."

My heart raced as I tried to think of something to distract Mrs. Olsen with. I wasn't good at this sort of thing! "I'm glad you're out here!"

Mrs. Olsen's lips pressed together as she folded her arms. "And why is that?"

"Because," I started saying, feverishly trying to think of something clever, "I had a question about last night's assignment."

"Oh really?" Mrs. Olsen asked, suspicious. "Last night's assignment is due today, and you have science… what period?"

"Fourth," I answered, "but I've got study hall before that so I thought I could ask you and finish it up during that."

Mrs. Olsen sighed as she waved her fingers toward herself. "Alright then. What is it?"

If I could remember what the assignment was, it probably would've helped. Instead of saying anything else, I stared at her as air slowly escaped from my throat. "It was abouuuuuuuuut…"

Sweat started to collect on my forehead, and was about to drip down my nose at any second. *Where was Maddie? There's no way I can stall Mrs. Olsen any longer!*

Thankfully, another adult came to my rescue, but I had no idea who it was. It was just a guy who came outta nowhere! He stepped out from behind me and held a slip of paper between his dainty fingers. I had to hold back a chuckle because the guy looked so goofy. He had a thick pair of glasses over a fat nose and a bushy mustache, and then I realized… it was *Maddie* in disguise.

57

"Hello, madam," Maddie said with a gruff voice. The way she changed her voice was both impressive and terrifying. "This *upstanding* student must have left my classroom *without* his hall pass."

"Wait," Mrs. Olsen said, leaning to one side. "Weren't there two of you out here?"

I shrugged my shoulders, playing along with Maddie's disguise. "Nope, it was just me. No idea what you're talking about."

"Hmmmmm," Mrs. Olsen hummed, stone-faced as she took the paper from Maddie's hand. "And who exactly, are *you?*" she asked the bushy mustached man.

Maddie's eyes darted back and forth. "My name is Misterrrrr…" she trailed off trying to come up with a name.

"Misterrrrrr?" Mrs. Olsen repeated as she cocked an eyebrow.

Maddie snapped her head up. "*Five!* The name is Mister *High Five!* I'm a substitute teacher today, thank you very much."

Mrs. Olsen curled her lip. "Oh really? *Mister High Five?*"

I stared at Maddie hoping she knew what she was doing.

"Are you going to make fun of my name as well?" Maddie asked, upset. "I'll have you know I get a lot of that, and you'd think I'd have developed thicker skin because of it, but I *haven't.* Go on then, make fun of me *all* you want, but at least have the decency to do it to my *face.*"

Mrs. Olsen's expression went from suspicious to sympathetic as she mumbled. "I'm sorry, I didn't mean to offend you. It's just a rather odd name, and…" Mrs. Olsen paused. "You know what? You're absolutely right. It's a *fine* name, Mister High Five."

Maddie lifted her chin proudly. "Thank you. Now if you'll excuse me, I must be getting back to my class, and I believe young little Brody Valentine should be as well?" she asked, bouncing her eyebrows up and down.

"Yup!" I snickered.

Pressing her lips together again, Mrs. Olsen waved

me away. "Fine. Get to class."

I took the hall pass from her hand and smiled. "Thanks, Mrs. Olsen. See you later."

The teacher nodded, and continued onward to her classroom.

I spun around, in awe of Maddie's quick thinking. "That was *brilliant*," I said.

"Ya think?" she replied. "And also – nice drawings."

My heart sunk. I didn't want her to dig through my backpack because I had a folder filled with doodles of superhero costumes that I only worked on during study hall. I've never showed them to anybody because it was a little embarrassing.

With a smirk, she added, "Don't worry about it. They're cool. It shows me that you really do dream of bigger things."

"A couple of lame drawings told you that?"

"Not exactly," she said, "but the superhero drawing that had an arrow to the words *'my costume'* did."

I slapped my forehead. "*Why* did I write that?"

"I said don't worry about it," Maddie replied. "Everyone daydreams like that. Nobody ever *talks* about it, but we *all* do it. Even me."

Taking a breath, I smiled. Instead of feeling embarrassed by her advice, I actually felt comforted. Madison was one of the more popular kids in the school, and to hear her admit something like that was pretty cool of her.

Another few minutes later, and we were standing in the middle of the gymnasium. Mr. Cooper, the gym teacher, was making his rounds as usual. And like always, he seemed distracted as he scratched the attendance off his clipboard.

He was so absentminded that when he approached Maddie and I, he didn't miss a beat. "Maddie... Brody..." he said, scratching checkmarks off the attendance sheet. I had no idea where he put the checkmarks because I knew our names *weren't* on his sheet of paper. We weren't even supposed to be in that class!

Mr. Cooper blinked slowly as he spoke. "Basketball in here, soccer and walking the track are outside. Do whatever, I don't even care anymore."

"See?" Maddie said, heading toward the gymnasium doors. "That man doesn't pay attention to anything. There's nothing to worry about."

"Where are you going?" I asked, jogging to catch up.

"To walk around the track and think," she answered. "Some fresh air might do us some good."

Just as Maddie stepped outside, I turned to make sure Mr. Cooper hadn't caught on to our scheme. He was already in his office, leaning back in his chair with his feet propped up on a desk. I guess Maddie was right. There was nothing to worry about.

Well, almost nothing. This whole situation was

something to worry about, wasn't it? I'm following a girl around the school searching for a journal that contains secrets that Buchanan's president is willing to *pay* for. Not to mention being followed by Colton and his hall monitor goons.

Maddie walked in front of me as she spoke quietly to herself. Should I tell her about Colton cornering me in the dungeon? Should I fill her in on the details of what he said just before Sibyl had come out of the bathroom? Was Colton even the *bad guy?* Before he disappeared like a vampire, he said he was working for the *good guys.* Could it be that Maddie and Linus were the bad guys in all this? Was I on the wrong team?

"You coming?" Maddie yelled, annoyed. She was almost twenty feet ahead of me.

I must've stopped walking. I sometimes do that when my brain is running a million miles an hour. It's like it can't do two things at once. "Yeah, sorry."

On the track, she walked next to me as she continued to repeat the strange fortune Sibyl had read. "*Lower* than a chicken's garbage..."

"Do chickens even *have* garbage?" I asked.

"Maybe? What's in a chicken coop?"

"Chickens," I answered. "And their eggs and stuff... I *think*."

"Do chickens eat anything that's packaged? The packages would need to be thrown away, right? So *that* could mean it was the chicken's garbage."

I chuckled at the thought of a chubby chicken

eating some cheese sticks out of a container, and then burping as they patted their belly filled with food. In my head, the chicken carelessly tossed the container over its shoulder.

"What's so funny?" Maddie asked.

"A burping chicken," I answered.

"You wanna grow up and join the real world for a second?" she snapped, lightly punching at my shoulder.

Her punch pushed me enough that my ribs ached. The smile disappeared from my face as I flinched. "Careful," I said. "I've got a killer bruise on my side."

Maddie continued walking on the track. "From what?"

I shook my head, trying to avoid the embarrassing story of my injury. "It's stupid. Some guys were just playing on the monkey bars the other day…"

"The monkey bars? Aren't those on the other side of the school? Where the first graders have recess."

I scratched at the back of my head. "Yeah, but we don't play on them or anything. I mean, we do, but not in the same way."

"You don't swing from them?"

I kept my pace with her as I replied. "No, we do, but not like them. You see there's a game we play called…" and then my brain connected the dots. "*Chicken*."

Maddie turned toward me. "That's a *dumb* game."

I ignored her biased opinion. "But I hit my side on the garbage can next to the monkey bars!"

Finally, Maddie understood. "Wait. You mean there's a garbage can next to the monkey bars?"

"A rusty metal one. It's like a giant barrel."

"A chicken's garbage," Maddie said, thinking. "It's a stretch, but I can't see what else that might mean."

"*Lower* than a chicken's garbage," I added. "So… *under* the garbage can maybe?"

Maddie punched my shoulder again, harder this time. With a confident smile and twinkling eyes, she said, "That's it. There's only one set of monkey bars over there. Let's go."

Ten minutes later, we were clear on the other side of Buchanan school. Mr. Cooper was still in his office, so he didn't notice that we had snuck away. Since it was only second period, none of the first, second, or third graders were outside, and the yard was completely empty.

The blacktop was warm, soaking the heat from the sun as it glared down from above in a cloudless sky. We followed the yellow paint markings of the outdoor basketball court as hoops lined the way to the other side of the playground.

Also littered on the ground were empty packages of chocolate bars and other sweets along with random dark spots of flattened chewing gum.

Maddie studied the pavement as she ran. "Looks like this whole candy problem has found its way to the *younger* students as well."

As we approached the monkey bars, we slowed down. The huge barrel was still sitting next to the playground equipment, nestled in a pile of woodchips.

Without hesitating, Maddie grabbed the sides of the garbage can and tipped it over on its side. It hit the earth with a thump.

Suddenly, I heard a buzzing sound all around me, and I freaked out. Sprinting away from Maddie and the barrel, I made it about twenty yards before I turned around. In a matter of seconds, I had traveled the entire course of the playground. Maddie had her hands on her hips and was glaring at me. At least I think she was – it was hard to tell because she was so far away.

"What's your problem?" she shouted.

I cupped my hands over my mouth and yelled.

"*Bees!* I'm allergic to *bees!*"

And seriously, I am. If a bee stings me, I can say goodbye to the rest of my day since it'll be spent in the hospital.

Maddie threw her arms out, angry. "You nimrod! It was just a bunch of fruit flies."

I slouched over, catching my breath, thankful that there weren't actually bees chasing after me. I could feel my heart pounding through my chest as I jogged back to Maddie.

Breathing heavily, I said, "It's just that bees scare me. Like, *really* scare me. Like, if you asked me what the scariest thing in the world is, I would say a giant bee chasing after me on a motorcycle, while his bee buddies scream my name from both sides of the road."

"What an *odd* thing for you to say," Maddie whispered.

I lowered my head, shamed.

Maddie sighed. "No, I understand. My little brother is allergic to them too. It's bad if he gets stung. I was only mad 'cause you took off like a shooting star and scared the daylights out of me."

I laughed. "Scare someone as tough as you? Yeah, right."

She slapped my shoulder playfully. "Whatever," she said, and then pointed at the spot that was under the barrel. "So look what we just found."

Half buried in the moist dirt was a soggy, oversized clear baggie, with something big on the inside, about the size of a textbook. It *had* to be the journal!

Maddie picked up the baggie and ripped it apart. A leather journal slipped out and fell into her hands. "This is it!"

My knees started to shake at the excitement of it all. Finally, after spending half the morning solving clues we were going to see what was inside that stupid thing!

Maddie flipped it over, but the look of delight disappeared from her face. "There's a lock on the front of it. Dang it, Linus!"

Disappointed, I took the journal from her hands and inspected the lock. There was a spot for a small key on the front. But then I noticed a slip of paper sticking out from the top of the journal. "What's this?"

Maddie pinched the paper, and pulled it out. It looked like there was handwriting on the front of it. She squinted, reading the next clue out loud. "The eagle's nest of Principal Davis's office at 9:00 PM."

I threw my arms out wide, frustrated. "Come on, Linus! How many breadcrumbs do you have to leave behind before you just give us the stinkin' answer!"

Crumpling the last clue in her hands, I could tell Maddie was fed up with Linus's little game as well. "Seriously, this kid might be taking it too far now. Whatever's inside this journal better be something *good*."

"Let's just break that lock apart!" I suggested.

Maddie studied the lock again, and then spoke. "This is a pretty heavy duty piece of metal. You couldn't break it open with a hammer. Trying would just hurt the journal itself, and I don't want to risk that."

"The passwords to Buchanan's computers might be worth a lot, but is it really worth all this trouble?" I asked. "It just doesn't make sense to me!"

"I think this journal could be sold for a ton of money if it got into the wrong hands," Maddie said. "Plus it could throw off the entire grading curve if it were released to the public."

"But that's just it," I said. "It's not like the teachers of the school couldn't create new passwords. As soon as everyone realized that *every single password* had been *compromised*, wouldn't you think that Buchanan would simply change them?"

Maddie paused. "You've got a point," she said, chewing her lip again. "All this trouble for a list of passwords *doesn't* make sense, which might mean there's more at stake than we know."

I pointed at Maddie's fist with the crumpled up clue. "Principal Davis's office is next up, right? Maybe we'll find the answer in there."

"I have a knot in my stomach about it," Maddie added. "If Linus went through the trouble of hiding his journal in the principal's office, then it could mean Principal Davis *himself* could be involved somehow."

"Isn't the principal a *good guy?*" I asked, feeling the same knot twist in my stomach.

"I don't know anymore," Maddie replied as she headed back toward the school. "Maybe this goes all the way to the top. That would explain Colton's involvement."

"But he said—" I coughed, realizing I said too much.

Maddie faced me. The look on her face told me she

wasn't going to let me stop talking. "*What* did Colton say? Earlier, you told me he didn't say *anything* to you."

I still didn't know who to trust, so I lied to Maddie. I didn't tell her that Colton had cornered me in the dungeon. "I mean, he just said his orders didn't come from the principal. I told you that earlier."

Maddie's eyes darted back and forth as if she were connecting invisible dots. "If Colton says his orders don't come from Principal Davis, then maybe the principal *is* in on it."

"Does it have to be connected?" I asked. "Could any of this be a coincidence?"

"Could be," Maddie replied softly. "But what if Colton is trying to bring the principal down?"

The knot in my stomach twisted harder. All of this searching had been a boiled down version of a treasure hunt, but now we were involving adults – adults with *power* – into the game. I didn't like that. "We're getting ahead of ourselves," I said. "It's still possible that the journal just contains passwords. If that's all that's in there, it's not that big of a deal."

Maddie turned around and started heading back toward the entrance of the school. "Only one way to find out."

I took a deep breath, and then followed behind her. This wasn't a game I liked playing anymore. Not one bit.

Several minutes later, we were standing outside the hallway to Principal Davis's office. The corridor was completely empty as we scanned the area. The hall monitors were nowhere to be seen, but that only meant it was a matter of time before their rounds brought them back this way.

"So what's the plan?" Maddie whispered.

"The plan?" I asked. "*You're* the one with actual secret agent experience! What do *you* think the plan should be?"

Maddie looked at me. "You're gonna have to go in there."

"*Me?*" I asked loudly. Cupping my hand over my mouth, I waited a moment before speaking again. "There's no way I'm gonna break into the *principal's office!* I'm already in *enough* trouble for the day! If I get caught doing this, then I'm probably looking at actual jail time!"

"Quit being such a drama queen," Maddie laughed.

"Why aren't *you* the one who's gonna break into there?"

"Because I'll be too busy keeping watch out here! You weren't too useful when Mrs. Olsen caught you earlier, and I doubt you'll be useful now! So if you're behind a closed door, you'll probably be just fine."

"Alone in there?" I asked. "Are you nuts?"

Lifting her wristwatch, she spoke. "I'll be with you through this. Remember that they're communicators."

All the fear washed away from my body as I remembered the cool spy watch on my arm. "Oh right! Okay, I'll *do* it!"

Maddie glanced down both ends of the hallway, and then walked to the principal's office door. Turning the handle silently, she pushed it open half an inch. She pressed her face against the open slit, and let the door shut again. "Davis isn't in there. You're good to go."

I handed her my backpack. "What do I do when I'm in there?"

"You'll tell me everything you see," Maddie said, pulling my bag over her shoulders. "Then I'll be able to walk you through the rest."

"What about the last clue?" I asked.

Maddie pulled a tight smile and shrugged her shoulders. "Without knowing what's in there, I can't help you. Once you're inside, maybe you'll understand the clue better," she said. And then she repeated the riddle. "The eagle's nest of Principal Davis's office at 9:00 PM."

"But it's not 9:00 PM," I said.

Maddie nodded. "Right. Like I said, once you're inside, it might make more sense."

"Should I worry about cameras and stuff?" I asked, putting my fingers on the handle of the door.

"Hope not," Maddie said, grinning as she handed me Linus's journal. "Take this with you."

Grabbing the leather notebook, I forced it into my back pocket. I shut my eyes and pushed the door open. Silently, I slipped into the office and let the door shut behind me. The light was switched off, but the room wasn't completely dark. I stepped across the carpet of the dead silent room, studying my surroundings.

In the entire time I've been at Buchanan, I had never once been to the principal's office, which was something I was quite proud of actually. The room was surprisingly larger than I thought it was going to be. A massive bookshelf stood against the wall at the back of the room. In front of that was the principal's desk, made entirely of wood. A leather chair was pushed into the desk.

The only light came from the computer monitor on Principal Davis's desk, but it was bright enough that I could easily see where I was walking.

Framed pictures hung on the wall next to me as I entered farther into the room. There was a small blinking red light at the ceiling. For a moment, I feared that there *was* a camera filming me until I saw that it was only a smoke detector.

The watch on my wrist chirped, and Maddie's voice spoke through the tiny speaker. "What do you see, Valentine?"

I studied the room again as I brought the watch up to my face. "There's a desk in the middle of the room, some pictures on the wall, and a huge bookshelf on the back wall."

"Do you see an eagle's nest anywhere?" she asked.

I looked at the bookshelf. "Nope," I replied. "I don't see a nest of any kind in here."

"Blasted!" her voice chirped. "Keep looking. What else do you see? Anything weird?"

I felt discouraged. "Nothing weird at all. It just looks like a boring office."

"9:00 PM," she said. "Maybe it's not referring to the time, but a direction. Face the principal's desk and look directly to your left."

"My left?" I asked.

"Yes, because if you were standing on a giant clock, 9 PM would be at your left."

Made sense, I thought. I faced the bookshelf and looked at the wall on my left, but it was the only wall that was completely empty. "Nothing," I said into my communicator.

I started walking to the bookshelf at the back of the room. The screen saver from the computer monitor glowed against the books making them easy for me to read. I spoke softly to myself as I studied each shelf. "9:00 PM… eagle's nest at 9:00 PM."

The communicator chirped again. "What're you doing? Did you find anything yet?"

"No," I replied. "Nothing yet. I'm looking at his bookshelf though. Maybe there's something on here."

"Okay, but hurry up," Maddie said. "I think I hear someone coming."

At the top of the bookcase, I saw a green light pulsing on and off. Curious, I started climbing the shelves to get a better look. I only had to pull myself up about a foot before I could see what it was.

Sitting on the middle of the shelf was a round clock with a green dot in the center. Every couple seconds or so, it would slowly glow on and then fade away. Weird, I thought.

I looked at the numbers on the clock, and saw that it actually had the wrong time on it. The arms were pointed in such a way that it was permanently on 9 o'clock.

Clicking my watch again, I whispered. "Wait, I think I might've found something."

Maddie's voice didn't reply.

I clicked the watch again. "Maddie? You there? I said I think I might've found something!"

The only answer I received was the sound of static as it shushed through the tiny speaker. Was she in trouble? I'd have to be quick so I could get back to her.

I looked to the left of the clock, to where 9:00 PM

was pointing. Staring right at me was a thick book titled *Eagle's Nest*.

A chill traveled down my spine as I grabbed the book and hopped back to the floor. Before I opened it, I spoke into my communicator again. "Maddie, I found it! I found the Eagle's Nest! It's a *book!*"

Again, the communicator remained silent.

I wanted to run into the hallway to see if she was alright, but I was too excited about opening Linus's journal. I flipped the book upside-down and shook it back and forth. A miniature golden key bounced on the carpet.

Dropping to my knees, I laid the journal down in front of me. I pushed the key into the socket of the lock, and turned it carefully until I felt it click. Taking a breath, I flipped open the journal and looked inside.

It was empty.

I mean, there wasn't any writing inside it. Instead, the pages had been cut so that a small space was in the center of the book. Linus had turned the journal into a container, and in the middle of the container was a small video player. It was like one of those music players my dad uses when he goes for a run, but it also had a two-inch full color screen on the front of it, doubling as a video recorder.

"What in the world?" I whispered as I held the recorder in my hands. I clicked the "play" button, instantly booting up the device. Were all the passwords on this little video player?

The screen blinked and started playing whatever it was that Linus had been so keen on hiding. In the middle of the dark principal's office, I sat on the floor and watched silently.

It was a video taken a few weeks ago. The date at the beginning of the movie showed me that. It was dark and grainy, but I could tell it was filmed in the lower levers of Buchanan, the dungeon. The person doing the filming was also hidden from view because I could see they were behind a stack of boxes. Linus must've been the one to film it.

The video suddenly started to get shaky as two boys entered into the frame. I didn't recognize the boy on the right, but I knew who the boy on the left was immediately. It was the school president, Sebastian.

My eyes were glued to the screen as the two boys in the video started speaking.

"The box of goods is in the room back here,"
Sebastian said. "There's enough candy to last you at least
a week this time."

The other boy looked nervous. "Here's the money
from all the candy sales. Four hundred bucks total."

"Excellent. This is all going according to plan. You
see? And you were worried this wasn't going to work."

"If you ask me now, I'd still say I was worried.
How long do you think before the school finds out you're
making money selling candy under the noses of the
teachers?"

"Ha ha! They'll never find out! The teachers at this
school have enough on their plate as it is. You think they
really care that kids are eating candy? They're adults
who are too distracted by their jobs. We're fine, and this

business is fine."

"It's really brilliant of you to sell candy to sugar craving kids."

"What can I say? I see where money can be made, and I go there. Maybe you can learn a little somethin' from it."

"The students here don't even have a clue either. That's the best part."

"I know, right? They freely hand over their cash for a chocolate bar. It's unbelievable that they're willing to pay two bucks for a candy bar that cost me fifty cents. Morons."

"Alright then. You say the candy is in the backroom, sir?"

"Yep. I've got, like, ten boxes for you this time. Hand them out so your guys can sell them, but remember – only keep sales of this stuff in the dungeon. Taking it to the upper levels of Buchanan is too risky."

"Right. I'll get the new guy to help me out with the boxes."

"New guy? What new guy? You're supposed to clear all your little goons through me!"

"He's cool. His name is Linus. Trust me. He's legit."

"Hmmm, I don't know. I'll look into him. You'd better hope he's legit, or it's on you."

"Seriously, Sebastian, if Linus was an undercover agent, I'd know it."

"You dolt! I told you to never use my name!"

"Sorry, sir."

"You can never be too careful of who might be watching."

"Right."

"As always, I'll have another shipment of candy for you on Monday. Bring Linus with you. I'd like to meet this kid."

"You got it, sir."

The camera started to get shakier. Linus must've lost his balance because the screen became a blur of motion. Sebastian and the other boy noticed it instantly. I couldn't see their faces anymore, but their voices were still coming through clearly. My eyes felt strained from watching the camera shake wildly. Linus must've been running at this point because he sounded like a dog breathing heavily.

"Don't let him get away!" Sebastian's voice cried out.

"You there!" shouted the second boy's voice. *"Stop him! Get in front of him!"*

The camera shook one last time before the video cut out.

The knot in my stomach returned and my mouth suddenly felt dry. I felt like I was going to puke. This *was* worse than we thought. In fact, I found myself wishing it *was* about a set of stolen passwords. At least, that way it'd be easier to deal with.

I brought the wristwatch back to my face and spoke into the mic. "Maddie, we've got a serious problem here."

She still wasn't answering. Now I was worried.

Hopping to my feet, I slipped the video player into my front pocket and started running to the front door, but I didn't get very far.

At that moment, I felt a sharp pain at the back of my head, and then my entire world went black.

When I opened my eyes, I felt as if my head was spinning. I had no idea where I was except I knew I wasn't in Principal Davis's office anymore. The floor was cold, hard, and damp… and my socks were *wet*…

This brings us back to the beginning of the story, and now you're up to speed with all the junk I've gone through today. Everything that happened has brought me to this point – *not* my best day ever.

I heard the boy ask his question from the shadows of the room, but my head was swelling with pain. "What did you say?" I asked.

The boy paused and then repeated himself. "I *said*, you know this is *over*, right? This little game you and your friends are playing? They've already ratted you out, Brody. You're *done*."

It was a bluff – it *had* to be. Maddie wouldn't do that, would she? Then again, I'm not exactly friends with her so I'm not the expert in what she *would* and *wouldn't* do.

The boy continued to speak from the dark. "Y'know, we were actually getting a little worried that you weren't gonna wake up before the end of the school day. Someone even suggested that we bring the school nurse to see you."

I felt confused. "How long have I been out?"

The boy chuckled. "Almost the entire school day. It was second period when we picked you up, but now it's seventh period – only about twenty more minutes before school is dismissed."

The entire school day? They hit me hard enough to knock me out for almost *five hours?* To be fair though, I *am* a heavy sleeper, and despite the pain in my head, I actually felt well rested. "Where's Maddie?" I asked.

"Where's the *journal?*" the boy replied.

I shook my head and shut my eyes tight. "What're you even talking about? When you guys knocked me out, I was *looking* at the journal!"

The boy paused. "But if *that* was the journal…"

I lowered my gaze.

The boy spoke again. "The book you were looking at *was* the journal we're all after isn't it?"

I didn't answer.

"But it had a large hole cut out of it," he continued. "Which can only mean there was something *else* inside the journal. Something that you *found* before we grabbed you."

Glancing at my jeans, I could see the bump in my pocket from the video player I slipped into it. Whoever kidnapped me never bothered to check my pockets for anything! I could feel a fit of laughter coming on, but I pushed it down deep into my gut and tightened a smile. What a bunch of *noobs!*

The boy LOL'd. "You totally just gave yourself away, you know that?"

"What?" I asked, dazed.

"You *looked* at your pocket!" he said throwing his arms out. "You might as well have just *told* me it was in your jeans!"

I licked my teeth, trying to come up with a bluff of my own, but I still couldn't think straight. I guess *I* was the only noob in the room.

Finally, the boy stepped into the light, and I saw his

face clearly. It was Sebastian, the president of Buchanan School. He held his open palm to me. "Hand it over, Mr. Valentine."

Defeated, I reached into my pocket and removed the tiny video player. I set it into Sebastian's hand, but not without glaring at him the entire time. Man, if only I had laser eyes, right?

Just then, I heard the muffled sound of someone struggling nearby. I glanced over my shoulder, to the spot in the corner behind me. The whole area was shrouded in darkness, but there was definitely someone back there. It *had* to have been Maddie.

"Let her go!" I cried, facing Sebastian again.

Sebastian laughed. "You think that's *Madison* back there?"

Baffled, I said, "Well, I *did*... up until you said *that*."

I watched as the president stepped around my chair and to the other kid in the room. He grabbed both sides of their chair, and started dragging it across the floor. As he pulled it into the light, I saw that it actually *wasn't* Maddie. "Linus?" I whispered.

Linus leaned forward in the chair as the president released it. The tape over his mouth prevented him from talking, but it didn't stop him from groaning loudly. Sebastian pinched a corner of the tape and ripped it off Linus's face.

Linus clenched his teeth, sucking air through them, making the sound someone does when they get hurt.

"*Sssssssssssssssssssss!*"

I felt a wave of emotion splash through my body, and I started talking rapidly. "Where have you *been* all day? Did you *mean* to run into me this morning? Why did you decide to involve *me* in any of this? Have you been *planning* it for awhile?"

Linus took a breath and licked his lips. Then he glared at me. "I can't believe you just gave up my video player like that."

"*Why* can't you believe it?" I shouted, angry. "I'm just a kid that goes to school here that never asked for any of this! I didn't *want* this! I didn't wake up this morning thinking, 'hey, I hope I get caught up in some secret agent conspiracy today!'"

Linus shook his head at me disapprovingly. Then he looked at the president. "So now that you've got the video player, what do you intend on doing with it?"

"This thing?" the president asked as he held it up. "You can bet your little video will get deleted. None of what you've filmed will come to light."

"The truth will come out sooner or later," Linus replied as he exhaled slowly. He was pretty badly beaten up.

"But why?" I asked. "Why sell kids a bunch of candy? It doesn't make sense!"

"Doesn't it?" the president replied.

"Wait a second," I said, feeling confused. "Where's the list of passwords then? What happened to all that?"

Linus shook his head, staring at the ground. He spit on the cement and spoke. "There was never a list of passwords," he whispered. "I only said that to get Sebastian and his goons off my trail."

"It didn't work out that way, did it?" Sebastian growled.

"No," Linus whispered. "It didn't."

I still wasn't sure exactly what Sebastian was after. "So then... candy sales, and money? That's what you're doing? Because I'd be disappointed if your only goal in all this was to make money. That's a pretty stereotypical 'bad guy' thing to do. I would hope that after all the trouble I've been through today, you'd prove to be a *real* villain. Unless your evil plan is actually a *long term* one.

Are you going to be a dentist when you grow up? Are you giving everyone a crazy amount of cavities so they'll come see you one day?"

The president found my questions funny, and laughed an evil laugh. "Most of the times, it's the obvious answer that's correct. I'm sorry to disappoint you, but this *is* about money. I have no desire to grow up to become a super villain dentist."

"How unoriginal," I hissed.

The president set the video player on the table at the side of the room. "It might be unoriginal, but look who has the most power. Me. *I'm* the one making money off unsuspecting kids at this school, and you know the best part? They *willingly* give me their cash for candy bars. I control the candy sales, and you know what that means?"

Linus and I sat silently, waiting for Sebastian to answer his own question.

"It means *power*," the president finally said. "*Money* brings *power*."

"But you're the president of Buchanan," I said. "You've already *got* power."

Sebastian straightened his posture and adjusted his necktie. "It wasn't enough for me. As president, sure, I control a few things, but now that I have everyone's money, I'm on a whole new level of *control*."

"A whole new level of *crazy*," I said, under my breath.

"In the land of the poor, the richest kid is king," Sebastian said.

The way he said it made me cringe, and I was beginning to think he actually *did* sound like a real villain. To me, the difference between bad guys and villains is that bad guys *don't* consider themselves as bad guys because they *think* they're doing something *good*. Villains, on the other hand, *know* they're doing something *bad*, but don't care because they *want* to do it. President Sebastian was definitely starting to *sound* like a *villain*.

Sebastian tapped his hand on Linus's shoulder. "And you almost foiled my plans, didn't you?"

Linus jerked his shoulder away from the president's touch.

Sebastian continued. "And I can keep this up all year. My parents have a membership at one of those 'buy in bulk' stores so I have them pick up a few boxes every week. The teachers have no clue what's going on under them. It's hilarious actually."

I didn't see the humor in it. Burping the alphabet is hilarious – taking money from kids isn't. Great, I thought. Just what Buchanan needed – a bully with power. I wonder if adults ever had to deal with people like this.

All of a sudden, there was a short clicking sound on the cement floor. Sebastian spun in place and stared at the concrete, looking for the source of the noise. Linus and I also scanned the ground, but couldn't see anything.

And then the worst smell in the history of all smells entered my nose. It smelled like a sewage plant had exploded next to a graveyard of fish, and the fish just finished having a dirty diaper fight, all in front of a pile of burning tires.

It. Was. Awful.

STINK LINES

Sebastian started hacking, as if he swallowed some water down the wrong pipe. He clutched at his throat and turned back to face us. "Which one of you let out that fluffy biscuit?"

I stared at the president, completely puzzled by what was just said.

"What's a *fluffy biscuit?*" Linus laughed.

Through his coughs, the president continued to point blame at us. "You guys are sick, man! Sick! I can't be in here! Oh man, I'm gonna *barf!*"

His reaction was hilarious, but I also felt like I was

about to puke all over the place. I looked at Linus, who had his hand up to me, telling me to wait a moment.

The president hacked again, and then sprinted toward the door. Without looking back, he flipped it open and jumped through. I could hear the pitter patter of his feet on linoleum as he darted down the hallway.

I pinched my nose shut and gasped for breath through my mouth. "What *is* that? OMG, it smells like my grandma's bathroom after we eat burritos!"

Linus jumped up from his chair and poked his head through the door. He stepped backward and snickered.

Maddie entered into the room with her hands over her mouth and nose. "Oh, that's awful!" she said, her voice muffled through her palms.

"What *is* it though?" I asked, embarrassed that my voice was a couple notches higher since I was pinching my nose shut.

"It's the stink bombs from the spy kit," Maddie said. "You stuffed them in your backpack, remember? But I've never used them before so I didn't know how many to set off... so I set *all* of them off."

My eyes were starting to water as I shuffled across the room. "At least it got Sebastian out of here, but he's still got the—" I shut my mouth, shocked as I looked at the table across the room. The video player was still there! I grabbed it and held it out to Maddie and Linus. "He forgot this! He left without taking it!"

Linus smiled. "We gotta get outta here before he comes back! And that'll be any second!"

"Yeah," Maddie said. "If it's not him, then you know he'll send some monitors our way."

"But what do we do with it?" Linus asked, stepping into the hallway. "School's almost out so we're running out of time! We need to show the student body this video, but *how*? How can we show *everybody* this video?"

And then I remembered the televisions Buchanan School had recently installed in the hallways. They were used to make announcements and were also hooked up to the school-wide speaker system. "We can use the televisions!"

Linus's jaw dropped as he slapped his thigh. "You're right! There has to be a way we can hook it up to those TVs! Where would the command center for that be though?"

"It has to be in the front office!" Maddie said. "I've made announcements a couple times, and every time I did, I had to speak into a little microphone in that office!"

"But do they play the videos there?" I asked.

"I don't know," said Linus, "but there's only one way to find out! Follow me!"

As Maddie and Linus sprinted down the hallway, I did my best to keep up with them, but that cramp in my side just wouldn't leave me alone. I slowed to a stop and rested my hands on my knees.

"Guys, wait!" I shouted.

Maddie stopped first. Linus ran a little more before he realized we weren't right behind him.

"What gives?" Maddie cried. "Are you alright?"

I nodded as I approached her. "Yeah, I'm fine," I said, holding the small video player out to her. "Take this though. I'm done. I just can't do this anymore."

Maddie's look of concern morphed into a look of anger. "What do you mean? You've been doing this all day and you wanna quit right before the finish line?"

I sighed, nodding. "I'm not like you guys. I'm not cool or popular or sporty or whatever… it's probably best if you two take off without me. I'm only holding you back."

"Right," Linus said, upset. "Because we're waiting around for you to make a decision right now!"

"I thought I could do this," I said. "But it turns out I can't. I just can't run around pretending to be something I'm not."

Maddie walked toward me. I could tell from the tone of her voice that she was still angry. "Let me tell you the truth about life – nobody is ever what they *pretend* to be. You probably look at all the cool kids and think they've got their stuff together, but they don't. They're exactly like you, but with one important difference – they know who they *want* to be, and they're working toward that goal. If you don't have something you're reaching for, then life is *safe* isn't it? And safe is *boring*."

I curled my lip and shook my head. It was like she could read my mind! Easy is boring, and boring is good... *used* to be good. The truth was that this entire day came out of left field... but I wouldn't have wanted it any other way.

Linus put his hand on my shoulder. "You were a secret agent with Maddie today, right?"

I nodded. "I was a kid helping a friend."

"Then *that's* who you are," Maddie said with a smirk.

Out of the blue, I heard Colton's voice speak sharply. "Isn't this cute. It looks like the three of you are dishin' out life lessons over here. Care to spoon a couple dollops into a bowl for me?"

At the corner of the hallway, I saw Colton and his two hall monitors blocking our path. The president was behind them, plugging his nose, and yelling with a high-pitched voice. "Get them! They've got something that belongs to me!"

Linus spun in place. He grabbed Maddie's hand and looked back at me. Then he moved his other hand toward my body and pretended to snatch the video player. With a smile, he winked at me, and I knew exactly what he was thinking. He wanted to act as if he had the video player in his hands so the monitors would chase after him instead of me. Pulling Maddie down the hallway, Linus started running toward Colton and the president.

Immediately, I took off in the opposite direction. I heard the president shouting from behind me and when I looked back, I saw the monitors chasing after Maddie and Linus. Their plan had worked!

I could feel the tiny rectangular video player in my hand as I neared the end of the corridor. The halls of Buchanan were designed almost like a flower, with the front lobby being at the center. All passages hooked long circles until meeting back at the center, which meant that if you followed your path long enough, you'd find yourself in the front lobby.

Maddie and Linus had run in one direction, and I was sprinting down the opposite path they took, but eventually our paths would cross again. I only hoped that they'd be smart enough to guide the monitors down another part of the school, and away from the front office. Of course they would... secret agents are smart like that.

My shoes squeaked on the freshly polished linoleum flooring as I bolted through the halls of Buchanan. The green lockers on both sides of me became a blur the faster I ran. In the entire time I've been a student here, I've never torn through a hallway like this – it was *exciting*. Without any teachers to order me to slow down, I felt as free as a bird. My side wasn't even cramping!

As the corner bent a little more sharply, I was forced to slow down, which gave me enough time to see if any of the monitors were following me. I was relieved to see they *weren't*.

There wasn't much time left before school let out. I only had minutes at most, so whatever was going to happen needed to happen fast. With the video player in my hand, it was my responsibility to get to the front offices and figure out how to get it to broadcast over the school's television sets.

Without Maddie or Linus to help guide me, I was totally on my own, and you know what? I *loved* it. For the first time in the entire day, I actually felt like *I* was in control of the situation. Buchanan's president was at the heart of a major scandal, and it was up to me to let everyone know about it.

Finally, the front lobby came into view as I took the last turn in the hall. I burst into the area and headed for the office. Pressing the handle down, I heard a click and pushed the door open. The motions lights flickered on overhead, which meant there wasn't anyone else in there. Good thing too because if there was, I'm not sure what I would've done.

There was a long rectangular counter that separated the front of the office from the back. I could see several computer monitors glowing, but no obvious place for me to hook up the video player. Sitting at the end of the counter was an old rusted microphone. I remembered that Maddie said she made the announcements through that a few times, so I knew I had to be close.

I pulled myself up on the counter and swung my legs around until landing on my feet on the other side. I heard my shirt tear and felt a pain as something scraped my arm. Along the side of the counter were plastic hooks that stuck out a few inches. Hanging from those hooks were sets of keys, probably for doors in the school. "Great," I muttered as I examined my torn sleeve. "Mom's not gonna be happy with *that*."

I turned around, and then I saw it – the area *under* the microphone had a small box hooked up to several kinds of video machines. There was a laptop computer, a DVD player, a CD player, and a cable that was hanging freely. It was the same kind of cable my dad used to hook our digital camera up to our television at home. That was it!

But before I could do anything, someone punched me right in my back. I keeled over against the counter, luckily missing all the hooks. Groaning in pain, I rolled to my back and saw Colton standing over me. "You punched me in the *back!*"

ANGRY COLTON

"You've become a real *thorn* in my side, you know that?" Colton growled.

I chuckled, scooting myself backward. "The school *deserves* to know the truth… the truth the president desperately wants to *hide!* These kids are getting taken advantage of by a bully in a suit, and I'm gonna make sure it doesn't happen again!"

Colton stepped forward. "Hand over the device!"

Holding my side, I scooted across the carpet, away from the crazy kid. "How can you take orders from Sebastian?" I shouted. "How can you choose to be on his team after all he's done?"

Colton wiped his lip as he stepped toward me. "I don't know anything about what you're talking about. All I know is that the school's president gave me the order to get that thing back from you, so that's what I'm doing!"

"So you don't even know what's on here?" I asked.

Colton shook his head. "It's none of my business, and by the bad day you've had, I'd say it was none of *yours* either."

Holding the video player in my fist, I kept inching my way closer to the hanging cable under the mic. "You're making a mistake," I said, noticing that Colton was next to the plastic hooks.

Colton's face clenched up as he grew angrier. "I'm afraid you're the one who's made a mistake!" he cried as he reached for me.

I dropped the video player and rolled to my feet. Just as I stood, Colton grabbed my shirt and squeezed his fists tight. I held his wrists as he pushed me backward, but I caught the counter with my foot and shoved back.

We struggled against each other until I finally managed to get my arms between us. With all of my might, I pushed against him, separating us completely. Colton fell against the counter, losing his balance. With my free hand, I grabbed the back of his leather belt and forced him back until I felt the exposed hooks. With the rest of my strength, I lifted him up until his belt was over one of the plastic hooks, and then I let go.

"Hey!" Colton shouted. "*What're you doing?*"

I caught my breath as I stumbled about. "*Hang out* and you'll see," I sneered in my best "action hero" voice.

Colton was half a foot off the ground, kicking his feet wildly. He was high enough that he couldn't touch the floor.

I turned around, and limped over to the video player. There were only a few minutes of class remaining so I had time. After I grabbed device from the floor, I connected the hanging cable into the socket at the top. The televisions in the hallway flashed on instantly. Shutting my eyes, I hit the play button. The speakers in the ceiling rasped as the sound of President Sebastian's voice spoke. Through the windows of the front office, I watched the footage all over again as it played through every TV in the school.

Colton's jaw dropped as he stared at the video feed. "I'll be a monkey's uncle…" he whispered.

The cafeteria was right across the lobby and through the windows, I could see kids raise their heads as the footage played on. Their faces were shocked as the president spoke on over the speakers.

Linus and Maddie suddenly appeared in the lobby. The hall monitors chasing after them slowed to a stop in front of the television and all four of them watched. Maddie hadn't seen the video yet, so she cupped her hand over her mouth, stunned.

Sebastian appeared jogging through the lobby and clutching at his side, probably from a cramp. His eyes were peeled wide open as he gawked at the television screen. I couldn't hear his voice, but I could read his lips as he said, "No no no no no…"

When the video finally finished, the television screens blinked, and switched off. It was done at last, and the weight on my shoulders disappeared.

For the last time, the speaker in the ceiling cackled. "President Sebastian, please report to the principal's office. Sebastian, please report to the principal's office. *NOW!*"

Through the window, I saw Sebastian glare at me. I was almost afraid that his eyes were going to crack the glass. The two hall monitors took him by the arms and marched him down the lobby, disappearing through the door to Principal Davis's office.

Maddie and Linus stepped into the room I was in. Maddie had a grin beaming on her face as Linus helped Colton off the hook on the counter.

"We're not going to have any more trouble, are we?" Linus asked the boy hanging from the plastic hook.

Colton sighed as the tension vanished from his face. "Nope. As far as I see it, this is over. I'm pretty sure my orders won't be coming from Sebastian anytime soon."

"What'll you do now?" Linus asked Colton.

Colton shrugged his shoulders. "I'm not sure," he said. "I think after all this, I'll need a vacation."

Maddie and Linus laughed. Colton nodded his head at me, and stepped out of the room.

Linus turned and spoke. "Looks like you saved the day, rookie."

"I couldn't have done it without you two," I replied, winking at Maddie. "But what about the principal? We still don't know if he's in on it."

Linus shook his head. "He's *not*. My orders came from *him*. They always do. He knew something was going on with the candy sales and ordered me to go undercover and look into it."

"But why was the journal hidden in his office then?" Maddie asked.

"Because Sebastian was already coming after me, and I figured that's the last place he would ever think to look," Linus replied. "I mean, who's crazy enough to break into Principal Davis's office?"

Maddie pointed her thumb at me. "*This* guy."

"You really proved yourself to be somethin' else today, Mr. Valentine," Linus said, putting a hand on my shoulder. "We could really use a kid like you on our team."

"You mean you didn't choose me on purpose?" I asked.

Linus laughed. "No, I *did* choose you. I've been thinking you'd be a good addition for some time now. I'm just glad it wasn't a mistake."

"But we never did anything together that would get you to think that," I replied.

"I could just see it in you," Linus said confidently.

"Sometimes it takes that extra little push to get people to do great things," Maddie added.

I scratched the back of my neck and took a deep breath. "I still think this might've been a little *too* much excitement for one day."

Maddie threw her arms out. "Oh, come on, Brody! You know this was probably the best day you've ever had!"

I stood thinking for a moment – now that I know there's a secret agency working in the shadows of Buchanan School, I'm not sure I could go on living the life of a normal student ever again.

Another smile appeared on Maddie's face. "The life of an agent is never dull."

"She's right," Linus added. "Sebastian's scandal with the candy was just the *tip* of the iceberg. There's more going on than anyone knows."

Now I was curious. "Like what?"

Maddie wagged her finger at me as she stepped toward the door. "That's classified information that only *agents* are allowed to know…"

Linus set a business card down on the counter. The only thing printed on it was an inkblot in the shape of a raven and some roman numerals. "If you're interested in what we're offering… you can find us there," he said, walking behind Maddie out of the room.

I stared at the business card – a raven with some roman numerals underneath it. It was obvious that the picture of the raven was a clue I had to solve in order to find the agency Linus and Maddie were a part of. I couldn't help but smirk at the idea of having to figure it out.

The bell to the school rang as I approached the exit to the office. As kids raced through the lobby, I could hear fits of laughter echo off the walls as they gossiped about Sebastian and the video they just watched.

It occurred to me that it wasn't so much the sugary treats that were a bad thing, but the idea that someone was ripping kids off by selling those treats in an underground market. The vending machines with healthy snacks weren't going anywhere anytime soon, but maybe Principal Davis would be open to the idea of having a few junkie items. I mean, the majority of students at Buchanan School *were* kids, right?

Leaning in the entryway to the front office, I tried to see where Maddie and Linus might've gone, but amidst the sea of students, they had completely vanished. I overheard some of the others laughing, joking about Sebastian's scandal, and how this was probably the most awful day Buchanan School had ever seen.

A smile broke on my face as Maddie's words slipped into my mind again. I glanced at the business card, and realized she was absolutely correct. While this might've been a bad day for Buchanan School, it definitely turned out to be one of the *best* days in *my* life.

I watched the faces of kids as they passed me, and then remembered the other thing Maddie had said. Nobody had their act together any more than I did.

But the difference between then and now was that now I *knew* who I wanted to be now, and I knew what I had to do to get there.

Shutting my eyes, I stepped out of the room as Brody Valentine, and into the hall as *secret agent* Brody Valentine. I was determined to do everything I could to find the answer to Linus's business card, and become the agent I was *born* to be.

...let's just hope there aren't any *bees* involved.

SECRET AGENT 2
6th GRADER
ICE COLD SUCKERPUNCH

There I was on the rooftop of the school, looking over the side of the building as the *entire* squadron of hall monitors closed in behind me. I glanced over my shoulder, trying to estimate how much time I had before they caught me.

Ten seconds at best.

I was completely cornered without a single escape option. I leaned my head over the edge and saw the grass two stories down. There were groups of students clumped together over most of the schoolyard and parking lot,

1

staring and pointing fingers at me. The wind picked up and blew my hair around, making my stomach queasy.

Looking to the sky, I did my best to push the dizzy feeling out of my body. If I stared at the clouds or something, maybe I could trick myself into thinking I *wasn't* on the rooftop of my school.

A small flock of flying birds caught my eye. I found myself wishing I had wings. How had my life come to this? I'm just a sixth grader in a boring school! My hobbies were video games, drawing, and blending into my surroundings! So how was it that every hall monitor was chasing after me? How was it that the principal wanted to throw me in detention for the rest of my life?

I gripped my hand around the canvas strap on my shoulder and pulled it tighter. The time capsule attached to the strap pressed against my shirt as it rose. The weight of the capsule surprised me. It was heavy – heavier than I expected, at least.

How could such a small container be the source of so much trouble?

I took a breath, listening to the footsteps of a hundred monitors circle behind me. I know, right? *A hundred* monitors for *me*. Seems like a bit of an overreaction for one kid…

But instead of being afraid, I smiled, confident that even a *hundred* of 'em couldn't stop me.

My name is Brody Valentine, and this is the story of the best *and* worst day of my entire life.

It started earlier that morning. I missed the bus so my dad had to drop me off at school, which actually meant that I was a little early since my bus was always late. With the extra few minutes I had to spare, my dad gave me a couple bucks so I could eat breakfast in the cafeteria before school started.

"Two dollars enough, Brody?" my dad asked through the rolled down window of his car.

"Yeah," I replied, stuffing the dollar bills into my front pocket. "It'll be fine."

My dad smiled at me. "Put that in your wallet!"

"I *will*," I said, "but my wallet is in my *locker* so I'll have to grab it from there first."

"Why don't you carry it around?" he asked.

"I don't know," I replied, trying to think of a nicer way to say that the wallet was uglier than a goat's butt. It was made of white leather and had little metal spikes that lined the outside of it. At the center of the spikes was a red "X" that my dad drew with a marker. He said it was punk rock, but I thought it looked like something a vampire would carry. "I just don't think about it after I toss it in my locker."

I saw my dad shrug his shoulders. "Well, get used to it," he said, and then he playfully added, "That's part of growing up!"

I smirked. A leather vampire wallet was part of growing up?

"Have a good day," my dad said. "Try not to break too many hearts, *Mr. Valentine*, okay?"

I hated when he joked about our last name like that. Just because it's "Valentine" didn't automatically make me smooth with the ladies. I shot him a thumbs-up and groaned. "Roger roger. Ten-four. Copy that."

My dad rolled up the window and peeled out of the parking lot. I'm not sure if it was on purpose to make me think he was cool or if it was an accident because he wasn't too great with a clutch. Anyway, it would've been embarrassing if there were any other students outside, but since I was early, there weren't. Lucky me.

I walked up to the front doors of the school and

glanced at the sign looming overhead. As a sixth grader at Buchanan School, I had walked under this sign every day since the first day of kindergarten, but never really looked at it until that moment.

The "B" at the beginning of "Buchanan" was nearly twice as big as my head. The rest of the letters were about half that size. As I studied the letters, I noticed the last "n" looked wonky, almost as if it wanted to run away. Oh well. That's what you get when you go to a school that doesn't really care for things like "maintenance."

After I stepped through the front doors, I immediately made my way toward the kitchen. I decided to skip my locker, which meant my wallet would have to stay in there for the time being. I didn't mind. The spikes made that thing uncomfortable in my back pocket anyway.

There were a couple kids in the breakfast line so I grabbed a tray and took my place behind them. As I looked over what the kitchen was serving for breakfast, I overhead some of the kids talking.

"That time capsule is getting dug up this morning, isn't it?" a boy asked.

"That's right, I forgot all about that," replied the girl he was talking to. "They're doing it right after the bell rings, aren't they?"

"Yeah," the boy said, pointing to a spot behind her. "And it's gonna get broadcast all over the school's television system."

I glanced over my shoulder looking at the television he was pointing at. Hanging from the wall was one of the large LED televisions Buchanan School used to make announcements. On the screen was a slideshow switching between images of sports games and random reminders of when a certain club was going to meet. I imagined the video of Sebastian playing on the screen and then chuckled quietly to myself.

It's only been a week since Sebastian was busted for the candy scandal, but he was already back at school. He got two days of detention for it, but since our school has a "three strikes," policy, he was still allowed to be the president of Buchanan. I guess that means he can perform two more "random acts of evil" before they decide he's not fit to be leader or something? Oh well, right? Not much I can do about it now, and actually there's not much I *want* to do about it anymore. Getting involved in the candy scandal was *more* than enough excitement for me.

It's strange to think the whole thing only took place a week ago. Sebastian was selling overpriced candy to the students of Buchanan. Most of the operation took place in the lower level of the school, which is also known as "the dungeon." I found a video of him talking about his plans and played it through the television system so everyone would know how much of a turd that kid was.

AGENT LINUS   AGENT MADDIE

But I didn't do it alone. There were two kids that got me caught up in that whole mess. A boy named Linus, and a girl named Maddie. The two claim they work for a secret agency located somewhere in the school, and after the events of last week, I don't doubt them for a second.

Did it completely change my life and flip it upside down? Nope. Mostly because nobody even knew it was happening. The only thing anyone saw was a video that started playing by itself at the end of the day. I'm pretty alright with that though. I'm a bit of a loner at this school – not cool, not *un*cool, but somewhere in the middle, which makes me more invisible than you'd think.

Once sixth grade started, everyone began separating into different groups while I sort of stayed in my own little world. There are other kids I talk to now and again, but I seriously doubt they'd know my name if you asked them. It's cool though. It doesn't bother me if I don't think about it.

Anyway, right after that mess with Sebastian ended, Linus handed me a business card that had an inkblot of a raven with the numbers 17 and 4 in roman numerals on it. He said if I was interested in what they were offering, I could find them there, which meant if I wanted to join their secret agency, I would have to solve the puzzle on the card.

I haven't tried to figure out the clue on the business card yet, but it's still in my wallet. I wanted to take it easy before deciding whether or not to follow through. It was a crazy and exhausting thrill ride that I couldn't say I'd like to experience ever again.

…but it doesn't seem to matter where I *hide* from trouble because trouble is super good at *finding* me.

After grabbing an orange juice and a biscuit, I

stepped into the cafeteria and scanned the room for a seat. Even though it was early, there were still plenty of students who were already at school. I guess a few of them have clubs or morning basketball practice they have to be at. I hope to have an ounce or two of athletic ability someday so I could be one of those kids at practice, but I think I need to fill out my scrawny little body first or I'll likely break a bone.

The cafeteria was a mess of confusion as I walked down an aisle. Metal curtain rods were scattered at various parts of the room and had black sheets draped over them. It almost looked like a crudely created maze. How anyone was able to find a spot was beyond me because I seriously almost forgot where I was as I peeked down every aisle. At one point, I thought I found the end of the maze, but instead I found myself back in the lobby of the school.

"Really?" I grunted, spinning in place with my tray in hand. I headed back to try and find a seat. After a few more minutes of frustration, I found my way out of the maze of sheets and stood in front of the open floor of the cafeteria.

Finally, I saw an empty table near the back that looked like a great spot for a quiet breakfast alone.

Setting my tray down, I took a seat on the bench. The table I chose was right next to the stage. And then I saw the reason for all the draped sheets. The drama club was using those sheets as a set for one of their productions.

I had totally forgotten about the play until I saw the rest of the stage. Watching from my spot, I saw a bunch of students hard at work moving random items around on the stage, preparing for a drama they were supposed to put on for the rest of the sixth grade class during lunch. It was about a football team that had to learn how to accept a werewolf as one of their teammates. Funny, right? Some kid named Brayden was in charge of it. Some say he's a werewolf fanboy, while others say he's just weird. Either way, the drama meant missing a few classes so I was all for it.

After scarfing down my biscuit, I glanced at the clock. There were only a few minutes left until homeroom, so I snatched my backpack off the floor and hopped into the lobby.

The sea of students was already splashing violently in the hallways of the school. I squeezed the straps of my backpack, kept my head down, and dove in, determined to make it to homeroom without drowning.

Luckily my class was just down the hall so all I had to do was basically flow with the blob of students until my door was in view. After getting lurched a few times by the current, I was able to slip safely into my classroom.

Just as I took my seat, I heard the bell ring. School had officially started.

Instantly, the television at the front of the room flickered on. It took a minute before anyone even noticed, but the hushed whispers from students slowly silenced as the school news started playing janky intro music.

I sighed, listening to the lead guitar and obvious electric drum machine play behind a cheesy jingle written by one of the younger gym teachers in the school. Once the music finished with a drum solo, some blue and white graphics appeared onscreen as the video zoomed in on a sixth grade reporter.

EARLY WORM NEWS REPORT
DEBBIE JOHNSON

"Good morning, Buchanan School," said the girl reporter as she held a microphone in front of her face. "My name is Debbie Johnson, and you're watching The Early Worm News Report."

I sunk into my desk and leaned back, settling in for a lame news update about some kind of time capsule.

Debbie continued as the camera followed her, shaking slightly from the cameraman. "As most of you already know, today is the day that Mrs. Olsen's science class has decided to dig up the time capsule that was buried back in 1999."

Was 1999 considered a long time ago? I guess it *was* before any sixth grader was born.

"And we're here live so you won't miss a second of it!" Debbie said, smiling. "Many years ago, back in the last *century*, Mrs. Olsen's science class filled a plastic tube with things that were considered popular and valuable to them."

One of the students off camera shouted. "The *real* news story is that Mrs. Olsen is old enough that she was still a teacher! That was like, last millennia or whatever!"

A bunch of kids in my homeroom class laughed.

Debbie laughed too, but ignored the comment as she walked through the schoolyard. "A time capsule, for those of you who don't know, is a container filled with items that are considered important during the year it was buried – items that tell the story of what life was like long ago. And a capsule from the year 1999 is sure to have some *super* old school stuff, such as VHS tapes or even CDs. Did you know if kids wanted to listen to music back then, they'd have to play something called a 'compact disc' or 'CD,' which was similar to a DVD, but wasn't able to play movies or anything. And what's worse is that those CDs only held about 15 songs and could only be played in a CD player!"

Some chuckling came from the front of the room. I have to admit that I laughed a little too. Debbie was poking fun at the idea that CDs were something we didn't understand.

Finally, Debbie reached the spot where Mrs. Olsen's science class had started digging. It was on the other side of the school, near the garbage bin that was next to the monkey bars. If you remember, that's where Linus had left his journal for Maddie and me to find last week. I'm *sure* it was just a coincidence.

Debbie turned back to the camera and put on her game face. "As you can see behind me, the digging has already started. Mrs. Olsen's entire first period science class is on the sidelines, waiting with teeth clenched as more of the dirt is moved away. Mrs. Olsen is here at the dig site along with Principal Davis and Coach Cooper," Debbie said as she moved toward Mrs. Olsen. Pointing the microphone at the science teacher's face, Debbie spoke. "Do you have anything to say to our viewers?"

Mrs. Olsen curled her lip. "I *heard* that joke about my age," she snipped.

Debbie stumbled over her words. "Uh, um, I uh… no no no. That wasn't *me.* That was some other student that shouted over me."

"Mm hmm," Mrs. Olsen hummed with her lips pressed together. "We'll see when I review the footage. That's fine, can we just start over? Walk up to me again and ask that same question."

Debbie looked confused. "Mrs. Olsen, we're *live* on air *right now.*"

Mrs. Olsen's face immediately flushed with rage,

but she did her best to keep it in check. Through her teeth, she sneered. "Would've been nice of you to say that to *begin* with," she whispered. The rage disappeared from her face as her mouth cracked a smile. "But yes, Debbie, we're all very excited to see what the time capsule from 1999 carries within it."

"You're so old that you forgot, right?" Debbie joked.

Mrs. Olsen bit her lip. It was obvious that she was about to explode, especially since the camera was slowly zooming in on the throbbing blood vessel on her forehead. "Funny," she said. "Just *wait* till you're in class, young lady."

All of a sudden the camera jerked to the side. There were shouts coming from the dig site, but because the video was shaking so violently, it was impossible to tell what was happening. It looked like a horror movie. The screams only made it *more* scary.

Mrs. Olsen's voice cut through the blurry footage. "What do you mean there's nothing there? That's impossible! The capsule should be there! What do you mean 'you think I'm *too old* to remember?'"

The image on the television was a green blur along with the heavy breathing of the cameraman. The green was probably from the grass. The heavy breathing was probably because he was chubby.

"It's not here anymore!" shouted a girl's voice from the television.

Debbie's voice answered. "What do you mean

14

'*anymore?*'"

At last, the camera focused in on the dig site. Most of Mrs. Olsen's science class was huddled around the massive hole they had dug.

The girl continued to speak as the camera focused on her hand pointing at the hole. "You can tell that something *used* to be buried there! See how the shape of the dirt looks like something had been pressed into it for several years? That must be from the time capsule, but it's clearly not there anymore! It's *missing!*"

The camera continued to switch between blurry and sharp as the image zoomed in closer to a dirty object at the bottom of the pit. I had to look away from the screen to keep from getting motion sickness. A boy hopped into the hole and started reaching for it.

Debbie spoke as the camera continued to go in and out of focus. "Hold on one second, viewers! It looks as though the time capsule has gone missing! *Stolen* from the dig site before anyone even dug it up!"

Everyone in my homeroom was suddenly interested, leaning forward in their desks. Even *I* was on the edge of my seat, shocked that someone would do such a terrible thing.

On the screen, the camera was still focused on the boy in the pit, studying the dirt covered object.

"What's that you have there?" Debbie asked, pointing her microphone at the middle of the pit.

The boy spoke loudly as he brushed off the object. "I'm not sure exactly. It looks like... like a *wallet* or something!"

Oh, buuuurn! The thief forgot their wallet at the scene of the crime! *Classic* dumb criminal mistake! I leaned back, put my hands behind my head, and waited for the news reporter to open the wallet and solve the crime already.

Debbie snatched the wallet out of the boy's hands and held it in front of the camera. The video was still shaky and blurry, but some of the features of the wallet were pretty clear. Most of the dirt had been scraped off and revealed that the leather was white.

Weird, I thought. Someone else besides me owns a white leather wallet? I shook my head, feeling sorry for the kid who owned the wallet because he was about to get called out on live television.

I watched the screen and noticed that the wallet in Debbie's hands had other similarities to my own wallet, which was in my locker. Along the edges were little spikes embedded into the leather, and at the center of the those spikes was… a red letter "X" that was drawn with a *marker*.

Uh-oh…

My heart sank into my butt as I stared at the screen. There had to be *two* of these punk rock vampire wallets in the world, right? Mine couldn't have been the *only* one in existence!

I watched the blurry video of Debbie's face as she fumbled about, trying to keep the microphone in her hand as she flipped over the wallet.

Everyone in the room started to whisper their own theories to one another as the news report played on. A couple kids suggested that a secret underground society of ninjas stole the time capsule. Someone even started ranting about how there was *never* a capsule to begin with and it's all some kind of crazy conspiracy. I even heard someone say it was probably time traveling cavemen. I mean, come on, really? Time traveling cavemen?

"Keep the camera on me," Debbie muttered as she flipped open the white wallet.

A voice from off screen shouted. "Who's wallet is it? Who would do such a shady thing?"

Debbie paused, holding the wallet up to the camera. The shaky video struggled to focus on the student I.D. that was tucked behind a plastic cover. Finally, the face on the I.D. was as clear as day.

"Brody Valentine! This wallet belongs to Brody Valentine!" Debbie shouted.

Everyone in the room gasped at the same instant as if they were trying to suck *all* the oxygen from the air. I think I was the only one who couldn't breath. I sat in my chair, completely stupefied and frozen in shock as the other kids looked at one another, puzzled and asking questions out loud.

"Who's Brody Valentine?"

"There's a kid at Buchanan with the last name 'Valentine?'"

"That name has to be a joke, right? No one here has a goofy name like that."

"Pretty sure that I.D. is fake. That sounds like a rock star's name."

Lucky for me, nobody in the class knew who I was. Or wait… was that lucky? Or just sad? Oh well, that one kid said I had a rock star's name, so I got over it pretty fast.

The television screen flickered. Another sixth grade news reporter was staring into the camera. Holding a few sheets of paper with his left hand and his finger pressed into his ear with his right hand, he spoke. "This just in for breaking news. The identity of the time capsule bandit has been made public, and Buchanan School hall monitors have issued a warrant for the arrest of sixth grader, Brody Valentine. I repeat, *Brody Valentine* is wanted for the theft of the 1999 time capsule *and* for having a weird last name!"

18

I gripped the sides of my desk. I had no idea what to do except sit helplessly in my seat. This all seemed to be escalating *way* too quickly.

"If you come into contact with Mr. Valentine," the news reporter said, "do *not* engage him. It's not known whether he's dangerous yet, but it's best to let the hall monitors do their job. Your cooperation is appreciated." The reporter swiveled in his chair, facing a girl wearing a fancy suit. "We have Lydia Steinburg sitting with us now to tell us what to expect, *psychologically*, from Valentine. She has no experience in psychology, but she's seen a few programs about it on television. Welcome, Lydia."

"Thank you," Lydia replied. "It's my pleasure to be here."

My school photo appeared in the corner of the screen with the word "WANTED" in red. I couldn't believe my eyes. This had to be a terrible dream!

"Lydia," the reporter said, "What do you think Valentine's next move is going to be?"

Lydia cleared her throat. "Well, if he's anything like the villains in the video games I play, then I believe *world domination* is next on his list."

"Are you kidding me?" I shouted, immediately slapping my hands over my mouth. I stared as the rest of my homeroom class turned in their chairs to face me. I was going to say something else, but was interrupted by some kids at the door.

Three hall monitors, wearing black suits and sunglasses, stood in the doorway. It was the same outfit that Colton and his monitors were wearing the week before, which meant these weren't your everyday normal monitors. They were part of the secret division of monitors, known as the "covert monitors."

"Brody Valentine?" said the largest monitor. "Come with us."

I took a deep breath and stood from my desk. I could feel the eyes of every student in my class burning holes right through my body. Grabbing my backpack off the floor, I tried to pull it over my shoulder, but the hall monitor yanked it from my hands.

"We'll take that, thank you," said the monitor.

I nodded, stepping out the door. My brain was still running in circles like a dog chasing its tail. Within minutes I had watched my wallet get dug up, a breaking news report that said my next move was world domination, and was arrested in front of an entire classroom of sixth graders.

This was *not* the greatest morning in my life.

As I walked down the hallway, I spoke. "Listen, I'm not the guy you're after."

"Save it for Principal Davis," replied the large hall monitor as he marched in front of me.

The other two monitors lagged behind, keeping their distance. One of the monitors was speaking into a walkie talkie. "We've got the package, and we're on our way. ETA five minutes."

The radio chirped, and a voice answered. "Happy holidays."

"I prefer the term, 'Merry Christmas,'" the monitor replied.

Again, the radio chirped. "All clear for package delivery."

I've never felt more confused about a conversation in my entire life.

"You're done, Valentine," the lead monitor said. "Game over."

"Seriously," I said, "I have no idea who took that time capsule, but I swear it *wasn't* me! I don't even know how my wallet got out there!"

The monitor laughed. "Right. Next thing you'll say

21

is that someone broke into your locker, took your wallet, and planted it in the ground where the capsule was buried. You were *framed*," he said, waving his hands in front of his body, mocking me.

"You *have* to believe me!" I pleaded. "I've been in homeroom the entire time!"

"The capsule was stolen *long* before school started, Mr. Valentine," the monitor shouted. "Unfortunately for you, you dropped your wallet and left some extremely hardcore evidence for us."

The monitors walked me down the hall, through the lobby and in front of the cafeteria. I saw the disappointed faces of children in study hall through the tinted glass windows. The students and teachers helping with the stage production stopped what they were doing to gawk at me. It made me sick to my stomach because they thought I was guilty.

So sick that I just about puked.

The lead monitor stopped and turned around. "You okay?"

I shook my head rapidly, pointing at my stomach. And then I glanced at the door to the nearby restroom that was connected to the school gymnasium. I clutched at my belly and started hobbling toward it.

"He's gonna pop!" said the monitor as he put his arm around me, keeping me from falling to the ground. "Help me get him to the bathroom!"

The other two monitors grabbed my other arm and rushed me to the door. The lead monitor pushed it wide open and allowed me to walk in.

"Puke your brains out in the toilet and get yourself cleaned up," the monitor said. "Don't try anything stupid because we'll be right out here waiting for you."

One of the other monitors spoke up. "I don't know, man. *Christmas* ain't gonna be happy if he knows we let him outta our sight."

Did that kid just say something about Christmas again?

The lead monitor tightened his lips as he pushed me into the restroom. "Then *don't* tell him."

The door shut behind me as I stumbled in. As soon as I heard it clunk, I stood up straight. My stomach *was* churning a second ago, but I knew I *wasn't* going to barf. I only faked it to buy some time in the bathroom. Those monitors would've never released me unless they were afraid of getting puked on.

Anytime I did anything crazy like that, I always wondered if I made the right decision. Could I have done something different back there? Said something else? My brain was racing with questions as I tiptoed around the room. What was I doing? Why was I even trying to escape? What if I went along with the monitors? Would that be smarter because I could simply explain that it wasn't me?

A weakness of mine is that I sometimes focus too much on what I *could've* done, you know what I mean? I waste a lot of time imagining situations play out with different endings, and at that moment I was having a hard time accepting what had already happened. What would I have changed if I could do it again?

Shaking my head, I returned my attention to the situation at hand. I grunted loudly, making noises to fool the monitors even more. As I did, I scanned the room. Since this restroom was connected to the gym, there was another exit on the other side, past the lockers.

I made one last gut wrenching sound to trick the guards into thinking I was violently ill, then I sprinted across the polished cement floor until I made it to the exit on other side.

Cracking the door open, I peeked into the gymnasium. Class was already in session with several students playing basketball. Over at the side of the gym, I saw the bleachers had been pulled out from the wall, which meant the space underneath was open.

Awhile back, my dad gave me a bit of advice on how to keep people from bugging me if I'm ever in a large crowd. We were at a church picnic and all these old ladies kept coming up to me to tell me how big I've gotten. You know the ones I'm talking about – they still pinch your cheeks even though you're not two years old anymore.

Eventually, my dad saw how frustrated I was that I couldn't even cross the room without getting stopped a bunch of times so he taught me this trick – walk as if your destination is *super* important. It doesn't even matter what your destination is! For the rest of the picnic, I followed his advice, and guess what? Not one single old lady tried to pinch my face. I kept imagining there was one slice of cheesecake left that I *had* to have, which translated to *"don't bug that kid 'cause he's on a mission!"*

My dad also said if that didn't work, then just run straight at the old ladies. They'll be so confused that they won't know what to do. They'll just stand there frozen in place!

Sucking up all my fear, I stepped into the gym and briskly walked toward the bleachers. My knees shook at first as I noticed a couple kids look in my direction, but my determined pace worked. They went right back to shooting hoops. I smiled at how skilled I was at keeping invisible. If there was a ninja clan at this school, I'd totally be the first in line to join.

Finally I ducked, stepping into the open space under the bleachers. It was dark since there weren't any lights there, which worked to my advantage. I expected the area to be filthy and littered with candy wrappers and sticky soda cans, but it was surprisingly clean. When I got to around the middle of the gym, I stopped and leaned against the wall. Through the small slits in the bleachers, I could see the shadows of other kids running around and playing. No one had a clue I was even there.

I sighed, trying to wrap my head around the facts. Someone stole my wallet, but I really don't have a clue *when* they took it. The last time I remember holding it was after Linus handed me the business card with the raven. I stuck the card into the wallet and tossed it back onto the top shelf of my locker.

But that *also* meant that someone got *into* my locker somehow, which isn't terribly difficult I bet. All they would need is a key or the combination. Figuring out the combination would take too much time and skill. Stealing a skeleton key that opened *all* the lockers would make it easy, almost like using a cheat code. Whoever did it *had* to have a key.

Let's not forget about the fact that I've been framed – been made to look like the thief that took the time capsule. Was the real criminal trying to frame *me* or was I just a random choice in a school full of students. Either way – *not* cool.

And actually, the fact that my wallet was taken and dropped off at the scene of a crime wasn't the most important part. The most important part was that someone stole the time capsule. Whatever Mrs. Olsen had buried back in 1999 was valuable enough to steal. So where *was* that capsule?

Suddenly, it hit me. I was going to have to find the time capsule if I wanted to clear my name of this mess. I'd have to find the *real* thief if I didn't want to stare at the walls of detention for the rest of my life. I hadn't planned on living out another day as a secret agent, but it looked like that's what was happening.

The only thing that really bothered me was the fact that I had no idea how long my wallet had been missing. It might've been taken last week or just yesterday, and I wouldn't have had a *clue*…

"That's it!" I said softly as I paced under the bleachers. "A clue! I could get back to my locker and search for a clue that might lead me to the real thief!" I paused, fully understanding that I was talking to myself like a crazy person. "But the monitors are probably swarmed around it already…"

I clenched my jaw, trying to shake the feeling of defeat off my shoulders. I knew it was dumb to search my locker, but I really had no other choice. That was my best bet at the moment, and even though the odds were stacked against me, I stepped out from the bleachers and headed toward my locker on the other end of the school.

The hallway outside the gymnasium was quiet and empty. Everyone was settled into their first period classes so I wasn't too worried about being seen. I just had to walk quickly by open doors if I was going to remain hidden.

As I rushed through the corridor, I heard my name from one of the televisions on the wall. When I glanced at it, I saw my school photo on the screen as a reporter's voice spoke behind it.

"Sixth grader Brody Valentine is wanted for the theft of the science class time capsule. After being apprehended by local monitors, Valentine overpowered the monitors and escaped. He is on the loose somewhere within the boundaries of Buchanan School. A reward of five *hundred* dollars has been offered for any information that might lead to the capture of Valentine."

Overpowered the monitors? All I did was walk into a bathroom!

"Principal Davis had this to say," the reporter said.

The image on the screen switched to a shaky camera of the principal standing in front of a dozen microphones. "The suspect was last seen being escorted by monitors outside the cafeteria. If you see him, do *not* approach him. Find the nearest adult and inform them that Brody Valentine is nearby."

What!? Now I'm *that* kid? Find an *adult* if you see me? *Seriously?*

I groaned as I started jogging through the hallways of the school. My locker was coming up, and the sooner this whole thing was over, the *better*.

Slowing to a stop just at the end of the hall, I

peeked my head around the corner. The next corridor was empty, and my locker was only a few feet away. I waited for a second, holding my breath and staring at a single spot on the floor. If you do that in a place that's completely still, you'll notice *anything* that moves.

When I was sure that no one else was around, I ran up to my locker and spun my combination on the dial. With a click, I lifted the handle and swung open the door.

Yep. The top shelf was completely empty. The wallet they had found *was* my wallet, which at this point, wasn't surprising.

I slid my hand across the top of the shelf, but all I felt was cold smooth metal. I started moving my textbooks around at the bottom of the locker, but couldn't find anything fishy down there either. The dial of the locker was totally fine too. There were no clues anywhere to be found!

I exhaled slowly, leaning into my locker, feeling completely defeated. My wallet was gone and the school thought I was a criminal. It was my word against the evidence. Out of frustration, I banged my head into the shelf where my wallet was supposed to be.

And then a second later I heard a clunk, as if a sheet of metal had fallen. When I looked up, I saw that the back wall of the top shelf was tilted, but only slightly. If I hadn't heard the sound, I wouldn't even have noticed something was off.

Reaching my hand in, I pushed against the spot behind the shelf. The instant my fingers touched the metal, the sheet slipped and fell back, revealing a *hole* in the wall!

I peered in, but couldn't see anything on the other side. The area was dark, but there was definitely a room back there.

Finally, I was getting somewhere!

I looked down both sides of the hall to see if there was a way to get into the room. Down the way and to my left, I saw a wooden door that was shut. The sign on front said it was a maintenance room.

I didn't waste any time. I walked to the door so fast that I completely forgot to shut my locker. No big deal, I thought. I'll just reach through the hole and shut it from the inside.

After opening the door, I slipped inside. It was dark and cold, and felt like the air was wet. It was noisy too. Along the walls were rusted pipes that probably moved water around the school. Some tools sat upon a wooden desk that was built into the side of the room. The walls weren't anything fancy – just exposed cinder blocks with bumpy cement that held them together. Before I took another step, I let the entrance shut behind me and made sure to lock it just in case.

And then I saw the hole in the wall. It was a few feet away and right at my eye level. I ran my fingers against the cinder blocks as I scanned the area below it for any trace of who might've taken my wallet.

I was surprised by the lack of cinder block dust below the hole. It almost seemed as though the opening had been carved long ago.

I took a peek through the small hole carved into the wall and then remembered that my locker door was still open. Without thinking, I reached my arm through the opening to grab the metal door.

At that instant, I felt two hands wrap around my forearm on the other side of my locker. My heart just about exploded in my chest as I tried to jerk my arm out, but whoever was on the other side had too good of a grip on me!

Propping my foot against the cinder blocks, I grabbed my caught arm with my free hand and tried prying myself away from the wall. It was like the locker had come to life and was trying to eat me!

"Let go!" I screamed.

A muffled voice shouted through the brick wall. "He's on the other side! Valentine is on the other side of this locker! Find a way through and arrest him!"

The voices I heard were of the hall monitors. Of course they were, right? Isn't that just my luck? Remember when I wondered if there was anything I'd change if I could do certain situations over again? Well, in this case, I *wouldn't* have blindly stuck my arm

32

through a hole in the wall.

"I didn't take the time capsule!" I shouted, still trying to regain control of my arm.

The monitor's grip on my wrist tightened and twisted like he was trying to give me a snakebite. "You've got nowhere to run, Valentine! Give yourself up and we'll go easy on ya!"

My face was getting hot as I struggled to free myself. The concrete edges of the hole was scraping against my arm. It *killed*. The door to the maintenance room pounded. The monitors were trying to break their way in.

I heard more muffled voices behind the wall. "It's locked! Who's got a key?"

"I forgot the key back at the pool!" answered another monitor.

Back at the pool? Were these guys kickin' back and relaxin' while catchin' some rays before they came after me? Strange, I thought. Even *stranger* because I'm pretty sure Buchanan *doesn't* have a pool.

"Then kick it down!" shouted the monitor with my arm.

Kick it down? Were they really going to try and— *BOOM!*

Yep, they were gonna kick the door down. My time was running short, and I was starting to freak out. Taking a deep breath, I held it in my lungs and kicked at the cement wall with all my strength. The force of my push finally freed my arm from the monitor, and I went flying into the wooden worktable behind me. Stumbling, I waved my arms out, regaining my balance.

The monitors kicked at the door again.

BOOM!

It was only a matter of minutes before they broke their way in. Spinning in a circle, I scanned the dark room, hoping for another exit, but I couldn't find one. The area was just a cold and dark prison cell that I had walked into willingly.

Dumb, Brody. Really dumb.

BOOM!

I ran to the door and pressed my body against it, like *that* was going to do anything. "I didn't take the capsule! You gotta believe me!"

"Sure ya didn't, Valentine!" shouted one of the monitors behind the door before they kicked it again. "Just turn yourself in and you can tell us the *whole* story!"

"Let me talk to Colton!" I pleaded. Colton was the leader of the covert monitors I had to deal with the week before. He was a tough kid, but I knew that he'd at least hear me out.

"Colton ain't on the force anymore!" replied the voice. "Turned in his badge and sash last week after the whole ordeal with President Sebastian!"

I grit my teeth, frustrated and more hopeless than ever. And just when I was about to give up, I heard a soft thump sound come from behind me, *inside* the room.

I turned to see what it was, but it was too late. The

monitors kicking at the door finally managed to break it open. The force of the blow knocked me across the room. As I staggered, I braced for impact, expecting the cold hard floor to slap me in the face, but it never did. Instead, I felt two arms catch me at the last second. I looked up fully knowing that it was a monitor that caught me, but I was wrong.

It was Maddie.

"Sup?" she said, smirking.

I would've responded, but a loud pop interrupted me. Instantly the room filled with a thick smoke cloud that made it impossible to see. It smelled like chalk dust.

"Climb," Maddie's voice whispered as she put a rope into my hands.

I couldn't see a thing, but I started climbing the rope that she gave me. A few feet off the ground, I felt another hand wrap around my own, and then it pulled me up into the space above the maintenance room. With less chalk dust up there, I could see that it was Linus that had helped me up.

He put his finger to his lips, telling me to keep quiet as he helped Maddie through the opening. Then he replaced the ceiling tile and gave me the most disapproving look I'd ever seen on *anyone's* face. It was even worse than the face my mom made when I told her I got an F on my math test.

We started crawling through the open space in the ceiling, which wasn't what I expected it to be. The walls were smooth and looked as though we were actually in a secret passage. Whatever this was, it was meant to be used as an escape tunnel.

I heard the muffled voices of the monitors again. "Where'd he go? You! Did you see him run out the door?"

"No, sir!" replied a boy's voice. "But I wasn't by the door when the smoke screen went off."

"Was *anyone* by the door? Did you guys just let him get away *again?*"

Nobody answered.

"*You're* the one that's gonna have to answer to *Christmas* then," the lead monitor said before I heard the door slam shut.

There it was again – *Christmas.*

36

"What's your *problem?*" Linus asked promptly.

I was confused. "What are you *talking* about?"

"Going to your locker like that was such a *noob* thing to do!" Linus said, shaking his head. "I thought you were smarter than that."

"Go easy," Maddie said. "He hasn't had the kind of training we've had. I think it was actually *smart* for him to check it out. You weren't down there just a second ago. I saw a hole in the wall right behind his locker."

Linus paused, still angry. "Really?"

"Really," Maddie repeated.

Linus continued crawling along the escape passage. "Fine," he said. "Follow us."

We crawled for another twenty feet or so before coming to an opening. A ladder was connected to the open spot on the ceiling so it was easier to climb down. The room we were in looked like one of the unused detention rooms that doubled as a storage space. Cardboard boxes lined the walls of the small room. The only open spot was the entrance to the hallway.

I rubbed my arm where the concrete had scraped against me. Wincing in pain, I took a seat at the long table in the middle of the room. Maddie sat on the other side and stared at me. Linus dropped a manila folder on the surface of the table and cracked his knuckles.

"Was it you?" Maddie asked right away.

"No!" I said, understanding what her question was referring to. "I didn't take that time capsule!"

Maddie folded her hands and leaned forward.

"Sorry. Had to ask."

Linus set his arms on top of the manila folder. "What do you know about this morning? Has anyone tried to contact you before any of this?"

"What?" I asked, confused. "No. Nobody contacted me about anything, and all I know of this morning was that they found my wallet at the dig site on *live* television."

"Did you put it there?" Linus asked flatly.

I shook my head. "You *think* I put it there?"

"So it was stolen," Linus continued. "When did you first notice it was missing?"

I exhaled slowly, rolling my eyes. "I don't know. I only saw that it was gone when I was looking for clues at my locker. I had no idea it was even taken!"

Linus nodded, staring me in the eye. "But your wallet was *in* your locker when it was stolen?"

Maddie interrupted. "Yeah, the hole in the wall can

tell you *that* much."

I was getting flustered. Throwing my arms out wide, I spoke. "*What* is going on here? *Why* was I framed for the time capsule theft?"

Linus glanced at Maddie, who nodded at him in return. It was a silent gesture of agreement.

Linus flipped open the manila folder and pushed the whole thing to my side of the table. There were three photos on top of a short stack of papers. One photo was of a girl with black hair. The other two were of the same boy. Strange that he would have *two* class photos.

"Recognize either of them?" Linus asked.

I tapped at the picture of the girl. "Her name is Sophia," I said. "I had a huge crush on her in third grade, but we never went out or anything."

"Right," Maddie said. "We believe *she's* the one who took the time capsule and planted your wallet."

"But *why* would she do that?" I asked. "I've never done anything to her! I mean, I probably acted like a dork and flirted or something, but is that really enough reason to *frame* a guy?"

"You'd be surprised," Maddie snipped. I wasn't sure if it was a joke or not.

Linus shook his head. "We believe Sophia is working with this kid. She's been known to pull heists for him in the past." He paused and looked at the class photos again. "Do you recognize *him*?"

I tapped at the table, studying the picture of the boy. "I don't know *who* he is, but I've seen him walking the hallways between classes. Kind of a big kid if I remember correctly. He has to be *new* at Buchanan, right? Because I've never had him in a class before, and I've gone here since kindergarten."

Linus tightened his lips. "His name is Christopher Moss, and he's what's known as a *super* sixth grader. Are you familiar with the term?"

I leaned back, floored by what Linus had said. "No way..."

"Yep," Maddie said. "He's in the process of *repeating* the sixth grade. He failed last year because he got all F's on his report card."

"A second year sixth grader," I said softly, staring at his photos. "That's why he's got *two* class photos. A *super* sixth grader. How sad."

"It's not sad," Linus said. "He did it to himself."

"Have a *heart*," Maddie groaned.

Linus continued. "Colton quit his position last week—"

"I heard," I said, trying to sound like I had my own sources for information even though I only knew because a monitor had just shouted it at me.

"And over the weekend, Christopher was somehow *given* Colton's old position," Linus said. "He's in charge of the secret service monitors now."

I flicked at one of the photos of Christopher. "But what's he got to do with me?"

Linus slid Christopher's photo aside and pointed at the sheets of paper underneath them. "Christopher *used* to be one of us. Last year he was the top agent in the agency we're a part of—"

"Which is called..." I interrupted, folding my arms and leaning back.

Linus looked up from his notes and glared at me.

I laughed. "You can keep it a secret all you like, but the fact that we're sitting here in this room, and you're telling me about all this means that I already have *some* knowledge about you and the agency you work for."

Maddie set her hand on his shoulder. "He's right," she said. "There's no reason to keep *everything* from him. Besides, *you* were the one who involved him last time."

41

Linus shut his eyes and exhaled through his nose. "Glitch," he said.

"Glitch?" I repeated.

"Glitch," Linus said again. "That's the name of the secret agency we work for."

I unfolded my arms and gestured for Linus to continued.

"Anyway," Linus said, returning his attention to the manila folder. "Christopher Moss used to be a part of Glitch last year, and was even the top agent in the field, but when he failed sixth grade, he got booted from the agency. It wasn't anything personal – the agency just frowns upon keeping super sixth graders as agents."

"Were the two of you agents last year?" I asked.

Maddie answered. "No. Glitch is only for sixth graders. We didn't know it even existed last year."

"We've been ordered to keep an eye on him this year though," Linus said. "Super sixth graders have been known to go bonkers from time to time, and it looks like Christopher just took some crazy pills. He's been busy creating an agency of his own here at Buchanan."

This all sounded so crazy, but I gotta admit, I was hooked. "Does his club have a name?" I asked.

"Suckerpunch," Maddie said.

"So he controls the covert monitors," I said, "*and* his own secret organization? This kid sounds dangerous."

Linus nodded. "He *is*."

I stared at the photos of Christopher that were on the table in front of me. He didn't look like an evil villain. He was clean cut, blond haired and blue eyed, and looked like he should've been the cool quarter back that everyone wanted to be friends with. Sure, he looked *slightly* older than a sixth grader, but not like a creepy teenager. As I studied the photos, a little light bulb clicked in my head, and I laughed.

"What's so funny?" Linus asked, annoyed.

"Christopher Moss," I said, smirking. "*Chris* Moss. *Christmas.*"

Linus and Maddie looked at one another. Linus twirled his finger around his ear to signal that maybe I was crazy.

"Those monitors were talking about someone they called 'Christmas,'" I explained. "Whoever they're working for goes by that weird name. It makes sense that Chris would go by *Christmas.*"

Linus leaned back in his chair, giving me the evil eye.

Maddie nudged him with her elbow. "Y'see? There's hope for Valentine yet."

Pushing his chair away from the table, Linus snatched up the manila folder and started walking to the door. He spoke as if I wasn't even in the room. "Valentine hasn't chosen a side yet, Maddie! He could be working for Suckerpunch right now, and we wouldn't have a clue! He could be playing *us!*"

I sat up, defending myself. "I'm not playing you!"

"Then why haven't you joined Glitch yet?" Linus asked coldly.

I paused, swallowing my pride. "Because that life isn't for me," I said honestly. "Sure, last week was fun and all, but this is serious stuff! I was *framed* today, and now the whole school is searching for me! When I got home from school after busting Sebastian, I was *happy* to go back to being a nobody!"

"That's *bogus*," Linus sneered. "Nobody's *that* much of a wuss!"

"No, I'm serious!" I said, throwing my arms out. "*I'm* that much of a wuss! I don't *want* to be the kid who chases after bad guys and gets caught up in risky situations!" Even as I said it, I knew it wasn't completely true.

"Then I can't and *won't* help you 'cause you haven't chosen a side yet," Linus said. "You think can float somewhere in the middle?"

"Isn't that what everyone else is doing?" I asked, irritated. "Aren't we all just staying off radars and out of everyone's lives? This isn't a movie! There isn't a *good* team or a *bad* team."

"Isn't there?" Linus whispered, glancing at the door. I knew he was referring to the students of Buchanan School. "*You* have the ability to be different from them! We *all* do! But it doesn't happen until we decide it does. You have to *choose* to be the kid that does the *right* thing or the one that does *nothing*. And if you choose to do the *right* thing, then you'd better stick to that decision and *do it* no matter what. Even when nobody else is doing it - no, *especially* when nobody else is doing it."

For the first time in my life, I actually felt speechless. I wanted to keep arguing because Linus was getting on my nerves, but deep down I knew he was a hundred percent correct.

Linus walked to the door, opened it a crack, and stopped. Without turning back, he said, "There's just no way of knowing without a doubt whether you're *with* or *against* us. C'mon, Maddie. We've got a school to save."

Maddie didn't move from her chair. "I think I'll stay," she said. "Brody could use a friend right now."

It was cheesy and a little embarrassing for her to say that, but it *did* make me feel better.

Linus shook his head, disappointed. With the pull of his arm, he yanked the door open and disappeared into the hallway.

"Sorry about him," Maddie said, rocking back and forth in her chair. "Sometimes the stress gets to him, y'know?"

"I can imagine," I said.

She looked me in the eye. "But he's right. Until you're working with Glitch, I shouldn't give you any help at all," she said, and then tightened a smile. "But I'm gonna give it to you anyway. *Don't* make this become one of the worst decisions I've ever made."

"That's what high school's for, right?" I laughed, trying to lighten the mood, but Maddie didn't seem to appreciate the joke.

"This is funny to you?" Maddie asked.

I coughed, containing my laughter. "No, sorry."

The bell started ringing in the hallway, which meant first period was over. Through the door, I heard the sound of hundreds of footsteps making their way to second period.

"So what do we do now?" I asked, standing from the table. "Go after Christmas?"

Maddie shook her head. "Christmas is harder to find than a monkey in the ocean."

I wasn't sure what she meant by that, but I went with it. "I know, right? Ocean monkeys are the *worst*."

"Right now, we only *think* Christmas is behind all this," Maddie said. "There's no hard evidence so we have to find the capsule first."

"Sophia then?" I suggested.

"Sophia," Maddie repeated, scratching at her eyebrow. "If we can find her, maybe she can give us some answers."

"So what class does she have?" I asked.

"Orchestra," Maddie groaned, annoyed. "*Hipsters.*"

In case you don't know, hipsters are kind of the new thing at my school. They're kids who are *too cool* to be cool. They spend half their lives doing the exact opposite of what everyone else is doing *just because* everyone else is doing it, and they try harder than anyone to make it look like they're not trying at all. They'll spend forever choosing their outfit so it looks like they just threw on a bunch of nerdy styled clothing. And then after all that, they throw it back in your face by talking down to you as if they're elite because of it! They're like bullies, but without the muscles!

The noise in the hallway slowly disappeared until there were only a few pitter-patters left. The bell rang again, which signaled the start of second period.

"C'mon," Maddie said unenthusiastically. "Better get going."

If Sophia had orchestra, then she'd still be in class. Students that had orchestra had it for the first two periods of the day. But any class that had anything to do with music was also in the lower levels of Buchanan.

"Wonderful," I sighed. "Let's go down to the dungeon."

Several minutes later, Maddie and I set foot back into the dungeon of Buchanan School. It felt weird because the two of us were doing the same thing just the week before.

Naturally, I made a lame comment about it. "So we're going to the same place for our second date, huh? Has the fire burnt out between us already?"

Maddie glanced back at me with an eyebrow cocked. I couldn't tell if she was annoyed or amused.

"Y'know," I said, stumbling over my words. "Because if we were on a second date and returning to a lame place then that'd mean we're a pretty boring couple and um... I uh..."

"I get it," Maddie said coldly as she continued down the hallway.

"Awkwaaaaaaard," I whispered, hopping a few

steps to catch up.

The dungeon was exactly in the same condition as it was the first time we were down there. The lack of sunlight made it so that fluorescent bulbs were the only source of light. There was a bluish green tint to everything, probably because the paint on the walls was moldy and chipping away. The wet concrete underneath the paint peeked out at us as if was begging to be seen.

The corridors were still filled with sugar addicts. President Sebastian's plot to sell sweets in the dungeon had been foiled, but it was going to be a few weeks before the problem was completely fixed. Principal Davis said all of Sebastian's candy had been confiscated, but that didn't mean it was totally gone. There were still students that had some leftover in their lockers and backpacks.

A bunch of shady kids had already tried bringing their own candy from home to sell since there was clearly a market for it, but teachers were quick to bust them at the first sign of it.

Still though... the few sugar addicts that remained in the dungeon scared the snot outta my nose.

"Where's the orchestra room?" I asked, rubbing my arms like I was cold, which was weird because the dungeon *wasn't* cold.

"Up ahead," Maddie replied. She looked back at me and snickered. "Someone afraid of the scary dungeon of Buchanan?"

My teeth started chattering, but I shook my head to

stop them. "They don't call it the *dungeon* for nothing!"

At that instant, a filthy hand waved in front of my face, nearly smacking my cheek. I cried out like a baby and hobbled backward, banging against the metal lockers on the wall.

"You guys lookin' to buy?" the owner of the filthy hand asked. His grin displayed a few missing teeth among some other rotten ones. In his other hand was an open canvas bag filled with chocolate bars. It looked like he had just finished trick or treating. "Got enough candy to last ya for a day! Whatcha want? Sugar-bombs? Choco-lattes? Sugar-shocks? I got it all!"

Maddie pushed the boy aside. "Stay outta our way, sugar head."

Kids had started using the term "sugar head" when referring to the sugar addicts in Buchanan's dungeon.

The boy with the candy licked his lips and frowned. "You'll be back," he sneered. "Ain't nobody comes down to the dungeon without pickin' up a few snacks before leaving."

As she walked past the boy, Maddie rolled her eyes and held her open palm in front of his face. She didn't say anything else.

The sugar head looked at me. "How about you? You don't seem to have a chip on your shoulder."

I leaned over and checked out his stash of goods. I saw all kinds of suckers and hard candy along with individually wrapped chewy candy that had a sugar coating. I'm not a "candy" kind of kid – I'm more into

49

chocolate bars, which was also lining the bottom of his bag. King sized chocolate bars and peanut butter cups were everywhere. I started reaching my hand out...

"Brody!" Maddie shouted from ahead.

Instantly I stood at attention and put my hands behind my head. Whenever I'm caught doing something I shouldn't be, my first reaction is to nervously laugh. "Hey, uh... I... ha ha ha!"

"Quit wasting time!" Maddie ordered.

I don't know why, but I looked at the sugar head and apologized.

Maddie and I walked down a few more dark hallways until we were outside the entrance to the orchestra room. You'd think the hallway would be filled with beautiful music coming from cellos and violins and stuff, but it wasn't. Instead, all it sounded like was a bunch of kids talking to one another.

Maddie touched my elbow and spoke. "Listen," she said. "While we're in here, just let me do the talking. These are *hipsters* we're dealing with. There's a very specific way of dealing with them so they'll cooperate, okay?"

I nodded.

"Seriously," she said. "Don't say a word! There's no 'good cop, bad cop' routine happening here. It's just *me* that's gonna talk."

Holding my hands up in surrender, I said, "Okay, I get it! I won't say a thing!"

Maddie turned around, took a deep breath, and stepped to the door of the orchestra room. I felt a chill run down my spine as I followed behind her. I wasn't sure what to expect, but Maddie's little warning had my knees trembling. Orchestra kids couldn't be *that* bad, could they?

The second we entered the room, it was like we stepped into another world. Kids were sprawled out on the floor listening to music on their headphones while others sat in chairs along the wall. Some of them mumbled about how "yesterday" my vest was. Only a couple of students had their instruments out, but they weren't playing them the way they were supposed to, probably as an act of rebellion to orchestras around the world.

Oh, and *everyone* wore thick black rimmed glasses *without* the actual glass part in the frames.

51

"Some kids wear glasses because they *need* glasses," I whispered to Maddie as she slowly walked to the center of the room.

She lifted her hand, gesturing for me to keep quiet, but she didn't scold me. "I know. Hipsters try too hard to make it *look* like they're *not* trying at all. Did you notice that nobody has their headphones plugged into anything?"

I laughed, realizing Maddie was right. All I could do was shake my head as I started scanning the room for the orchestra teacher. Why wasn't he out there? Where could he even be? And then I saw that he was in his office, reclined in a chair with his feet up on his desk. He was wearing a checkered shirt with a scarf so tiny that it was pointless. His mustache looked like something from a western movie and on his head was a brown knit cap. I almost made the mistake of thinking he was wearing jeans, but then I saw that they were sweatpants with a denim print. How awful. No wonder these kids were allowed to do nothing. Their teacher was a hipster too!

"Looks like you're in the wrong classroom," said one of the hipster girls, reclining in a seat. Her voice was chill as if she didn't care. Of course she didn't. She was a hipster.

Maddie stopped directly at the center of the room. She set her hands on her hips and spoke. "We're looking for a girl named Sophia."

The hipster girl made a smack sound with her lips as she raised her eyebrows. "Sophia is such a lame-wad name," she sighed. "It's so yesterday."

The hipsters around her nodded and mumbled in agreement.

Maddie paused as her face grew red with anger. "There's a girl named Sophia somewhere in this class. I don't care about the weirdo hippy names you've given yourselves because your *real* names are all that matter. Now tell me where we can find *Sophia*."

Another boy sat forward in his chair and wagged his finger at me. "You're the kid that stole the time capsule, aren't you?"

I started to answer, but he interrupted me.

"Way to go, man," he said, smiling. "Everyone was too into the capsule anyway, right? Time capsules are so *yesterday*."

"Right?" the hipster girl groaned.

Maddie took a step forward. "Of course time capsules are yesterday! That's the point of them!"

Everyone in the room casually glanced at each other. I heard several of the students whisper the phrase, "*Played out.*"

Abruptly, Maddie snapped, pointing at the girl in the chair. "Tell us where Sophia is or else!"

The hipster girl blinked slowly. It looked like she was falling asleep. Tipping her chair back, she finally spoke. "Your clothes are so *yesterday*," she whispered.

Maddie stormed forward and swept her foot under the girl's chair.

"Aaaah!" the hipster girl screamed as she fell backward.

Faster than lightning, Maddie caught the hipster by her shirt and pulled her back to safety. The metal legs on the chair clamped down on the hard floor.

"You see my partner over here?" Maddie hissed, pointing her thumb at me. "He's *crazy.* He *eats* hipsters for breakfast so if you don't tell me where I can find Sophia, then I promise that your future children will *weep* when you tell them stories of what happened after I leave him alone with you guys in this room!"

I stood there with my eyes wide open, stunned by what Maddie was threatening. Obviously it was a bluff, but I hoped the hipsters couldn't see it. I did my best to look menacing by furrowing my eyebrows and chomping my teeth together. I was trying to imitate a rabid dog, but probably looked more like I had something stuck in my cheek.

The hipster girl bought my act. She sat up straight and ran her fingers through her frazzled hair. "Ugh," she grunted. She nodded her head to point at a spot across the room. "Sophia's over there."

In that instant, one of the students jumped up from the floor and sprinted toward the exit. She moved so quickly that she was a blur, but I knew it had to be Sophia. Why else would anyone freak out like that? Kicking her foot out, Sophia knocked the door wide open and dove into the dark hallway.

Maddie took the lead, taking off like a dog after a bunny. As she jumped through the door, she held her wrist next to her mouth and spoke into the watch that was strapped on it. I couldn't hear her, but if it was the same watch she wore the week before, then I knew it had a built-in communicator.

Without hesitating, I ran through the orchestra room, following Maddie into the hallway. I paused outside the door to see which direction she had taken off in, and when I saw her shadowy figure to my right I immediately returned to the chase.

Sophia was already halfway down the hall, running as fast as she could. Maddie kept after the hipster, but stumbled over a small stack of boxes. Rolling across the floor, I heard her grunt as she slid against the wall. I almost stopped to help, but I didn't want to lose Sophia so I jumped over the boxes and continued.

The squawks from my sneakers bounced against the lockers as I kept my eyes on Sophia. She was running deeper into the dungeon, and not toward the stairs like I thought she would. Common sense said that she'd try to escape to the upper levels of Buchanan, but that wasn't where she was headed.

My side was starting to cramp, but I pushed harder because if she got away, then my name would *never* be cleared. Surprisingly I was catching up to her. At that point, I was only about ten feet away.

Just then, Sophia ran past a random sugar head, grabbing his sack of sweets.

"Hey!" the kid cried. "That's mine!"

As I ran past the same boy, I saw Sophia make it to where the hall turned the corner. She kicked her foot against the hall and instantly shot herself into the opposite direction. While she was still in the air, she tossed the sack of candy at my face.

I responded the way I did in gym when someone throws a ball at me. I flinched, raising my hands to my face and then dropped to the floor. I was moving so fast that my body slid against the polished tiles until I bumped into the lockers.

"Nice," said Maddie as she slowed to a stop beside me. Grabbing my hand, she helped me off the floor.

I remained silent, feeling pretty embarrassed. Dusting off my jeans, I wiped the bit of spit off my lip and stayed close to Maddie's side.

Maddie took the lead again, but this time she didn't run. Catching her breath, she stepped around the corner carefully just in case Sophia was waiting there with a surprise attack.

The fluorescent bulbs flickered and buzzed as we walked under them into the next hallway. I was expecting a long, dark, and scary corridor that we were going to have to explore, but to my surprise, the hall ended almost immediately after we turned the corner. There was about fifteen feet of hallway that was surrounding by lockers. Against the back wall was another set of lockers. There was no sign of Sophia.

Maddie pointed at one of the tiles on the ceiling. It was cracked and moved out of place. "There," she said through heavy breaths. "She must've climbed up to get away."

"Then let's follow her!" I said, jumping as high as I could while reaching my arms out. Even at my highest, my hand only reached about eight feet up. The ceiling was a good twelve or thirteen feet high.

Maddie leaned against one of the lockers against the back wall, still trying to catch her breath. She rubbed the spots on her knees where she had fallen. "Unless you got some rope or something I don't know about, she's as good as gone."

I clenched my jaw, frustrated and angry that Sophia had gotten away. Grunting, I started pacing around the small area. "So what now? She's just *gone* and I'm dead meat? How about we try to figure out where she's gonna jump out from?"

"It could be anywhere," Maddie said softly. "She could be on the other side of the school already."

"You can't just give up like this!"

"Stop yelling at me!" Maddie shouted. "Man! Just give me a second to think! Which one of us is the secret agent again?"

I pinched the bridge of my nose. I could feel a headache coming on from shouting so much. "I'm sorry," I said. "I just thought we had her for sure, and now I'm back to square one."

Maddie shook her head, but kept quiet.

Folding my arms, I started rubbing them up and down again like I was cold. Don't ask me why, I just was. Staring at the open ceiling tile, I tried to imagine how Sophia had gotten herself up there. It was possible this was always an available escape spot for her, and a rope was always waiting for the day she'd need it. Walking over to Maddie, I stood for a moment, and then leaned against the locker next to her.

CLICK!

"No!" shouted a girl's voice from inside the locker.

I about jumped out of my skin as I stumbled away from the locker until I realized the voice was Sophia's.

"Ha!" Maddie said, pointing at the metal locker door. "You tried to fool us into thinking you got away through the broken ceiling tile!"

Sophia started pounding at the door. "You nimrod!" she cried. "You leaned against my locker and shut it! Now I'm stuck in here! Let me out! Let me out *now!*"

Maddie kicked the locker once, but hard enough that the clang echoed through the halls. "Not until you tell us what we want to know!"

"Never!" Sophia screamed. "I don't have to tell you a thing! Now let me outta here!"

"Then *we're* outta here," Maddie said as she started walking away. Her footsteps slapped against the cold floor loudly.

I stood still, unsure of whether Maddie was going to actually leave or not. It was the most intense five seconds of my life. It seemed a little harsh of Maddie to just leave Sophia stuck in a locker like that – almost bully-ish, but then again, Sophia *did* frame me for the theft of the time capsule. Two wrongs didn't make a right, did they? No, there was no way Maddie was going to leave. She *had* to be bluffing, right?

Finally, Sophia hit the locker door again and shouted. "Wait! I'll tell you everything! Whatever you want! Just don't leave me in here! It's dark!"

Maddie turned around, smiling at me. "That's more like it."

I swallowed hard. I could feel my muscles relax as Maddie walked back to the locker. I decided the best thing to do was to say nothing, while trying to soak the information in.

"Let's start with the time capsule," Maddie said. "Did you take it?"

Sophia paused. I could tell she didn't want to confess, but finally, she spoke. "Yeah," she said softly. "I took it."

"Why?" Maddie asked.

"Because I was told to."

"And you just do anything you're told to do?"

Sophia chuckled through the locker. "When it involves a huge payday, then yeah."

"So you were *paid* to take the capsule? By who?"

"Yeah right, like I'm gonna tell you that."

"We already know it was Christopher Moss," Maddie said, shooting me a look. The truth was that we *didn't* know it was Christopher, but hopefully Sophia wouldn't be able to tell.

It worked. I heard Sophia sigh as the locker bumped once, probably from her resting her head against the inside.

"Yup," Sophia said. "Christmas left me an envelope of cash with some instructions in my locker... *this* locker."

"How much?" I asked, curious.

"Hundred bucks," Sophia replied.

"*Hundred bucks?*" I cried. "How's this kid got that much money?"

"I don't know!" Sophia shouted so loudly that the metal locker trembled.

Maddie scratched at her chin. "What's Christopher want with the capsule? What's inside?"

"I don't know that either," Sophia said. "All the instructions told me to do was to take Brody's wallet, dig up the capsule, bury the wallet into the hole, and then drop the capsule off in the garbage can next to the science labs on the second floor."

61

"*When* did you take my wallet?" I asked.

"This morning," Sophia replied. "The note said there was a hole in the wall in the maintenance room, and that on the other side of the hole was the wallet I was supposed to take."

The fact that my wallet had only been missing since earlier that morning made me feel better, but the idea that the hole in the wall was *already* there didn't.

Clapping her hands together, Maddie spoke cheerfully as she walked away from the locker. "Onward to the second floor then!"

Walking briskly, I caught up to her before she turned the corner. "What about Sophia? We can't just leave her in—"

"Agent Madison?" came a gruff voice from down the opposite end of the hall.

"Down here, agent Donavan," Maddie said.

A boy dressed in normal street clothes stepped around the corner. Another girl that had the same style clothing accompanied him. When they saw me, they both flinched.

"He's innocent," Maddie said.

The two agents immediately relaxed.

"Sophia's stuck in her locker," Maddie continued. "She wants out bad so she'll give you the combination. Take her directly to the principal's office. She confessed to stealing the capsule."

"Great," Donavan said. "Where is it?"

"We're on our way to retrieve it right now," Maddie

said. "I'll keep the agency in the loop as soon as we find it."

Donavan and the girl nodded, and then walked past us to help Sophia out of her locker.

Maddie walked to a closed door in the hall and opened it. She waved her hand at me to step through first. I watched as the two agents opened Sophia's locker. Sophia stepped out, drenched in sweat. She slowly lifted her chin until she made eye contact with me. Her eyes were cold, and felt as if they pierced my soul. They were hypnotizing.

"C'mon," Maddie said.

I clenched my eyes shut and shook my head, trying to get the image of Sophia out of my thoughts. This whole thing had me more frazzled than I realized. Finally, I stepped through the door that Maddie held open.

Inside the dark room, I heard the bell ring again, signaling the end of second period. It was amazing how fast time flew by when we were chasing after criminals.

Maddie approached a television that was mounted on the wall and switched it on. My class photo was on the screen. I was still a wanted criminal in the school.

In the dark room, Maddie took a seat. "We'll wait here until third period starts. Everyone's still looking for you so it wouldn't be the smartest thing to walk the hallways now. I mean, unless you *want* to go detention."

I sat in the desk next to her, but remained silent. I was breathing heavy from the chase we just had and still felt a little embarrassed by it.

"So…" Maddie said, trying to make conversation. "Why *haven't* you tried to find Glitch yet?"

I shrugged my shoulders. "I already told you. I don't think I'm cut out for it."

Maddie laughed. "Are you kidding? You've already escaped from hall monitors, chased after a thief, and helped find the location of the missing time capsule, and it's not even *noon* yet."

"I don't know," I said, uneasy.

"Remember what I said to you last week?" Maddie asked.

"Fake it till you make it…" I said.

"No," Maddie said, angered. "You *are* what you *think* you are. You were successful in busting Sebastian last week because you knew who you wanted to be, but it sounds like you let that dark shadow in again, didn't you? The one that tells you to stay quiet and out of trouble because life is easier that way, right? It's easier to be invisible, isn't it?"

Weird how she even used the word "invisible."

"I wish you *did* try to find Glitch," Maddie said. "It would've made *this* situation a heck of a lot easier."

I shook my head. "Doesn't matter. That raven card was in my wallet anyway, and my wallet is locked up in evidence somewhere."

Maddie smirked suspiciously. "There wasn't much on it. I bet you've got it memorized."

I stared at the floor. She was right. I *did* have it

memorized, but I wasn't about to give her the satisfaction of knowing me so well just yet.

The bell outside the door started ringing out. Third period had officially started. Maddie peeled the door open. Together, we made our way out of the dungeon and headed to the second floor of Buchanan.

About ten minutes later, we made it to the second floor, where most of the science and math classes were held. Science needed a few extra rooms because of the lab work that was needed. Toward the center of the second floor, there was an open courtyard filled with hundreds of different plants for the botany portion of class.

The garbage can Sophia had talked about was just at the end of the corridor and was easy to find. It was built into a container in the wall so it was less of an eyesore. Plastered all over the brick walls were wanted posters with my face on them.

"How do they do that so fast?" I asked.

"It's likely that Christopher is behind it," Maddie replied. "This all happened so quickly that it makes me doubt the principal had anything to do with it. Of course a bunch of wanted posters sprouting up would be considered a good thing so nobody really asks *where* they came from. I bet Christopher had the posters printed up *before* today."

"Who *is* this kid?" I whispered. "How does he have this much pull?"

"Good question," Maddie said. "I have a feeling he's gonna be a real problem for Glitch in the future."

As we approached the garbage can, Maddie glanced over her shoulder to see if we were being followed. When she was sure that we were alone, she went ahead and pulled the container out of the wall. Ripping the plastic bag from the metal, she stared into the empty bin and chewed her lip.

The time capsule *wasn't* there.

"Of course," I groaned.

Maddie pushed the container back into the wall, and then pointed to a spot over my head. "Don't worry," she laughed. "Looks like we might have a little good luck coming our way."

I turned around to see what she was pointing at. On the wall, over our heads, was a tiny camera with a little blinking red light on the front of it.

"Um," I said, "Is that something *we* have to worry about right now?"

Maddie shrugged her shoulders and grabbed my hand to follow her. "No, because Sophia already confessed. If Principal Davis reviews the footage, he'll know we were just looking in the spot she said it'd be. This is proof that you're helping."

"Okay then," I said, relieved. "Where can we watch the footage? I bet we'll see Christopher taking the capsule from the garbage, right?"

"Hopefully," Maddie said as she walked swiftly down the hall.

She pulled me along until we got to another closed door that had a keypad on the outside of it. After punching in a set of numbers, the pad blinked red and green, and I heard it unlock. Pushing the door open, Maddie stepped through first.

Inside the new room, I saw dozens of small television screens blink with black and white videos of random spots around the school. Apparently there were cameras mounted everywhere in Buchanan.

Maddie sat at the empty swivel chair in front of what looked like the command center for a spaceship.

"Is this the Glitch headquarters?" I asked, walking around the tiny room. There was barely any space for two people so if it *was* the headquarters, it was a little disappointing.

"Of course not," Maddie said as she jabbed her fingers at the keyboard in front of her. "This is just the hub for the surveillance cameras."

"Cool," I said, setting my hands on the back of Maddie's chair and leaning into it.

"Computer," Maddie said flatly. "Show me the video for the science lab hallway starting at 7:45 AM this morning."

No way! A voice controlled computer system? Was Glitch *actually* a legit secret agency in the school?

The televisions all blinked once. Then they showed the video feed from the morning across all of the screens at the same time creating one giant image in front of us.

Maddie folded her hands and rested her chin on

them. As she studied the video, she tapped her finger on the tip of her nose. "Fast forward at double speed."

I watched in awe as the video instantly obeyed her command. Little squiggle lines bounced around as the video showed the entire morning at double the speed.

"There! Computer, pause video!" Maddie said, pointing at the screens. "Sophia is dropping the capsule off in the garbage can."

I stared at the frozen image of Sophia standing next to the garbage can. The timestamp on the video said it was 8:23 AM, which meant it was between homeroom and first period. It was clear that she had dug up the capsule before school, but didn't deliver it until *after* the school discovered it was missing. On the paused screen, I could see a hallway filled with students walking to their next class.

"She dumped it in front of a hallway of kids!" I said. "That's *crazy*."

"*Bold* is more like it," Maddie said. "Computer, continue fast forwarding at double speed."

As the timestamp fast-forwarded, I felt my heart start to race. This was it. We were about to see Christopher Moss, A.K.A. *Christmas*, snatch the capsule from the garbage can – the last bit of evidence I'd need to clear my name. Sophia and Christopher would *both* get busted and I'd be free to go back to living my boring little invisible life.

And then everything I knew to be true spit in my face again.

Maddie and I stared at the television screens, our jaws dropped open, totally in shock of what we were watching.

"Computer," Maddie managed to whisper. "Play video at normal speed."

On the screen was a boy, digging through the garbage. He was facing away from the camera. Every time he looked over his shoulder, I had to squint to make sure I was actually seeing things straight. "That's not..." I whispered, but trailed off.

"It is," Maddie said. "It's Linus."

The video played on. My brain was jumping hurdles trying to understand what was happening. Linus pulled out the garbage can, dug his hands around the bottom, and removed the time capsule. He had a nervous look upon his face as he glanced over his shoulder every couple seconds.

"What's he doing with it?" I asked.

Maddie's voice was cold. "I don't know, but we're gonna find out."

I watched as Linus dropped the capsule into his backpack and shut the garbage can. But before he disappeared off camera, he stopped right in front of it, staring into it for an uncomfortably long time, as if he was surprised that it was even there. As an agent, shouldn't he know where *all* the cameras are?

"Computer," Maddie said as she spun her chair. "Resume normal recording."

The televisions all blinked again like they did before. One by one, each monitor flipped back to the video feed of whichever camera they were attached to.

I wasn't sure what was next. "What now?" I asked.

Maddie snapped to her feet, pushing the swivel chair away with the backs of her knees. "I don't know, okay? I don't have all the answers so quit bugging me for them!"

I lowered my gaze, embarrassed. "I'm sorry... I just..."

Maddie pushed me aside and stepped through the door. "Would you just keep your mouth shut? Just let me think for a second!"

Standing in the doorway, I didn't say another word.

Maddie paced back and forth in the hallway, occasionally picking her head up and looking at the camera that had caught Linus. Mumbling nonsense under her breath, she shook her head as if she were arguing with herself.

At last, she stopped and made eye contact with me. "We're gonna go straight to Suckerpunch."

"What about Linus?" I asked.

Maddie folded her arms tightly and tapped her foot, annoyed. "There's no point in trying to find him. We could look at his locker for clues, but there won't be any. He's too good to leave behind any evidence."

"But he left that video," I said.

"Whatever," Maddie said. "If Linus switched teams and is working for Suckerpunch, then he'll be there with the time capsule."

"What if he *didn't* switch teams?" I asked, trying to remain hopeful.

"Doesn't matter!" Maddie said. "Either way, he'll be with Suckerpunch right now, which means he'll have *a lot* of explaining to do. What period are we in again?"

I thought for a moment, and then answered. "We're halfway through third period now."

Maddie placed her hands on her hips and nodded. "We've only got a period and a half until lunch and that ridiculous school play about the football werewolf or whatever. I thought we'd have the case solved by then, but it doesn't seem to look that way."

I leaned against the lockers feeling that same sick feeling in my stomach as I thought about going to

71

Christmas himself. "Great," I said. "So where's Suckerpunch?"

"I don't know," Maddie said. "They've been one step ahead of Glitch when it comes to their hideout. Every time we think we've found them, they're not there. And they're snooty about it too, almost like they're kickin' back and relaxin' about the fact that we can't find them."

I paused. "What did you just say?"

"I said we don't know where their hideout is."

"No, the part after that. You said something about kickin' back and relaxin.' It's funny because when those monitors were taking me away earlier, I had the exact same thought," I said, trying to remember *why* I thought that. "What did they say?"

Maddie stared at me, holding her open palms out. "How would I know what you said?"

And then it came back to me, flashing across my mind. "It was when I was in the maintenance room! Someone said they forgot the key to the room back at the pool, and I thought it was *weird* 'cause Buchanan School doesn't *have* a pool!"

Maddie's eyes glistened as a smiled spread apart on her face. "But it *used* to."

Like the cool kid I was, I remained calm, and replied with, "Huh?"

"Buchanan School *used* to have a swimming pool," Maddie explained. "The rumor is that it got shut down back in the 90s because it was never cleaned or something. So they drained it and closed off that section of the school. It's mostly used for storage now I think. The entrance is *in* the gym. There are a set of double doors with a 'do not enter' sign taped to the wood."

The light bulb clicked on in my head. "You're right! And that actually makes a *ton* of sense. At least it explains why the boy's locker room always smells like steamed broccoli."

"That whole *area* smells like steamed broccoli," Maddie said, frowning. "So gross."

I followed Maddie to the edge of the stairs. Before she took a step, she looked back at me with her big brown eyes. "Are you ready for this?"

Was she kidding? After the morning I'd already had, I just wanted to go home and play some video games with a steaming cup of hot chocolate! Of course I wasn't ready for this, and I'm almost positive that I'd *never* be ready, but I couldn't bring myself to look away from her *humongous* brown eyes! Her eyelids fluttered and her good looks got the better of me. I grinned like an idiot, and said, "I was *born* ready."

Nearly ten minutes later, we were sneaking around the side of the gym, using the technique my dad taught me. The gym teacher, Mr. Cooper, even gave us a nod when we walked in front of his office. He either thought we were in his third period gym class, or he didn't care.

"Coach Cooper has that earring now," Maddie said. "Is that weird?"

73

"Very," I said. "He's an old dude. He shouldn't be getting his ears pierced. I mean, I *guess* he shouldn't. Who am I to say?"

"Still," Maddie said. "It's just the one tiny gold hoop, like he *wanted* to look like a pirate, but couldn't afford anything larger."

"Couldn't afford it?" I asked. "He's a *gym teacher.* That means he's loaded with money, doesn't it? Don't they make *tons* of money?"

Maddie frowned. "I don't know."

"Well, when I grow up, I know what I'll be spending all *my* money on."

"What's that?"

"Comic books," I said. "You know how many comics I'd have if I spent my yearly salary on them?"

Maddie didn't say anything.

"A lot," I said, answering for her, but instantly felt like a dork. Out of embarrassment, I tightened a smile and repeated myself. "I'd have *a lot.*"

The rest of the walk though the gymnasium was silent between us. I hoped it was because the situation we were walking into was one to be nervous about, and not because I embarrassed myself only seconds ago.

"Brody!" came a voice from behind me.

My heart dropped, afraid we were caught, but when I turned around, I saw that it wasn't anyone to be worried about. It was my friend, Chase. He had the same last name as Coach Cooper, but I was pretty they weren't related.

"You're definitely *not* in this class," Chase said, smiling and pointing at me.

"Uhhhh," I said, trying to come up with something clever.

"We're here on business," Maddie said flatly.

Chase smiled. "Hi," he said, holding out his hand. "My name's Chase."

"I know who you are," Maddie said as she took his hand, shaking it like a businesswoman. "But more importantly, I know *what* you are."

Chase's smile melted away as he continued to shake Maddie's hand. I wasn't sure what Maddie had meant by saying she knew *what* Chase was. Apparently he had some sort of secret. Maybe when this whole ordeal was over, I'd ask him about it.

Maddie's stiff face cracked, and she chuckled. "You have nothing to worry about," she said to Chase. "I know you're one of the few good guys at this school."

Yeah, I was definitely going to have to remember to ask him about Maddie's comment.

"Thanks," Chase said, looking rather uncomfortable. He turned his attention to me and spoke, worried. "So what's up, man? I saw that news report this morning on the television... was it... you?"

"No!" I said, louder than I meant to. "That's actually what we're doing here. We think we've found the person behind the whole thing."

Chase furrowed his brow. "*Behind* the whole thing? What do you mean?"

I knew I said too much. I always did whenever I was nervous. "It's nothing," I said as cool as possible, scratching the back of my neck. "I just mean that we're trying to help them find it."

"Who's them?" Chase asked.

"Why all the questions, Chase?" is what I *wanted* to yell, but instead I just shrugged my shoulders. "Y'know... *them.*"

Another voice cracked from across the room. "There he is! Brody Valentine, stop right in your tracks!"

Chase spun around. "What? You're still running?"

"Dude, you gotta believe me," I pleaded. "I swear it wasn't me that took the time capsule!"

Maddie stepped forward. "Brody's innocent, and we're about to bust the guys behind it, but we need some

76

time."

Chase's eyes grew fierce. He nodded once. "Go," he said. "Quickly before those monitors get over here. I'll hold them off as long as I can."

I tightened a smile at him. Chase was a good kid, but even more, I considered him an actual friend. "Thanks," I said.

"Thank me when this is over," Chase said, turning around.

Maddie started sprinting to the far end of the gym, to the double doors with the "do not enter" sign. I ran as quickly as I could, looking back at Chase every few seconds. He was able to distract a few of the covert monitors by running circles around them, but the rest of the monitors were still coming after Maddie and me.

"Faster!" Maddie shouted.

I was feeling good, running like a cheetah across the gym floor up until my side cramped up on me. It hurt so bad that I stumbled.

Maddie pushed open the double doors that supposedly led to the abandoned swimming pool and Suckerpunch's hideout. She turned and reached her hand out to me. "Come on, Brody!"

Hobbling, I did my best to keep my pace.

"Stop right there, Brody!" the monitor shouted.

Most of the kids in the gymnasium were staring at that point, watching to see if a fight was going to break out. I was trying my best to keep it from coming to that.

"Grab my hand!" Maddie shouted one last time.

I choked down my pain and launched myself forward at the double doors. Maddie caught my wrist and pulled me into the next room through the doors. Instantly, she sprang up and pushed the doors shut. Grabbing an old broom, she wedged it between the handles of the double doors, locking it.

The monitor on the other side slammed into the door with all his force, but the broom didn't budge. His muffled voice came filtered through the cracks. "You can't run forever, Valentine!"

Rolling to my feet, I arched my back as I stood up, trying to stretch out the cramp in my side. I listened as the monitor jumped into the doors again. He was a big kid, and I was surprised that the broom wasn't breaking.

"We'd better hurry," Maddie said as she walked across the floor.

The room we were in was just an entrance to an entrance. It was the area where people would gather to pay for a ticket to see the swim competition.

On the far right wall was a huge boarded up window that probably served hot dogs and soda back when Buchanan used to have swim meets. On the far left was a bench against a wall where pictures of swimmers hung. At the end of each side, there was an opening in the brick wall that probably led to the boy's and girl's locker rooms. I never noticed a sealed door from inside the locker room, but I bet I'd find it if I looked.

And at the far end of the room, directly in front of Maddie and me, was another set of double doors. The words "Buchanan Swimming Pool" was painted on the frosted glass portion of each door.

"There it is," I said, taking the lead.

"Wait," Maddie said, snatching my elbow.

I turned around. "What?"

"I didn't really think this through," Maddie admitted with a shaky voice. She reached into her pocket and pulled out a red object. Holding it out at me, she said, "Here. Take this. It's my last one. It's a custom smoke shell – no need to light anything. Just pull the string on the end of it to pop it open, and slam it on the ground as hard as you can. The chalk dust will burst from it, creating a smoke screen…y'know, in case you need it. In case things go… *wrong*."

Taking it in my fingers, I grinned. "More spy stuff. Cool." I paused, realizing neither of us had actually talked about a plan. "What if something *does* goes wrong?" I asked.

Maddie took a deep breath, and stepped past me. When she got to the second set of double doors, she looked at me, knocked on the glass, and said, "If something goes wrong, follow the raven."

Follow the raven? Was she talking about Linus's business card he gave me last week? Before I could ask, the double doors cracked open an inch.

A voice from the other side hissed. "Happy holidays."

Maddie shot me a look, totally confused. She paused, lifting her hands up toward me and shrugging her shoulders. She wasn't sure how to respond. "Ummm....."

"Happy holidays," the voice said again, a little more gruff.

"I don't know what he's talking about," Maddie mouthed to me.

And then I remembered that earlier in the day, I had heard one of the covert monitors say the exact same thing. It had to be a code they used to make sure they were dealing with other Suckerpunch agents! I jumped forward and nearly squealed. "I prefer the term 'Merry Christmas!'"

There was silence as Maddie and I stared at each other. Had I said the right thing? Were we busted? Was my side going to cramp up again from another chase? I hoped not, because I wasn't sure I could handle it another time.

Finally, the door creaked open. The boy on the other side was hidden in the shadows. I heard him breathing heavily, as if he were a chubby kid that just finished running the mile. And then I realized that it was *me* that was doing the heavy breathing. The Suckerpunch doorkeeper didn't say a thing as he waved us in, allowing us to enter their base of operations.

I wish I could tell you that it was a room filled with awesome spy gear and agents training with crazy science fiction stuff, but I'm sad to say it wasn't that at all. Instead, it looked exactly how an abandoned swimming pool would look if sixth graders were seated around it looking at their laptops and cell phones. It looked like a LAN party, where each kid was playing the same videogame with each other, but on different screens. And if you've ever seen a LAN party, then you'd know there wasn't anything exciting about it unless you were actually playing one of the games.

"How disappointing," I said.

"I promise Glitch has a cooler base," Maddie said. She held her arm out, and whispered. "Look!"

Not even five feet away, the time capsule was resting on a rickety table, right next to us. I was so excited that I had to keep myself from jumping at it. Curling my toes in my shoes, I grit my teeth, and whispered softly. "Let's just grab it and go before we're caught."

Maddie acted like she didn't hear me. She stepped farther into the room with determination as if she knew exactly where she was going. When her walk turned into a run, I knew she was after something, and I knew it was only seconds before the Suckerpunch agents saw that we were there. "Linus, you traitor!" she shouted as her feet stomped on the concrete.

Across the room, I saw Linus jump up from a table. On the other side of the table, I saw the figure of another sixth grader who I've only seen in passing between classes. It was Christopher Moss, or as I've come to know him, Christmas.

"You're so dead!" Maddie shouted like a warrior as she dodged enemy agents that dove after her.

My knees felt weak as I watched her run away, shrinking against the backdrop of the abandoned room. I wanted so badly to run after her because I *knew* she was going to be in trouble in just a second, but the time capsule kept screaming for attention on the table beside me. The agent covering the door ran after Maddie, leaving the exit *and* the capsule unguarded.

"Forget it!" I grunted as I snatched the time capsule. I stuck my arm through the strap and pulled it up to my shoulder. The sounds of footsteps echoed across the empty concrete of the pool as I darted back to the exit.

Slipping through the door unnoticed, I leaned against the wall, listening to the door click shut. Maddie screamed at Linus, her muffled voice vibrating against the frosted glass until spilling into the room I was hiding in. I felt terrible.

But I did my best to shake the feeling of abandoning Maddie off my shoulders. Now that I had the capsule on my shoulder, I couldn't waste any time wondering if I could help her. She was a highly trained secret agent! She could handle herself, right?

I heard her muted shout one last time. "Follow the raaaaaven!"

I balled my fists out of frustration, knowing that she was telling me what to do, but I also knew it was only a matter of seconds before Suckerpunch's agents realized the time capsule was gone. I had to act fast.

The hall monitor in the gymnasium was still pounding against the double doors so that exit was blocked off. I wondered if Chase was still doing his best to keep the other monitors occupied. I slipped into entrance to the boy's locker room instead, hoping there wasn't a sealed door. Lucky for me, there wasn't.

I was beginning to really appreciate how many exits there were to boy's locker room. I was able to bypass the gymnasium completely and jump right into the hallway of the school, near the lobby.

I stood in silence as more thoughts bounced around my noggin. Was there anything I could change about what just happened? I sighed, knowing the answer was that I probably shouldn't have run out on Maddie. My guilt sunk like a brick in my stomach.

At that moment, the bell rang. Third period was over and students were about to pour out of their classrooms. My face was still plastered all over the walls of the school so there wasn't any chance that I could stay invisible. Was this how super cool kids felt? Like they couldn't go anywhere without people knowing who they were?

Shoving the time capsule under the front of my shirt, I moved to a water fountain and stepped on the pedal at the bottom. Water began shooting out of the spout as I bent over to take small sips. The ice-cold liquid made my teeth hurt as I listened to students walk by me, engaged in their daily gossip.

"Did you hear they haven't caught Brody yet?"

"I heard he escaped the school and flew the coop! Headed to Mexico or something. Hope he knows how to speak Spanish."

"Did they ever find the time capsule he took? What was in it?"

"I don't think they did. I heard it was filled with millions of dollars worth of pirate treasure though – probably how he could afford to escape the country."

I kept sipping the water. Did they really just suggest that the time capsule was filled with pirate treasure? My classmates at Buchanan weren't exactly the smartest bunch, I'll be the first to admit that.

"Hurry up, man!" said a boy behind me as he nudged my foot with his own.

I slurped at the water and coughed because I

accidentally inhaled some. Covering my mouth, I managed to squeeze out a "sorry" before stumbling down the hall. Another kid bumped into me, tossing me back toward the fountain. After a few more steps, I found myself in the middle of the hallway, deep in the flowing river of students.

I kept my hand over my face as I coughed, but after I noticed that I was getting *more* attention from coughing, I stopped. If I kept covering my face, it would've looked weird so I stared at the ground instead and stopped trying to walk *against* the crowd.

After a few steps, I found myself swept up by the rush of kids. They weren't even paying attention to me! Keeping my head down, I walked as if I were going to my next class. A wave of cold air washed over my body and my walk suddenly felt very familiar. I sighed with each step, feeling a numbness in my limbs, like I was an undead zombie walking the halls.

The time capsule remained under my shirt the entire time. Both my hands were on it, making sure it stayed that way.

As I marched with the other students, I remember the last thing Maddie said to me. *Follow the raven.* She was obviously talking about the raven on the business card Linus handed me the week before, but the business card was still in my wallet, and only the monitors at Buchanan knew where *that* was at.

Good thing I had it memorized.

I'll confess it wasn't hard to memorize. It was just a business card with an inkblot of a black raven with the numbers 17 and 4 written in roman numerals under it. The problem was that I didn't know what the raven *or* the numbers meant.

But wait… *why* was I even bothering with the time capsule anymore? Why not just take it to the principal's office and be done with the horrible day I've had? Maddie was *probably* going to be fine. Sure, she was with Suckerpunch now, but that was just a group of sixth graders. What were they gonna do?

…what *were* they gonna do? I felt my stomach turn as I imagined them cutting Maddie's hair or something.

No way. Linus wouldn't let them do that. Linus might be fighting for the bad guys now, but Maddie was still his friend… wasn't she?

The truth was that I had no clue. About *any* of it, and it was getting on my nerves so bad that I didn't even notice that my hands were stinging from the kung fu grip I had on the time capsule through my shirt.

The right thing was to help Maddie. I *knew* it was the right thing because my stomach settled down as soon as I made the decision to do it. For the second time in my life, I had to make the decision to do the *right* thing instead of the *safe* thing.

And I felt alive again.

I snuck a peak at the time on one of the clocks on the wall, trying to see how much longer I had until fourth period started. I was in the lobby of the school where there was a clock hanging above the tinted cafeteria windows, and two other clocks at opposite ends of each other, hanging above the east hallway and the west hallway.

The clock I checked was above the west hallway, but for some reason, I glanced back at the clock above the cafeteria. I'm not sure why – maybe something in my brain told me to do it – maybe it was a coincidence. But when I did, I saw a familiar image.

The logo on the bottom part of the cafeteria clock was a symbol in the shape of a raven. When I checked the west hallway clock again, the raven logo *wasn't* on it. Of course, I naturally spun in place and looked at the east end clock. I wasn't surprised to see that the raven *wasn't* there either.

Follow the raven.

Alright, Maddie. I hope you knew what you were doing. I sifted my way through the other students until I made it to the cafeteria doors. Through the glass, I saw the drama team setting up for the play that was supposed to be performed during lunch, the one about the werewolf football player.

I opened the door, and snuck into the cafeteria, keeping as close to the wall as possible. The black sheets were still draped on coat hangers just like earlier that morning so it was like walking into a maze, which was great because I didn't have to worry about being spotted.

The only thing I could see was the area above the black sheets, but that's all I *needed* to see. I looked for another clock and was surprised to find two of them in there. One was directly above the stage, and didn't have a raven. The other clock was placed above the kitchen doors.

And that one *did* have the raven logo.

I won't lie. I had a goofy smile on my face. Wouldn't you? I was super excited about finding the path!

Creeping against the wall, I kept myself outside of the maze of black sheets. There wasn't much sense in trying to find the way through the maze rather than around it. When I got to the kitchen doors, I paused to collect my thoughts.

What was going to happen when I found the Glitch headquarters? Would they even listen to me? What if they locked me away in detention forever? I shook my head. No. I wasn't going to stand in my own way this time. Maddie was in trouble. Linus was a traitor. I had to get in there and just tell everyone what I saw. They were agents and they'd be able to handle it from here.

I pushed down on the handle and opened the door, proudly taking another step into the unexpected.

The kitchen lights were switched off, but the stainless steel shelving had a glow that illuminated enough of the room for me to see. I carefully walked over the polished flooring, my shoes squeaking with each step.

A shadow suddenly rose up from behind me. I nearly jumped out of my skin as I fell against one of the shelves. I was afraid for my life until I figured out it was just my eyes playing tricks on me. The thin slit from the kitchen doors allowed a small amount of light into the room. Because of that light, shadows loomed and danced all around me.

I turned around and scanned the clock above the inside of the kitchen doors. No raven.

As I stepped farther into the room, I saw an object twinkling near the back of the room where it was the darkest. Squinting, I allowed my eyes to adjust a little more and could see the faint outline of a circle. It was another clock, glinting at me like it was trying to get my attention so I slid over the counter to see what it wanted.

I had to put my face right up to the clock to see it clearly in the dark. On the bottom portion, I saw the same logo of the raven that the other clocks had. A smooth metal door was standing next to the clock, and on the other side was a glowing number pad. The roman numerals must've been the code I had to punch into the pad.

I smiled. "Like candy from baby," I whispered.

"But candy from a baby is bad and um… what I'm doing is good. Uh… like *giving* candy to a baby – no wait, that's probably not a good thing either. Whatever."

I stopped messing around and punched the numbers into the pad. It beeped after every digit.

"One…"

Beep.

"Seven…"

Beep.

"Four…"

Beep.

After the last beep, the number pad blinked red and white. I heard a rush of air as the smooth stainless steel door sunk back an inch before sliding open. I took another breath, and stepped through the door to the Glitch headquarters.

Just like the rest of my morning, what I saw disappointed me. I walked into a massive room, but there was *nothing* inside. It was just an empty room with a bunch of empty desks. To be fair, it *looked* like something *used* to be in the room.

I was about to turn around and give up until I heard the sound of slow clapping echo off the glossy walls. I'm not the kind of kid that enjoys surprises, especially when it involves being alone in an empty room made of brushed metal. I've seen enough horror movies to imagine how these situations end.

Spinning in place, I dashed back to the open door of the kitchen, but I was too late. There were two boys blocking my path, staring at me with their arms folded. They weren't dressed as covert monitors. The only other thing I could think of was that they were agents of Suckerpunch.

I stared through the two boys, listening to the slow clapping that continued. I shut my eyes and shook my head. Way to go, Brody. You just walked into a trap. I turned around to see who was on the other side of the room, but as I did, I already knew it was Christopher Moss. *Christmas.*

Christmas laughed and clapped one final time. "If it isn't Mr. Brody Valentine himself!"

"Christopher Moss," I hissed.

"Oh, come on," Christmas said. His voice was a little higher than you'd expect from a super sixth grader. He sounded the way someone does when they're joyful.

"Only my friends call me *Christopher*. My enemies call me *Christmas*. I guess we're about to find out which name *you'd* like to call me."

CHRISTOPHER MOSS

AKA CHRISTMAS

Placing my hand on my chin, I cracked my neck. "I got a couple names I'd like to call ya."

Christmas stopped in place. He pressed his lips together and wagged a scolding finger at me. "Nice burn," he said. "But you seem to forget who has the power in this room."

At that moment, one of his bodyguards behind me kicked at the back of my knee. I lost my balance and dropped to the cold metal floor. I tightened a smile as I tried to pretend it didn't hurt. The time capsule slipped out from under my shirt, but I caught it just before it hit the floor.

Christmas frowned. "*That's* what you *get* when you run your mouth. Can we try this again, but without the sass?"

Staring at the floor, I didn't speak.

"I see you have the time capsule," Christmas said joyfully, pointing at the container in my hands. "I won't even take the thing away from you, alright? This will be a *peaceful* conversation."

"Where's Maddie?" I asked coldly.

"She's been…," Christmas paused, folding his arms. "*Dealt* with."

"If you hurt her in any—"

Christmas put his hands up and patted at the air. "She's *fine* for now, alright?"

I didn't answer.

Christmas's dress shoes clopped on the floor as he restarted his walk. "Even a quiet guy like you has to admit that today has been pretty fun, no?"

Still on my knees, I stared at the floor, making sure I didn't make eye contact with him. If he used to be part of Glitch, then I knew I had to work extra hard at hiding my fear.

Christmas held his arms out and spun in a circle. "Do you like what I've done with the place?" His laugh bounced off the metal walls. "This room used to be filled with pests, but I think I've done a bang up job of clearing them out!"

"So Glitch *used* to be here?" I asked.

Christmas curled the side of his lip, trying to form what I thought was a smile. "Correct. They *used* to be here," he growled. Then with his high-pitched voice, he laughed. "I guess they got *spooked* or something, right? And all I wanted to do was say hello, but by the time I got here this afternoon, they had already packed up. Headed south like a bunch of ugly ducks afraid of the cold weather that Christmas brings."

Ew. Was this boy really going to use his name as a pun?

Christmas continued to speak. He was a smooth talker, that much was for sure, but he was also very animated in the way he gestured with his hands when he talked. With his fingers pressed together, he almost danced as he made his way toward me. "It's really a shame you didn't see this place when it was at its prime, *last* year."

I chuckled. "That's right. I almost forgot you enjoyed sixth grade so much you decided to come back for seconds."

Christmas's face flushed with red. I heard one of the bodyguards move behind me again so I braced for another kick, but Christmas snapped his hand out and shook his head. It was his way of ordering the bodyguard to back down. He had power, and he knew how to use it.

I watched as Christmas took a deep breath and cracked his knuckles. I really hoped he wasn't thinking of introducing his fists to my face. My nose can't talk, but if it could I bet it'd say something like, "I really enjoy not being broken!"

"Brody," Christmas said softly. "What's your role in all this?"

I paused, confused. "What do you mean?"

Christmas smiled as if he felt sorry for me. "Your *purpose*," he repeated. "Why are you even here? What are you looking for?"

Still unsure of what Christmas meant, I said, "I was looking for the Glitch headquarters. Duh."

Christmas let out a small laugh. "But *why*? Is it because you think you're secret agent material?"

"It's because—," I started to answer, but he interrupted me.

"Is it because you're crushing on Maddie?" Christmas said. "Maybe you think all this is going to mean you guys will go out someday?"

"No," I said, my voice cracking.

"Then what?" Christmas asked. "Surely it's not because you think you're Glitch material because you'd make a *terrible* agent."

His words cut like a knife. I didn't think I had crazy awesome spy skills, but I *was* beginning to think I was *sorta* good at this. Was it possible I was utterly wrong? Maybe. It's happened before.

"I can see that doubt in your eyes," Christmas said, finally standing before me. "I look at you, and I can tell you're the kind of kid that *doesn't* crave adventure. Am I right?"

"Maybe."

"And yet here are you in the middle of one. Trouble *found* you, didn't it?" Christmas asked, holding his open hand out to me. I think he wanted me to shake it.

"...maybe," I replied, ignoring his outstretched hand.

Clasping his hand shut, Christmas drew it back. "Listen carefully, Mr. Valentine, because I'll only offer this once."

I rose from the floor, feeling the weight of the time capsule in my palms.

"Join us," Christmas hissed. "Join Suckerpunch. You've shown that you want *more* in life, but Glitch isn't going to get you anywhere anytime soon. I can't say that Suckerpunch will get you there quicker, but what I *can* tell you is that Suckerpunch promises to bring chaos to Buchanan School. Complete and utter chaos."

"You created Suckerpunch just to cause trouble?" I asked.

"I spent all of last year trying to bring peace and keep things safe," Christmas said. "But safe is *boring*. I think this time around, I'll introduce a little *madness*."

Safe is boring. Funny how Maddie said the same thing to me.

Christmas continued his rant. "After all, Glitch has *abandoned* you! Instead of helping you today, they've tucked their tails between their legs and buried themselves in a hole somewhere, leaving you completely on your own to deal with one of *their* problems – *me*."

"That's not true," I said.

Christmas hopped backward, acting shocked. Raising his eyebrows, he opened his arms up and waved them at the empty desks. "Do you *see* them? Because I sure don't!" His shoulders sunk as he turned to face me. "Are they just voices? Do the voices tell you to do things, Brody? Do they keep you awake at night?"

"I don't hear voices," I said, annoyed. I wasn't sure if Christmas wanted me to like him or hate him. He was nuts! Impossible to read!

Out of nowhere, Christmas dropped to the floor and crossed his legs, rocking back and forth like a child waiting to open presents. "You were like a flame to a moth," he murmured. "A *fish* that couldn't resist the bait."

I narrowed my eyes, watching the super sixth grader on the floor. "Bait?"

Christmas clapped rapidly, excited by his own words. "You're predictable, Brody Valentine! A predictable sixth grader that did exactly as I wanted you to! Of course I have to give myself a *little* credit, after all, it was *my* genius brain that made the plan. Boy, if my brain could scream gleefully, it totally would!"

I shook my head. I was beginning to feel embarrassed, but I wasn't sure why. "What are you talking about? *I've* got the time capsule now. You've lost! My name is as good as cleared!"

Without warning, Christmas sprang to his feet and screamed like a maniac. "*Look around you, Valentine! You're on your *own* now! Glitch isn't around for you to *hide* behind, *is* it? You're just a *nobody* that the whole school thinks is a thief!"

"But when I return the capsule, I'll tell them what you've done, and what you're *planning* on doing!" I shouted.

"Who's going to believe a *thief?*" Christmas replied. "You really think Principal Davis is going to believe you if you waltz into his office and return the time capsule he thinks *you* stole! Yeah, right," Christmas said nodding, rolling his eyes and tossing me a thumbs-up. "Good luck with all *that*."

I could feel my blood boiling again.

Christmas spoke to me like he was scolding a child. "You really goofed up this time, didn't ya? Getting Sophia to set you up was the hardest part of this whole thing, but as soon as you took the bait, the dominoes all fell over perfectly. You escaped from the covert monitors in the morning and created your own mission to find the capsule. I just had to dangle it far enough for you that you couldn't resist the challenge of finding it."

"You're insane," I whispered.

Christmas grinned and continued his monologue. "When Sophia was caught, I *knew* she'd rat me out to Glitch. Being a member of Glitch last year, I also knew they'd see me as more of a threat than they had before. I didn't expect them to move their base so quickly," Christmas said, spinning in a circle, "but as you can see, they sure did! Glitch is running around like a chicken with its head cut off! Plus the amazing Brody Valentine

100

will be locked away in detention until college, and *I* got what I wanted from the time capsule."

I swallowed hard, feeling a knot in my throat. He just said he got what he wanted from the capsule. Had my entire morning been a waste of time? If I could go back and change things, I totally would've followed Linus so I could've caught him when he took the capsule from the garbage can. Blast!

"Check out the best part," Christmas said, laughing and patting at the air again. "That time capsule has *your* finger prints all over it. You're done, Brody. I've *won.*"

He was right. Even as he laughed, I was rolling the capsule around with my fingers, which is where most fingerprints are located, just sayin'. I could've tried tossing it at Christmas, but he'd stay away from it like it had cooties.

Christmas stepped past me and mumbled some words to his bodyguards. I stood in place with my fingers aching from the heavy time capsule. What was I going to do? What *could* I do?

The two bodyguards were blocking the exit to the kitchen. Christmas had entered the room somewhere on the other side, but there was no way I could tell if he had other bodyguards stationed there.

Christmas thinks he's giving me a choice by offering me a place in Suckerpunch, but what he didn't know was that it was *never* an option for me. Linus was the one that said if I was going to do the right thing, I'd have to do the right thing *no matter what*. In that moment, I became a firm believer of that, even if the person who said it had chosen the *wrong* thing.

As slowly as possible, I reached into the front pocket of my jeans and felt the smoke shell that Maddie had given me earlier. Easing it out, I held it in my palm. Just as I was about to yank on the string, I overheard the conversation Christmas was having with his bodyguards.

"Hand me the CD, please," Christmas's voice snipped.

Both of the bodyguards mumbled back and forth to each other until one of them finally said, "Uh, boss, we thought *you* had it."

Christmas's voice became a whisper. "*What are you talking about?* I *told* you to remove it from the time capsule back at headquarters. Remember? I said take the CD out and put the capsule on the table by the door! *Now which one of you has the CD?*"

"Not me," the first bodyguard said.

The other spoke softly. "Me neither."

"You mean…," Christmas sighed. "*The disc is still in the capsule?*"

I took that as a sign for me to set off the smoke shell. Clutching the small object in my hand, I pulled the string apart from the other end. I did as Maddie had instructed and slammed it into the floor by my feet. A blast of white chalk dust swallowed the entire room. I dove forward to gain speed, making sure I made a ton of noise so Christmas knew I was trying to escape.

"After him!" shouted Christmas's voice.

I rolled over one of the desks and stood perfectly

still in the thick cloud, listening as the two bodyguards and Christmas ran right past me without a clue. Their heavy footsteps led away until I couldn't hear them anymore.

As the dust thinned out, I spun around to savor the fact that I had fooled those bullies, but apparently I was too quick to celebrate. I was wrong – Christmas was still in the room, staring right at me.

With fire in his eyes, he shouted. "Give me the time capsule, Brody!"

Spinning in place, I dashed for the other end of the room. Wonderful, I thought. At some point, those two bodyguards were going to realize I wasn't in front of them and turn around, which meant I'd be completely surrounded.

The entrance on the other end of the room came into view and was wide open. Jumping through the doorway, I found myself in what looked like a back alley, but with a ceiling over the top. Metal pipes stretched down both walls on either side of me with breaks in the places where other corridors met the one we were in.

The walls became a blur as I raced through the narrow hallway. I could hear Christmas's footsteps and shouts behind me, but I never bothered looking back. All I wanted to do was get to safety without smashing my face against one of the brick walls.

Faster and faster I ran, cutting sharp corners and tearing my way through the hidden back section of Buchanan School. I had a firm grip around the time capsule, keeping it close to my body. After a minute of sprinting, I glanced behind me to see that I was alone, but I continued to run in a circle of confusion until I was absolutely sure Christmas wasn't on my tail anymore.

Catching my breath, I studied the concrete walls, trying to make sense of where I was in the school. Without a map or anything, it was impossible for me to tell. All I knew was that I was somewhere *way* behind the kitchen.

Feeling the stress of what little time I had left, I started jogging down the corridor through the humid air, passing small openings that looked like offices for the maintenance people.

"Brody!" shouted a girl's voice just as I ran past one of the openings.

I slid to a stop and spun around excited. When I walked into the small office, I saw Maddie. She was sitting on a chair, but wasn't tied down or anything.

"What gives?" I asked. "How come you're sitting back here?"

Maddie jumped to her feet and threw her arms around me. "Christmas told me that if I waited here, then he'd bring you back so we could all talk it out!"

"And you *believed* him?" I asked, confused. Nodding my head, I tightened a smirk. "No, I get it. That kid's a smooth talker, isn't he? I would've believed him too."

"You have the capsule!" Maddie said.

I held up the container. "Yep."

"Did he say why he wanted it? What's inside that thing?"

Poking my head into the corridor, I checked to make sure we were still alone. "No, he never said why he wanted this. What about Linus? What happened back there?"

Maddie shrugged her shoulders. "I dunno," she grunted. "Those Suckerpunch goons got to me before I could get to him."

"Mega bummer," I said.

"It is," Maddie said, taking the lead down the corridor. "Come on. The exit's down this way."

Maddie's wristwatch chirped loudly, and then Christmas's voice came through. "Hello there, Maddie," Christmas said over the tiny speaker. "I'm sure Brody is with you by now so would you be a doll and give him this message for me? Tell him I'd like that time capsule back, please and thank you."

Maddie jogged up to a metal door and pushed down on the handle. The carpeted hallway of the school was right on the other side. "Don't listen to him," Maddie said. "It's time we went straight to Principal Davis with it."

The wristwatch chirped again. "Tsk, tsk, tsk," Christmas scolded. "The two of you are being very *very* naughty! Now bring me that time capsule, or *else*."

Maddie stopped in the open door. "Or else *what?*"

"This," Christmas said.

Immediately, the school's fire alarm blasted overhead. The horn was so loud that I covered my ears in pain. I could see Maddie say something to me, but I couldn't hear her.

Classroom doors flipped open as students filed out of the rooms. Because the fire alarm was activated, every single person in the school had to make their way outside.

Just when I thought my luck couldn't get worse, I saw a team of covert monitors stop in their tracks and point at me. One of them put his finger to his ear and spoke, probably alerting all the other monitors that I was spotted.

Maddie pushed me back through the door. The fire alarm was still going off, but it wasn't as loud in there. "There's a ladder to the roof back in that room I was waiting in! Get to the roof! I'll hold the monitors back!"

"But what about you?" I cried.

"I'll be fine!" Maddie shouted. "Get to the roof!"

Once she pulled the door shut, I started racing back to the small office we had just walked out of. I wasn't looking forward to climbing a ladder all the way to the roof, but I was so freaked out that I wasn't thinking straight. It probably wasn't the smartest thing I'd ever done, but again, my brain was wonky.

The ladder was exactly where Maddie said it was. On the back wall of the small office, metal loops stuck out from the walls and reached through a small opening in the ceiling. I was thrilled to see that it wasn't just a wooden ladder resting against the wall, but a solid passage to the rooftop.

Securing the strap of the time capsule around my shoulder, I grabbed the first metal loop and started making my way up.

On the rooftop, I slid away from the opening I had climbed out of, letting the rusted hunk of metal fall back into place. I heard a dull clunk and knew that the opening had locked itself. So much for climbing back *down* the ladder.

I hopped to my feet, sliding against the loose gravel under my sneakers. When I got to the side of the building, I looked over the edge and saw that most of the students had gathered in the parking lot. A few of them noticed me, and pointed.

Flinching, I dropped to the ground and started crawling across the gravel. There had to be another way down, there just *had* to be! A door or another opening that was locked tight had to be *somewhere* up there.

And then I heard the sound of kids shouting at me, but it wasn't coming from the parking lot. It was coming from across the rooftop!

"Great," I groaned as I stared at what looked like *every* covert monitor at Buchanan gathering at the other end of the roof, spilling from of an open elevator behind them.

"Turn yourself in, Valentine!" shouted the lead monitor. "You've got nowhere to run!"

"Just my luck," I said, exhaling slowly. I rose to my feet, and made my way back to the edge.

There I was on the rooftop of the school, looking over the side of the building as the *entire* squad of the school's monitors closed in behind me. I glanced over my shoulder, trying to estimate how much time I had before they caught me. Ten seconds at best, I thought.

I was completely cornered without a single escape

option I could think of. I leaned my head over the edge and saw the grass two stories down. There were groups of students clumped together over most of the schoolyard and parking lot, staring and pointing fingers at me. The wind picked up and blew my hair around, making my stomach queasy.

Looking to the sky, I did my best to push the dizzy feeling out of my body. If I stared at the clouds or something, maybe I could trick myself into thinking I *wasn't* on the rooftop of my school.

And then I saw a small flock of birds flying in the distance, making me wish I had wings. They were black, like the raven logo I had searched for earlier. Seeing them somehow comforted me.

I gripped my hand around the canvas strap on my shoulder and pulled it tighter. The time capsule attached to the strap pressed against my shirt as it rose. The weight of the capsule surprised me. It was heavy – heavier than I expected, at least.

I took a breath, listening to the footsteps of a hundred hall monitors circle behind me. I know, right? *A hundred* monitors for *me*. Seems like a bit of an overkill for one kid…

But instead of being afraid, I smiled, confident that even a *hundred* of 'em couldn't stop me.

I remembered my dad's advice and imagined the monitors as old ladies trying to grab a handful of my face. I dug my shoes into the gravel, and bolted directly at them – I think it's called a "blitz" in football.

A few of the monitors panicked, diving out of the way. In all the confusion, the rest of the monitors stumbled about, trying to make sense of what was happening. I think they were trying to figure out if someone had grabbed me or not.

I felt a hand snatch the strap on my shoulder and jerk me to the ground, but I instantly dropped and rolled away from the monitor. My quick moves caused a couple other kids to jump over me to avoid getting hit.

Once I was clear, I jumped to my feet and continued to run right through the heart of the squadron of monitors. I couldn't believe it was working! My dad's advice was working! They were so confused that a bunch of them could only watch as I ran by them.

Finally, I emerged on the other side of monitors, totally surprised that I had gotten out with barely a scratch. Hobbling the last few feet, I entered the open doors of the elevator. I turned and pretended to tip my hat at the defeated monitors. "It's been fun, boys, but it's time we part ways," I said sarcastically as I punched the "G" button for "ground floor." The doors slid shut, and I was left in silence.

Smooth jazz flowed from the speakers as I caught my breath. The time capsule was still safe in my bag, and for the moment, I was safe too. The elevator ride was so calm and quiet that it almost felt like I was dreaming. I even found myself whistling along with the music as I watched the numbers above the door switch from "2" to "G." When the doors opened, I knew I'd be in the lobby of the school. That meant all I had to do was make it to the offices and this whole situation would be over with.

The elevator beeped as it came to a stop. Just before the doors slid apart, I felt a knot in my throat. If there were any other monitors that weren't on the rooftop, then it was possible that they'd be right on the other side of the doors. In all my excitement, I hadn't thought that part through.

When the doors opened, I wasn't surprised to see that the situation was worse that I thought – it always was. Christmas was standing there, and he looked furious.

"How perfect!" he sneered. "The universe has smiled upon me after all."

I was going to say something witty, but went with something a little more physical. Jumping from the elevator, I pushed against Christmas. As he tripped over his feet, I immediately leapt off to the side to keep him from grabbing me.

"Get back here!" he shouted as he reached his hand out.

His fingers brushed against my shirt as I barely slipped away. I saw the entrance of the front lobby not even ten yards away, but I knew I would never make it there with Christmas so close behind me, so in my panic, I took a hard right turn, jumping into the cafeteria.

I scampered across the floor, hoping I didn't fall over on any of the folding chairs. The drama team already had the room set up for the play they were putting on. The black sheets that were draped across curtain rods were near the stage, so I made my way toward them. If I could just get into the confusing maze, I thought maybe I'd have a shot at losing the psycho behind me.

I heard Christmas's footsteps clap across the floor just as I glided into the maze of sheets. Without paying any attention to what I was doing, I made my way down random paths and just hoped for the best.

I heard the heavy breathing of Christmas as he searched for me. "You can't run forever, Valentine! What do you really think is going to happen here?"

I remained silent.

Just then, the bell rang out with three short bursts. It was the signal for the end of the fire drill. Almost instantly, I heard the footsteps of students slap on the floor of the cafeteria. Since fourth period was just about over, everyone was gathering for the play instead of getting back to their classes.

I knew there was no way I'd make it out of the

cafeteria without getting caught so that idea was out. If only I could find my way to the back of the maze, I could probably sneak out that way.

Turning right, and then left, and then right again, I found myself more confused than when I started. I had no idea what direction I was facing, but then I remembered the clocks! If I could see which clock had the raven logo on it, I'd know where the kitchen was and all I'd have to do was go in the opposite direction!

At that moment, the lights in the cafeteria dimmed in preparation for the play. Even if I *could* still see the clocks, there's no way I'd be able to see a tiny raven logo without any light.

Frustrated, I began running through the maze, turning down any corner I came to. At that point, I didn't care if I jumped out in front of a thousand students. I just didn't want to get caught by Christmas.

I ran without thinking.

Turn left.

Turn right.

Turn left.

Turn left again…

Until I couldn't go any farther. The last turn brought me to a wonky looking wooden door with a metal sign that read "Boy's Locker Room Entrance 6B."

Finally, my luck was turning around. Again, I felt thankful for the fact that Buchanan's locker rooms had so many entrances. I pushed against the door, sliding it open slowly. The small rush of cold air felt good against my face as the opening split apart to reveal more of the locker room.

As I took my first step, I heard Christmas growl behind me. "Oh no you don't!"

Jumping into the dark room, I ran down a couple aisles, keeping on eye over my shoulder. The time capsule bounced on my back as I darted back and forth, trying to find a good hiding spot.

The door clicked shut, and all I heard was the sound of Christmas catching his breath. It reminded me of the type of horror movie where the bad guy was right around the corner.

Pushing myself against one of the cold metal lockers, I waited to see what he was going to do. My plan was to make sure I knew exactly where he was in the room before bolting back out into the lobby.

I stared at the spot above the lockers. The room was nearly pitch black except for a few spots that seemed to glow with yellow light. I'd never seen the boy's locker room like that before, but I've also never looked above the lockers. Weird how you notice those kinds of things when you're hiding from a psychotic secret agent.

"Come out, come out, wherever you arrrrrrre," Christmas crooned softly.

I held my tongue, keeping quiet. If I could redo *this* situation? I wouldn't have stopped running after I got into the locker room. I should've just kept going until I found another door.

"Would you just give up already?" Christmas asked. "I'm growing bored with all this running! If I wanted to run so much, I'd have joined the track team!"

"Sure," I said. "All you have to do is leave me alone and I'll stop running."

Christmas laughed. "You're in no position to negotiate. You're at the end of the line, and I think you know that too."

I heard Christmas jump. I couldn't see him, but he was probably trying to surprise me into flinching and making noise, giving away where I was hiding. Breathing slowly, I remained as still as possible.

"Look, bro," Christmas said. "Can I call you 'bro?'"

"No," I immediately answered.

He didn't care. "Bro, we got off on the wrong foot. If you'd just give me the time capsule, then maybe we can work something out. How's that sound?"

My fingers were shaking as I heard his footsteps grow closer. "What kind of deal? The same deal you made with Sophia?"

"Sophia?" Christmas asked. "If all you want is money, I can arrange that. In fact, I'll give you twenty bucks right now if you just hand it over."

"Is that how much you paid her to frame me?" I asked, even though I knew how much he paid her.

Christmas laughed. "I *wish.* She got paid a lot more to drop your wallet off and steal the capsule, plus a little extra because she did it *over* the weekend."

"But what about her now? She confessed and gave herself up," I said.

"Not my problem," Christmas replied. "She knows better than to snitch on me. If she serves time in detention, then it'll be because she stole the capsule. I won't have anything to do with that."

I felt the capsule against my back as I leaned against the lockers. Christmas's footsteps were getting closer. It was only a matter of seconds before he cornered me down the aisle. I sighed, feeling defeated. "What do you want with this capsule anyway?"

Christmas's long shadow appeared on the floor

outside the aisle. There was a good thirty seconds until he spoke again, but it felt like an eternity. "I feel like I *do* owe you an explanation since you won't be seeing daylight until you graduate. At least it'll help *me* feel better about the terrible morning you've had. Not that I *care* though."

"Thanks," I said sarcastically.

"The capsule was buried in 1999," Christmas explained. His shadow continued to creep across the cement. "It was filled with the typical boring stuff like baseball cards and newspaper clippings, but the *brainless* Principal Davis decided to include a few *extra* items. He grabbed a couple of CDs from his office and tossed them in there. I honestly think it was a mistake, but a copy of the school's computer operating system was among the discs."

"How do you know?"

"Buchanan buries and digs up a time capsule every year," Christmas said. "And Mrs. Olsen, the science teacher, keeps a list of items buried with each one."

I was confused. "But why would Principal Davis throw CDs in there?"

Christmas shrugged his shoulders. "Probably because he figured nobody would use them anymore in the future. Maybe he thought we'd open the capsule and say, '*Whoa, what are these shiny round things?*'"

"So all you want is the school's operating system?" I asked, crawling away down the aisle. "What good is *that* going to do you?"

Christmas laughed the kind of arrogant laugh you'd expect from a super villain. "Because I'll install it on my laptop. I'll fail *every* sixth grader at Buchanan. Every one of them! They'll *all* have to repeat the sixth grade because of it. What's more chaotic than an entire *school* of *super* sixth graders? I don't think *anyone* is gonna make fun of me after *that!*"

For a second, I thought I heard someone gasp, but ignored it because I was pretty sure we were alone in the locker room.

Hopelessness washed over me as I stared at the insane super sixth grader's shadow. Last week when Maddie and I were trying to bust Sebastian, we thought we were dealing with this exact thing. I was relieved to find out it *wasn't* that, but it's funny how the universe works sometimes. I guess it decided to deliver an uppercut to my chin, making the situation terrifyingly real.

Thanks, universe. *Thanks*.

As I crawled to the other end of the aisle, I glanced over my shoulder once more to make sure Christmas's shadow hadn't moved, but when I looked, it wasn't there. Gulping, I started my army crawl forward again, but my head bumped into something hard.

"Season's greetings," Christmas snarled.

Before I could respond, he grabbed the time capsule's strap on top of my shoulder and lifted me off the ground. As a kid who was only a year older than me, he was as strong as an ox!

When I was on my feet, he let go of the strap and pushed his foot against my stomach, slamming me into the lockers. I watched as he raised his fist.

Shutting my eyes, I braced for impact, hoping that he would punch my cheek instead of my beautiful nose. A gust of wind blasted against my face, tossing my hair around just before I heard what sounded like a heavy blanket falling to the floor.

All of a sudden a bright white light flooded my vision, swallowing the world around me. I wasn't sure what was happening, but it couldn't have been good. Don't people see white lights when they die? I wasn't in any pain, but was it possible that Christmas punched me *that* hard?

I heard Principal Davis's voice erupt in the distance. "Let him go, Christopher! Put him down this instant!"

Still scrunching my face, I cracked open an eye. The light was intense, making it impossible to see. And just as quickly as it appeared, it disappeared. The room fell dark again, but only for a second. The lights in the locker room switched on and I could see everything.

I saw the faces of all the sixth graders at Buchanan staring at me. Christmas was frozen in shock with his fist in the air, poised and ready to smash my face in.

"What?" Christmas whispered. "What is this?"

Looking to my left, I saw the locker room we had been running around in. The lockers weren't made of metal, but of painted cardboard. The floor we were standing on wasn't actually polished concrete either, but old wooden boards.

We *weren't* in the gym. We were still in the cafeteria!

The play that Brayden and the drama club were supposed to perform was about a werewolf on the football team! Of course there'd be a fake locker room as a set piece! The sound of a blanket falling was the curtain dropping. Across the room, I saw a boy standing next to a giant spotlight. Yes! The bright white light! I wasn't dead after all!

I laughed joyfully. I'd never in my life felt so happy to see the drama club.

A bit of drool fell from Christmas's lip. He was still in shock. I don't think his brain had caught up to reality yet.

"Busted," Brayden said from the side of the stage. His arms were folded and he looked unhappy. "Now get off my stage so we can put on this play!"

Principal Davis stepped onto the stage and approached us. "Christopher, you've got *a lot* of explaining to do."

"B-b-b-b-but I," Christopher mumbled.

Principal Davis's eyes bulged with anger as he pinched his fingers together. "Neh! *First*, you called me brainless. *Second*, you just admitted to everyone that *you* set it up so the time capsule was stolen. *Third*, you framed Brody for theft. *Fourth*, I don't have proof yet, but I bet you pulled the fire alarm. *Fifth*, you call yourself 'Christmas.' *Sixth*, you held Maddie prisoner… should I go on?"

Christopher hung his head and whispered, "No, sir."

Principal Davis took Christopher to the side of the stage where Coach Cooper met them. Together, they escorted the super sixth grader out of the room. The students in the cafeteria watched with wide eyes as the leader of Suckerpunch was taken away. I overheard a few kids talk about how they were glad Christopher's plan to fail everyone wasn't successful. Duh, right?

Maddie ran to the stage, hopping up in one athletic leap. She threw her arms around me for a second time that day. Can't say I didn't like it.

"Look at you," Maddie laughed as we walked backstage and out of sight from the rest of the sixth graders. "Saving the day again like it's no big deal."

Linus stepped out from behind one of the props. "Well done," he said.

I stepped in front of Maddie to protect her. "What are you doing here?" I asked, angry.

Maddie held her fist in the air. "You no good backstabbing son of a jackal!"

"Let me explain," said another student's voice.

Maddie turned, and straightened her posture. "Sir!" she said, surprised and saluting.

"It's alright," said the boy. He was shorter than me with brown hair. His brown eyes looked weary behind his thick rimmed glasses. Holding his hand out to me, he said, "The name's Jacob, but you can call me Cob. I'm the leader of Glitch."

I glanced at Maddie who nodded at me in return. Taking Cob's hand, I squeezed it tightly. "Valentine," I said. "Brody Valentine."

Cob put his hand on Linus's shoulder. "Linus was working as a double agent today, at *my* request."

"But why?" Maddie asked.

"You saw the video of Linus taking the capsule, right?" Cob asked.

Maddie and I nodded.

"Well we were there when Sophia dropped it off," Cob explained. "Since we already knew where it was, I sent Linus in to retrieve it."

Linus stepped forward. "I made a deal with one of Christmas's agents that I'd hand deliver the time capsule if I could join Suckerpunch. The agent asked Christmas, and he was gleeful about it."

"Apparently Christmas was excited at the thought of getting the capsule *plus* a Glitch agent on his team," said Cob. "In his arrogance, he let Linus right in."

"That's why I saw you talking to Christmas at the abandoned pool," Maddie whispered.

"Exactly," Linus said. "But it's also why I couldn't do anything to help you at the time. If I tried to protect you or help you escape, my cover would've been blown."

"My *mind* is blown," I joked.

"Now we know where the Suckerpunch hideout is," Cob said. "Plus Linus got a look at some of their plans for this year."

"Trust me," Linus said, folding his arms. "This *isn't* the last we've seen of them *or* Christmas."

Cob looked right into my eyes. "What d'you say?" he asked. "Can we consider you a member of Glitch?"

I tried to keep a straight face, but my smile finally snuck out. "Darn tootin'," I said, embarrassed at my lame choice of words.

Nobody laughed. They just looked at me like I was the strange one in the bunch, which I knew I was.

Maddie and Linus continued talking. I handed Cob the time capsule from my backpack. I literally felt relief at having the weight of the capsule off my shoulders. I almost asked if I could open it, but at that point in my day, I just didn't care anymore. I already knew what was inside anyway, so it didn't matter.

Before he disappeared backstage, Cob tossed my white leather wallet back to me. I caught it, actually happy to see it.

Stepping to the side of the stage, I joined Maddie and Linus. The lights in the cafeteria dimmed once again, and the room grew silent. The spotlight switched on, pointing directly at the center of the stage where Brayden was standing.

As the play started, I wondered what would've happened if I would've stayed out of the way today. Would I be in detention? Would I be safe? Would I have to repeat sixth grade next year along with everyone else? What else could I have done? If I could go back, would there be any part of it that I would've changed?

I shook my head, wondering if I made the right decisions.

The crowd laughed at a joke Brayden made on stage. Maddie and Linus laughed too. I never thanked Maddie for saving my butt for a *second* time in my life, but that was okay. Now that I was an official member of Glitch, I was certain I'd get the chance to return the favor someday.

For now, all was well within the walls of Buchanan. Christmas was busted, the stolen time capsule was returned, my name was cleared, and there was a werewolf cracking jokes onstage. I laughed, realizing how weird that sentence sounded.

Maddie glanced back at me and smiled softly, her eyes twinkling.

I returned the smile, feeling the best I'd ever felt in my life.

Nope, I finally decided. There wasn't a single thing in my day that I would've changed if I could.

SECRET AGENT 3
6th GRADER
EXTRA LARGE SODA JERK

A tiny baby trying to choke me to death with his tiny baby hands – *that's* how I would describe the way a tuxedo felt.

Don't ask me how spies wear them all the time. Mine was tight in the arms and made the back of my knees itch. It was like an alien symbiote from outer space was slowly crawling across my body, trying to bond with me because it needed a host to survive. I feared that soon I would be more *tuxedo* than I was *human.*

Seriously, I felt like a giant man-penguin. If I were a superhero, I'd be called Penguinman. They (the penguins) would crown me their king and I would rule over them with a frozen fist! No wait, superheroes don't

1

rule over anyone. Only bad guys do that, and I'm pretty sure there was *already* a villain like that…

Man, I should cool it on the comic books for awhile.

As if wearing a tux wasn't bad enough, I was also sitting in the middle of a bamboo forest, even though only moments ago I was in the hallways of Buchanan School.

BRODY VALENTINE

I'll be the first to admit I often zone out when walking the halls between classes only to find myself in the wrong room when the bell rings, but it's never been so bad that I've ended up in a *bamboo forest.* I think I even heard a monkey howling in the distance – uh-huh, that was *definitely* a monkey.

I mean, yes, up until a minute ago, I was wearing a blindfold, but the *clown* said I *had* to put it on if I ever wanted to see Maddie again!

Aaaand I'm just *now* realizing how *bizarre* that

2

all sounded.

"Where the *heck* am I?" I whispered as I stood from the creaky old chair.

A quiet little *clink* sound hit the ground. When I looked down, I saw that it was the broken pair of glasses I had placed in the front pocket of my tux.

I picked up the glasses and inspected them. One of the lenses was completely missing, while the other had a crack down the middle of it. Both hinges were bent out of shape, but still connected to the frame. Opening the glasses carefully, I pulled them over my face.

"Linus?" I said softly, stepping away from the rickety chair. "Linus, can you hear me?"

The sound of shuffling feet answered.

"*Linus?*" I asked again, speaking a little louder.

Just then, Maddie stumbled through the bamboo trees.

MADDIE!

She looked disheveled and stressed out. Her hair was tied into a frizzy ponytail on top of her head, and her cheeks were covered in dirt. She stopped at the edge of the forest, struggling to keep herself upright.

Immediately, two goons stepped out from behind the trees. They both had rubber bands pulled tightly back on their thumbs, aiming right at me.

"Where's the Horseshoe, Brody?" asked a thin and menacing voice from the trees.

I said nothing.

A third kid walked out from the forest. He was taller than the two minions aiming rubber bands at me. The boy was dressed in a white button down shirt, and had a white hat on top of his big head. At his neck was a fat black bowtie that looked like something out of a 50's movie. He stopped when he was standing next to

Maddie. "*Where's* the Horseshoe, Brody?"

Feeling a little dizzy from the insane scenario, I shook my head. "What're you talkin' about..?"

The boy in white lost it and shouted like a maniac. "*Don't play games with me, Valentine! You think I look like someone who likes playing games? I* know *you* know where it is, so you'd better give it up 'fore I do somethin' *crazy!*"

I gulped and took a seat on the antique chair again. I thought for a moment, feeling lost and confused. "*You* have it," I said. "I already *gave* it to one of your men!"

The boy in white raised his eyebrows and sighed, pulling a pair of scissors from his back pocket. With his other hand, he took Maddie's frizzy ponytail and started rubbing it between his fingers. And then he spoke, softer than before, as if he didn't hear what I had said. "I'm going to ask you one more time. The Horseshoe... *where* is it?"

Maddie's gaze met mine, and we stared at each other for a moment.

A glint from the scissors distracted me, and I looked back at the maniac holding Maddie's ponytail.

"Don't," I said, surprised by the crack in my voice. "*Please...* don't..."

The scissors flinched slightly. I heard the metal squeak against itself.

"Wait!" I cried out.

The boy in white opened the scissors.

Shhhhhhhhhk...

The sound was awful and inside my head, like when the dentist scrapes at your tooth right after drilling it.

Maddie's ponytail was in the boy's grip. The scissors were in his other hand. His two goons were standing on both sides of him with rubber bands pointed right at me. I was at least fifteen feet away from all of them. Even if I was the fastest kid in school, I wouldn't be able to reach Maddie before she got her hair cut.

I looked into her eyes. They were intense, like she was born to be a secret agent. I, on the other hand, probably looked like some kind of doll with doughy eyes, hardly intimidating at all.

My jaw started to ache. I had to force myself to blink. All this stress had me flexing every muscle in my body without knowing it. I even had to gasp for air because I was holding my breath.

I spoke, my voice cracking the same as before. "Please, I'll get it for you, okay? I don't know why you never got it, but I'll *find* the Horseshoe, and I'll hand it to you personally. Just please... *don't* do this."

The boy in white paused, grinding his teeth while staring into my soul.

And then the scissors snipped.

Maddie's scream was the last thing I heard before my world went dark… or it might've been my own scream. Either way, it definitely sounded like it was from a girl.

My name is Brody Valentine, and I'm a secret agent.

That morning started like any other. There was nothing weird or off-putting about it at all. I had arrived to Buchanan School around 7:35, give or take a few minutes. All the students were clustered at the front doors of the school, waiting to get in and away from the chilly morning air. Personally, I love it when I can see my own breath in cold weather.

Most of the kids around me were wearing long sleeved t-shirts or hoodies – typical fall weather apparel. A few of them were even wearing beanies. As we all piled through the doors, I glanced up and saw the broken Buchanan School sign. The last N was still hanging by a single nail. When were they going to fix that? Seems dangerous to let fate decide when "*Buchanan*" was going to become "*Buchana.*"

It had been a couple weeks since my last great adventure, which was fine by me. If I grew to be an old man, and the only thing I could say about my life was that I foiled an evil plan concocted by an evil dude, then I think I could die happy.

For anyone new to my life, here's a quick blurb to catch you up – imagine you're watching a movie, and the narrator says, "Previously, in Brody's life…"

It all started when I was thrust into the secret agent life because a friend of mine, Linus, thought I could make the cut. On my first "unofficial" case, Linus sent me on a treasure hunt to find evidence he had hidden away – evidence that the school's president, Sebastian, was secretly up to no good. With the help of another agent, Maddie, we were able to bust the bad guy and save the day.

Linus and Maddie are members of a secret agency called "Glitch." They're part of a team of agents operating behind the scenes of Buchanan School, working to keep things peaceful.

My second "unofficial" case had me running around the school trying to clear my name because someone had *framed* me for stealing a time capsule. That *someone* turned out to be a kid named Christopher Moss, who also goes by the name "Christmas."

Christmas is known as a "*super sixth grader*," which means this is his *second* year at Buchanan in grade six. That's right – he *should* be a seventh grader, but was held back for some reason.

He used to be an active member of Glitch, but the agency had to boot him since it doesn't allow super sixth graders as agents – it's probably because Glitch would be flooded with failing students who just want to remain secret agents.

And so, because of getting canned, Christmas started *his own* agency called Suckerpunch. His agency exists just to cause chaos in the school. I think it's his way of getting back at the system that failed him.

In both cases, Sebastian's and Christmas's, I came out on top. Exhausted, but victorious.

My third "unofficial" case was just last week. If you've kept up with my story, then you'll notice that I haven't mentioned it before. The reason for that was because it was uneventful and ultimately a failure.

Glitch got word that President Sebastian was up to no good again so the agency wanted to throw me into the field, "off-the-record," to see how I'd handle myself. The rumor was that Sebastian was working with a team of *ninjas* to make sure his plan worked. I know, right? Like ninjas even exist anymore.

Long story short, Glitch dressed me up in a wolf costume during Buchanan School's career fair, and then paired me up with some kid named Brayden. I was working undercover, trying to gather evidence of Sebastian's wrongdoing, but before I could get anything good on him, someone *else* had already blown the lid off the case.

It wasn't my proudest moment, and definitely not the most action-packed. But whatever, right? Such is life.

Finally, I made it through the front doors and into the lobby. I cupped my hands around my mouth and blew air into the small chamber I made out of my palms, trying to get the blood flowing to my fingers again.

I paused for a moment, watching all the students flow through the hallway, imagining them as microscopic red blood cells traveling through a vein, like they were the blood that kept Buchanan School alive.

Messed up, right? That's what happens when I watch one too many sci-fi movies.

I held my breath, clutched the straps of my backpack, and dove into the mess of kids, headfirst. I'd been through enough at Buchanan that walking the halls wasn't such a big deal anymore. If someone shoulder-bumped me, I could handle it. If someone tossed an insult my way, I could let it slide. The confidence came from knowing that I had a greater purpose in life, and that no matter what the school threw at me, I could handle it because—

It was at that moment when something caught my foot, and someone shoved me from behind. I tripped so fast that I face-planted into the carpet. I hit so hard that for a moment, I thought I saw stars. I heard giggling coming from some of the kids as they walked by me.

Wonderful. Just wonderful.

"Have a nice trip!" said a voice from above me. "See ya next fall!"

I glanced up to see who pushed me. Standing over me, with a bunch of his friends, was a student named Gibson. I didn't know too much about him, only that he was a bit of a jerk that had his sights set on me. I wish I could say I didn't know why, but that wouldn't be true.

Here's what happened – on the first day of school this year, I got to Buchanan with, like, a *minute* before the tardy bell rang. Because of that, I slid my bike into the railing and hooked my bike lock around the frame and latched it shut. As it turns out, my bike lock hooked Gibson's bike frame too.

When school was dismissed that day, I ended up staying an extra thirty minutes because I got duct taped to the lockers in one of the empty corners of the school. When I finally managed to free myself from the sticky situation (see what I did there?), it was only so I could walk outside to Gibson and a few of his friends fuming at the fact that his bike was locked to mine. Not my best moment, but that was the reason I stopped riding my bike to school.

Gibson and his friends didn't beat me up or anything like that, but every couple weeks I *do* get picked on a little more than usual.

"Hey, Gibson," I said, picking myself off the floor. The bottom of my chin burned. I tried to rub it, but it stung when I touched it.

"Lock up anyone else's bike recently?" Gibson asked, glancing at his friends so they knew when to laugh.

"Nope," I said, raising my voice slightly. "I've been extra careful about it."

Gibson laughed as he pushed right through me. His friends followed behind him like he was their king.

I sighed, doing my best to ignore the stares from other kids in the hallway. You'd think life would be different after working with a secret agency for the past month, but surprisingly it wasn't. It was kind of like being a superhero with a secret identity, except a superhero's secret identity isn't a sixth grade kid getting pushed around in school.

Avoiding eye contact with *anyone*, I continued my way down the lobby and into the hallway where my locker was located.

As I passed the front offices, I could see Principal Davis through the window, speaking with the school nurse, Mrs. Duvall. She had only been the nurse at Buchanan for a couple of weeks since the last one mysteriously disappeared. Sounds scarier than it was – the old nurse probably just retired… or died.

Mrs. Duvall was a younger woman, probably fresh out of college. And she was cute too – everybody saw it. Brown hair and brown eyes with a smile that could stop you in your tracks.

At any given time during the day, a line of boys would be waiting outside her door, claiming they felt sick. I *might* or *might not* have been one of those boys at one point in time. Let's just say if she were a clerk at a video rental store, I'd probably rent movies from there every single day.

She was friendly, smart, and always had a smile on her face, except for today. She had her arms folded and looked upset about something. Obviously through the window, I couldn't hear her conversation with Principal Davis, but I saw them shaking their heads at each other, occasionally glancing back at her office door.

Weird. Hopefully she wasn't thinking about quitting.

The first bell started ringing through the halls. Instantly, everyone switched directions, knowing they only had five minutes before school started.

"Did you see all that stuff outside?" someone asked, close enough for me to hear.

"Yeah, man," a student replied. "I can't believe they got all that stuff today. This school just worked itself up a couple notches in the coolness factor."

I glanced down the hall, at the glass doors at the end. Through the windows, a flurry of colors moved and danced about. After seeing the activity, I realized I could hear music thumping from the massive speaker system that the staff was busy setting up outside. Everyone was getting ready for a killer party for the school.

"Nice," I whispered.

Buchanan School had officially turned one hundred years old over the weekend. Can you imagine that? Students were walking on the same campus one *hundred* years ago, probably dealing with the same problems that kids do today. Well, sort of. I'm sure kids today didn't worry about getting eaten by bears while walking to school. Wait… did kids worry about that a hundred years ago?

Every year, the staff at Buchanan plans something special for the birthday of the school, but year one hundred was entirely something different. For the last half of the day, the school was going to basically turn into a carnival, with games and rides, and everything. And to top off the celebration, there was going to be a concert at the end of the school day, which parents and alumni of Buchanan were also invited to attend. The band that was chosen was called "Annee Mu." I have no idea why they called themselves that, but I'm sure they had their reasons.

The rumor was that the staff was going to throw out free hats during the show.

It was going to be crazy awesome.

At last, I made it to my locker. Spinning the combination on the dial, I lifted the metal handle up and swung the door open. My books were sitting at the bottom, but I ignored them completely. Instead, I reached my hand up and pushed against the back wall at the top. Thankfully, it didn't budge.

During the case with the time capsule, a student had gained access to my locker through a hole they made in the back. It was how they stole my wallet and planted it at the scene of the crime. After the case was cracked, Maddie had personally seen to it that the hole was sealed up, but I still felt the urge to check it every morning. It became such a ritual that if I ever *forgot* to check, the rest of my day would feel crummy.

I flipped my backpack upside-down and dumped everything onto the floor of my locker. A few kids looked my way, confused as to why I wasn't putting any textbooks into my bag. I shrugged my shoulders at them, but didn't offer any answers. Once I was finished, I shut the metal door and strolled away.

The halls were becoming empty as kids filed into their homerooms. Glancing at the clock, I saw that I only had about a minute until school started, so I sped my pace. My homeroom was only a few doors down, which meant I could make it there on time... but that *wasn't* where I was going.

"Mr. Valentine," Principal Davis said. He was standing outside the front office doors with his hands on his hips, watching the lobby clear out. I guess he was done talking to school nurse. "Move those feet, young man, or you're gonna be late. That'll earn you a *week* in detention!"

Principal Davis was always tossing out orders, but everyone knew it was in good fun. He was never seriously threatening anyone.

"Got it, sir," I replied, carving a path through the lobby.

"Hold on," Principal Davis said, pointing his thumb down the hall I had just walked out of. "Isn't your homeroom the other way?"

Some muddled words spilled out of my mouth as I tried to think of an excuse as to why I was walking in the *opposite* direction of my class. Finally, I spoke. "Oh, I gotta see about... a *thing* upstairs."

The principal frowned, taking a step forward.

I felt a thin layer of sweat form on my forehead.

Principal Davis chuckled as he patted the air in front of him. "Relax, I'm kidding. Do whatever you need to do, and then get to your homeroom."

"Aye-aye, sir!" I said, saluting. I snapped my hand down, embarrassed. Sometimes when I'm nervous, I do dumb things, like talk like a sailor and salute people. Yeah, I'm awkward like that.

I hurried down the hallway and turned the corner, glad to be away from the principal. The clock on the wall said I only had about forty five seconds until school started so I had to hurry if I didn't want to get caught outside of class.

At the staircase, I glanced at the steps going down into the dungeon of the school, which was the nickname everyone used when talking about the lower level. The steps going up were on the left side. I ran up the stairs, skipping every other one with each leap.

The second floor of Buchanan was nearly deserted. All the homerooms were on the first floor so I didn't have to worry about anyone seeing me, except for the teachers who had classrooms up there.

I jogged down the hall and glanced over my shoulder one more time before stopping in front of a heavy wooden door that was shut. Turning the metal handle, I pushed it open and stepped into the dark room.

Inside the classroom were stacks of cardboard boxes filled with all kinds of random items. Some boxes had shirts with the old *wildcats* logo printed on them. Other boxes were filled with shirts that had the new *moose* logo on them.

Along the walls were old chalkboards that weren't being used anymore. You know the kind – the ones with wheels at the bottom so people could move them from class to class. After getting replaced with dry erase boards, these antiques could only be found in gym locker rooms.

16

At the far back of the room, I walked up to one of the ancient boards that had a bird drawn in white chalk on the front of it. The broken wheels at the bottom made it so the board itself had to lean against the wall in order to stand up.

Once more, I looked behind me, making sure I was alone. I set my hand on the eraser that was sitting on the bottom rack and slid it all the way across the wood until I heard it click.

The entire chalkboard jumped forward an inch, but it didn't scare me. Really, it didn't. I totally didn't flinch because of the chalkboard. I flinched because… um, I don't know, but it *wasn't* because of the chalkboard.

Wrapping my fingers around the edge of the *not*

17

scary chalkboard, I pulled it back, revealing a hidden
door with a keypad right in the center of it.

I punched in the secret code without realizing I
was whispering the numbers as I did it. "Two, zero,
one, five."

The green dot appeared at the top of the keypad,
blinking rapidly.

"Hope that means it worked," I said.

The metallic door hissed like it was some kind of
pressurized space ship door. And then it slowly opened
on its own.

A female voice greeted me over the speaker
mounted to the wall. "Welcome to Glitch. The time is
currently 7:46 AM. The temperature outside is forty
seven degrees Fahrenheit, eight degrees Celsius."

I couldn't help but smile. A welcome message
with the time and temperature seemed like a bit of an
overkill.

I stepped into the secret room, which was much tinier than I expected. There was a security guard seated at a circular desk with the name of the agency on the front of it. The rest of Glitch was behind him, but I can't say it looked impressive.

The same kind of portable chalkboards from the previous room were being used as makeshift walls in the Glitch headquarters. It was like looking at a bunch of second-rate cubicles. A few kids were working on laptops, clearly dying of boredom, while others laughed with each other near the water cooler.

It didn't matter to me how frumpy the Glitch headquarters looked. I was still excited to be in on the action. "Awesome," I whispered.

The guard didn't look up from his newspaper, but acknowledged that I was there. He was another sixth grader at Buchanan that I recognized, but I'd never spoken to. Actually, I'd never spoken to about 99% of the students at the school.

"You got anything you ain't supposed to have?" the guard asked.

I chuckled like I was the excited "new kid" on the first day of school. "Nope!"

Setting the newspaper down on the counter, the guard took a honkin' huge bite from an apple, and then spoke with a mouthful of food. "Alright then, you're clear. Give me a sec to deactivate the security system first."

Security system?

Leaning over, the guard snatched some kind of plastic sheet off the floor. It was bubble wrap, and there were yards of it between the desk and the first wall of portable chalkboards. If anyone stepped on the sheet, it would pop like crazy, alerting the guard to the fact that someone was trying to sneak into the agency. Cheap, but effective.

"The security system," the guard stated, "is *deactivated*."

Stepping around the guard, I took a deep breath. This was it. This was the first time I was going to officially enter the Glitch headquarters as an agent.

A few weeks before that moment, I had entered the old Glitch headquarters, which used to be in a hidden room behind the kitchen. At that point, Glitch had already disappeared because Suckerpunch knew exactly where they were. This new upstairs headquarters was put in place after Glitch was forced to

20

abandon their old one.

With one foot forward, I took a step and walked into the new base of operations.

It would've been perfect too, if I hadn't tripped on the welcome mat just beyond the guard. I stumbled forward, but caught myself before falling completely to the floor. I already fell once, and didn't feel like doing it again.

Everyone, and I mean *everyone*, in the agency stopped what they were doing to look at the goon who just hobbled into their headquarters. Even the guard spun in his chair to stare at me.

I held my hand up. "I'm alright," I sputtered. Great. First impressions aren't one of my strengths.

Many of the kids shook their heads at me as if I was just an annoyance to them. I felt my heart race as my face grew hot with embarrassment.

Suddenly, the feeling of being the "new kid" was back again, but not in the excited way like it was before. This time it was an overwhelmingly stupid feeling that was slapping my face. I wanted to turn around and just go to my normal homeroom. At least there I could disappear at the back of the class.

"Don't mind them," a girl's voice said. "They just need some time to warm up to you."

I looked up, hoping it was Maddie, but it wasn't. It didn't matter though because her short sentence already helped me feel a little better. Funny how a tiny bit of kindness can change the way someone feels. "Thanks," I said, forcing a smile.

"No bigs," the girl said, smirking with the corner of her mouth.

Just like most of the kids at the school, I'd never

talked to this girl before, but I recognized her from some classes we had together. She wasn't exactly the kind of person that was hard to miss though.

From head to toe, she was dressed in bright colored clothing, and was probably the trendiest person I'd ever seen in my life. On any other kid, her outfit would look gaudy, but she wore it with such confidence that it worked on her.

She wore thick-rimmed glasses – the kind that hipsters wear, but they didn't look "*hipster*" on her. I think they were prescription. A pink unzipped hoodie was draped over her shoulders, covering a black t-shirt with a tiger image printed in metallic ink. Her skinny jeans were tucked into her boots, which went halfway up her shin. Finally, around her neck was a set of metallic headphones – the kind that were huge and went all the way around the ear. I could hear music coming from the speakers.

"The name's K-pop," the girl said.

"K-pop?" I asked. "That's a weird name."

She narrowed her eyes. "My *real* name's Caitlyn, but my friends call me K-pop."

"Why K-pop?" I asked.

Sighing, she answered. "It stands for 'Korean pop music.' I'm obsessed with it. I love it *so much*. It just makes me feel alive when I listen to it. You oughta give it a chance."

"Oh, are you Korean?" I asked, because after she mentioned the bit about Korean music, I noticed that she looked Asian.

"Actually," K-pop said with a wink. "I am, but only half. My mom's Korean, but my dad's Norwegian."

"Nice," I replied. "So that makes you *Kor-wegian*."

K-pop laughed at my dumb joke.

K-POP

"I like your clothes," I said, accidentally making myself sound like a creep. For some reason I started talking a mile a minute. "I mean, I like your style. I think they're *cool*. Your clothes! Your *clothes* are cute. You look *cute* in them. No, I mean your clothes look *cute* on you. Not that *you're* cute, no wait, you *are* cute, but your clothes are cute. That's what I'm talking about!" I forced myself to stop and speak slowly. "Your clothes… are cool… and I like them."

K-pop stared at me, confused.

"I'm just gonna be done talking now," I said, staring at the floor. "Forever."

"You're weird," K-pop stated.

Again, I felt dumb.

But then she smiled. "I *like* weird. Glitch could use a little *weird*."

I scratched the back of my head. "Thanks, I think."

"Cool cool cool," K-pop said. "So you're the *great* Brody Valentine, I presume?"

I nodded. "You've heard of me?"

"I have," K-pop said, taking a seat on a nearby desk. She talked really fast while moving a piece of gum around in her mouth. "Everyone in Glitch has. You're all they're talking about these days."

I felt nervous. "What kind of things are they saying?"

K-pop shrugged her shoulders. "Everything that *can* be said. That you'd make a good agent, that you'd make a terrible agent, that you got lucky, that you'll become the head of Glitch one day, that you'll fail on your first day here. *Everything*."

"Good to know that *some* people have confidence in me," I said.

"Do you know what kind of agent you're going to be?" K-pop asked. "You seem kinda gangly, not that that's a bad thing."

I paused. "I didn't realize they were different kinds. What kind are you?"

"I'm a computer person," K-pop said. "I'm a computer person that's out in the field, but you better not call me a nerd or I'll karate chop you into next week!"

The half Asian, half Norwegian girl in front of me was so animated that I felt a little intimidated. "What do you do as a computer person?"

K-pop gestured at some of the kids around us, working at their laptops. "All these guys are computer people *here* at the Glitch headquarters. I work with a computer on site, *during* a mission. Power needs to go out for a minute? That's my job. Electronic locks need to get hacked? That's me."

"Sounds cool," I said. "I guess I don't know what kind of agent I'll be. Hopefully I'll be... what did you call it? Out in the field?"

"Yeah," K-pop said. She pointed a thumb at other kids at their computers. "These guys live boring lives. If you're gonna be an agent, might as well get a little dirty, right?"

"Uh, right," I agreed. I glanced at the clock again. It was already 7:50.

K-pop hopped off the table and got closer to me. "So what kind of things do you like?" she asked, her face almost a foot away from my face, clearly breaking my personal bubble.

"I, uh, like sci-fi stuff," I said, inching away.

"Coooooool," she said, chewing her gum loudly. "Like spaceships and stuff? Time travel? Different dimensions?"

I laughed, still moving slowly away. "Yeah, all those things. Comic books, space operas, things like that."

"Spy movies?" K-pop asked.

"Definitely," I said.

"Wait," K-pop continued. "You're not here 'cause you're an action-junkie, are ya? Lookin' for some sort of action and adventure, huh? A Jedi craves *not* these things."

"No, no," I said, putting my hands up. "Nothing like that."

K-pop slapped the table and stared me in the eye. *"Then why are you here? Who sent you? What agency are you with? Why won't you look me in the eye?"*

"K-pop!" shouted a boy. "Go easy on him!"

I looked past K-pop to see who shouted. It was the leader of Glitch, a boy named Cob, and he was glaring at us from across the room.

K-pop turned around and laughed. "Just messin' with him. You know, some rookie hazing."

Cob stood by a desk that had been blocked off by a few of the portable chalkboards. "Get back here," he said to me, waving his hand.

I started walking down the aisle, between the desks. K-pop grabbed my elbow before I got too far.

"Hang on, duder," she said. "You seem like a cool kid." She flipped a business card out at me. For half a second, I wondered how kids our age would even go about getting their own business card. She continued. "If you find yourself in trouble, just call that number on the card. Don't text dumb junk either. No jockin' me, okay? Don't make me regret this. Don't make it weird. Okay? Because I'll block your number in a heartbeat."

"What's jockin' mean?" I asked.

K-pop sighed. *"Flirting.* Don't *flirt* with me over text message, or I will *end* you."

"Oh, right," I said, trying to sound cool. "I *knew* that. I thought you said something else."

K-pop smiled. "No, you didn't."

"Valentine!" Cob called out angrily like he was the chief of police in an 80's movie. He even had his cell phone pressed against his chest so whoever was on the other end of the line couldn't hear him yell. "My office! *Now!*"

I slipped K-pop's business card into my back pocket. "Thanks for this," I said. And then I turned and swiftly walked back to Cob's section of the room.

"You're *late*," Cob said, pointing at the chair in front of his desk, motioning for me to take a seat. He put the cell phone back to his ear and continued his conversation with whoever was on the other line.

His choice in clothing was unique to say the least. While everyone else wore brightly colored trendy shirts and jeans, he chose to wear clothing that looked like it came from his grandfather. A brown cardigan was pulled over a blue polo shirt. His shoes were leather loafers that perfectly matched his brown colored khaki slacks.

He was also the only sixth grader I knew who had a receding hairline. He looked like a really short 50-year-old man. Maybe he was one of those guys who age backwards! That's a real thing, right? I think I saw a documentary about it once.

On the wall behind him were all kinds of printed sheets of paper and notes, pinned to corkboard. Several of the pins were connected with red or blue thread, probably because the papers were related to each other in some way.

"That's horse radish!" Cob said sternly. "How do you expect me to run the agency based on that? C'mon, man, you gotta give me a *little* more slack!"

I tried not to be rude by acting like I couldn't hear him and continued studying the corkboard behind him.

A bunch of class photos were also tacked up, including President Sebastian and Christopher Moss. Several pictures of other kids, who I also knew, but had never spoken to, were hanging too – a chubby kid glaring at the camera, a scrawny girl who was wearing a black hoodie, and even one of a kid in a white hat wearing a white button down shirt with a fat bowtie.

And then there was a photo of the vice president, a student named Wyatt. On the other side of the vice president was a picture of another kid, who I *had* spoken to before, named Chase Cooper. I was surprised to see his name on Cob's board. Chase had a red thread tied around his pushpin that led back to Wyatt, and then back to Sebastian. Weird… why would *Chase* be on Glitch's radar?

CHASE COOPER — WYATT (VICE PRESIDENT)

Cob nearly exploded. "Why are you even telling me all this if there's *no other way* around it? Quit wasting my time!" he shouted, holding the cell phone in front of his face. Seething, he jabbed at the "end call" button on the cell phone screen. If this were an old action movie, he would've hung up the phone by slamming it on his desk. Too bad cell phones didn't work the same way.

Falling into his chair, he leaned back, repeating what he had said earlier. "Valentine, you're *late*."

I glanced at the clock on the wall. It read "7:58."

"I'm not late," I said defensively. "You told me to be here at *eight*, so as a matter of fact, I'm two minutes early."

Cob folded his hands and leaned forward, acting as if he were a parent trying to maintain patience with their child. "If you're not early, you're *late*. If I say to be here at eight in the morning, then you show up fifteen minutes *before* that. Understand?"

A girl's voice spoke from behind me. "Cob's one of *those* guys."

I turned, happy to see that Maddie and Linus were taking a seat on the bench that was against one of the chalkboard walls.

"What kind of *guy* is that?" Cob asked, cocking an eyebrow.

"Lighten up a little," Maddie said. "It's Brody's first day, alright?"

Cob swiveled back and forth in his chair, waving his hand at me. "Brody's first day was during the career fair last week, and he botched that up real good."

I sunk in my seat, but didn't say anything.

Linus sat forward and defended me. "That wasn't *Brody's* fault. You sent him out there in a wolf costume without *any* kind of instructions on what he was supposed to do! All he knew was that he needed to keep a close eye on Brayden, but as it turns out, we sent him to spy on the wrong kid!"

"If you ask me," Maddie added, pointing at Cob, "It's *your* fault for putting all your money on Brayden, when it *should've* been on Sebastian, *just like I told you!*"

Cob pinched the bridge of his nose. He set his hands back down on the desk and spoke softly. "You're right. The wolf costume was my mistake." He held his open hand at me. "Which is why you're still here. That case flopped because *I* sent you after the wrong kid."

I was stunned because it was the first time I didn't feel responsible for what happened at the career fair. "Okay," I said.

Cob raised his eyebrows. "You're still late though, got it?"

31

I started to defend myself by pointing at K-pop, who was dancing with her headphones on. "If that girl didn't stop me then—"

"Nuh-uh! You have nobody else to blame but yourself. Accept responsibility and don't let it happen again."

I faked a smile. "Put your nose to the grindstone, right?"

Cob paused, his beady eyes staring at me through his glasses.

Maddie covered her face, shaking her head disapprovingly.

Finally, Linus broke the awkward silence. "Who were you chewing out over the phone? Or were *you* the one getting chewed out?"

Cob sighed. "Funding for Glitch is getting cut by 80%."

"*What?*" Linus and Maddie exclaimed simultaneously.

Cob lowered his head. "Yup. We're gonna have to let a bunch of good agents go. It's been a long time coming, and frankly, I'm surprised I was able to keep our heads above water *this* long. At an 80% loss, they're basically shutting down the agency!"

"Who's '*they?*'" I asked.

Cob chewed on his lip and answered simply. "The powers that be."

"That doesn't seem fair, does it?" I asked. "Especially because you're adding *me* to the mix."

Cob smiled, pointing his finger at me. "No, *you're* the exception. You busted Sebastian a few weeks back, and then busted Christmas. No agent here has that kind of a record, not even Linus, and he's the best we got."

I felt my pride swell in my chest.

Linus folded his arms. "Beginners luck," he huffed. "It could've happened to anyone."

Aaaaand with that, the pride I felt quickly disappeared back into the hole it climbed out of.

"Christmas made the *classic* bad guy mistake of saying too much," Cob said. "He's a pea-brained dinosaur who got arrogant and thought he had already won."

"Exactly!" Linus said. "Which is why he started running his mouth when he thought he was alone with Brody!"

"There's something about those moments before victory," Cob said. "It seems to make villains do dumb things, like *explain* their whole plan."

Maddie chimed in. "It's because they want recognition. They want *someone* to know how their carefully crafted plot went off without a snag."

"Any criminal *daft* enough to do something like that *deserves* to get busted," Cob added. "If Christmas held his tongue a little longer, he *might've* gotten away with it."

Running my finger across my eyebrow, I tried my best to act like I didn't care that everyone in the room was trying to downplay my role in busting Christmas.

I think Maddie noticed because she sat forward in her chair. "Let's not forget that Brody kept him talking," she said.

"None of that matters anyway," Cob replied. "Glitch is still losing money, even though we saved the day."

"But what about Christmas?" Maddie asked. "He's still around, and you know he's the most ruthless kid we've ever encountered, especially because he created his own agency called Suckerpunch to combat ours!"

"Ain't nothin' we can do about that now," Cob said. "Besides, Christmas *and* Suckerpunch have been off the grid since Valentine busted them. For all we know, he's done playing games."

"He's *not* done," Maddie sneered. "Christmas is still in his classes so we know he's still here at Buchanan. It's safe to assume he's up to no good. There's a reason why his agency is called *Suckerpunch*. They're gonna hit us when we're not looking."

"This conversation is over," Cob said flatly. "Glitch isn't shut down *yet*, and we still got a job to do. We best stick to what we're good at. What're we good at?"

Maddie and Linus answered at the same time, with the same unenthusiastic tone in their voices. "Catchin' bad guys."

"Right," Cob said. He pointed at Maddie and Linus. "Go ahead and give Brody your cell numbers in case he needs to call or text you. Brody, you give them yours."

All three of us swapped numbers, saving them into our phones.

Cob opened the metal drawer on his desk and pulled out a manila folder. He tossed it toward me. "There's a kid who keeps flushing cotton swabs down the toilets – keeps backing them up. Your job is to find him, and tell him to *knock* it off."

"Clogged toilets?" Linus asked. "I haven't heard of any pranks like that."

"Trust me," Cob said. "It's happening, and it ain't

pretty."

"*Really?*" I asked. "That's *it?* Stop someone from plugging the toilet? What kind of lame case is *that?*"

"Not every case is the end of the world, cowboy," Linus snipped, annoyed.

"A clogged toilet is a disaster," Cob said. "Whoever's responsible is doing it on purpose as a prank. Slippery bathroom floors are dangerous and can hurt people, so this *thug* needs to be stopped." Cob folded his hands and sat forward, speaking softer. "Brody, let me explain something first. Glitch doesn't exist to save the day in glorious fashion. Glitch exists to keep everything on a straight path, do you understand?"

I shook my head.

"Our goal," Cob continued, "is to keep things normal, without anybody knowing what happened. We take credit for nothing because we basically don't exist. Got it?"

"Got it," I said.

"Good."

"What are we supposed to do if we find the toilet clogger?" I said sarcastically. "Ask him to leave the toilets alone?"

"That sounds about right," Cob replied.

"*Borrrring,*" I sang under my breath.

Cob stared at me. I could tell he wanted to get angry again, but he didn't. "Glitch works to maintain the status quo. You know what that is?"

"It means you try to keep things the same."

"We try to keep things the same," Cob said, repeating the lesson. "We keep things running like a well oiled machine. No hiccups or snags. Our best days are when we *save* the day without a single student at

Buchanan knowing the difference. Keeping the toilets from overflowing is all part of it."

"That's the *janitor's* job though," I mumbled.

Cob lifted an eyebrow. "Are you too good for the assignment, Brody? Because if so, we got enough agents who would be more than happy to take the case.

"No," I said. Catching someone clogging the toilets didn't sound exciting, but it was better than sitting in homeroom. "No, it's cool. I want to do this. Let's go find this kid."

Pushing the manila folder toward me, Cob continued. "This folder has all the info you need for the case, but there's barely anything in it since we don't know anything about who's doing it. All you really need to know is that the bathroom on the second floor is the one the criminal is focusing on."

"The one just down the hall?" Linus asked.

"That's right," Cob said.

Maddie stood from the bench and walked to the open space between the chalkboards. "After you," Maddie said to me, holding her hand out.

I stepped out of Cob's makeshift office of chalkboard walls. The other agents of Glitch were still at their desks, typing furiously on their laptops. It was hard to believe that I had been going to school here for a few months while all of *this* was going on behind the scenes. I wondered what other crazy secrets Buchanan School held.

Outside the Glitch headquarters, in the classroom used for storage, Maddie and Linus took a spot by the entrance. There was still about ten minutes left until homeroom dismissed.

Linus spoke quietly. "Look, rookie, I don't want to have to babysit you today, alright? I didn't ask to train you."

"I didn't ask to be trained by you," I replied, annoyed.

A couple months back, before I knew anything about Glitch, Linus was kind of a friend. I say "kind of" because we only sat together a few times during lunch, talking about sci-fi dweeb stuff. Ever since I learned he was an agent, his attitude had shifted to a more serious and aggravating person. To put it bluntly – he was kind of a jerk.

"If this whole thing goes south, just stay outta our way, alright?" Linus said.

"Have you forgotten that this was the kid who busted Sebastian's plan?" Maddie said, grinning. "*And then* busted the lid off Christmas's plan *along with* finding Suckerpunch's base of operations?"

"Doubt it's even in the abandoned swimming pool anymore," Linus said. "If they were smart, they'd have switched locations just like Glitch did."

"Don't change the subject! My point is that Brody has every right to be here with us."

Linus looked at me with narrow eyes. "Just stay outta our way," he said again.

Maddie huffed, folding her arms. "Where do we start? The bathroom is right down the hall from us. Should we just sit here and wait until we see someone go in?"

"No," Linus said. "That would take too long, and would be a waste of time if they never showed up."

"I seriously can't believe we're taking care of a prankster," I said, checking behind me to make sure

Cob wasn't there to hear me whining. "Aren't there better things to do?"

Surprisingly, it was Maddie that defended the job. "It might be *just* a prank, but it still needs to get taken care of. Now quit your belly achin' and try to be helpful."

I sighed, rolling my head back. And then I had a thought. "What about those surveillance cameras you showed me last time? The ones in the room down the hall?"

In our previous endeavor together, Maddie took me into a room filled with monitors displaying video feeds from all over the school. It was my first real evidence that Glitch was a legit secret agency.

"See?" Maddie said to Linus. "The kid's fulla good ideas."

Linus opened the door to the hallway, shaking his head. "Go on then," he said. "Let's get there before the bell rings."

Several minutes later, we were in the dark room that housed all the surveillance screens. Maddie took the seat at the command center and started typing on the keyboard in front of her. The only sounds in the room were of the monitors humming, and Maddie's frantic typing.

I had to break the silence. "So… how long you been in the business of being a secret agent?" Small talk? Really? Way to be interesting, Brody.

Linus stared at the screens. "Since the last day of fifth grade. I was recruited by Glitch at that time, telling me I could be an agent in sixth grade."

"And you?" I asked Maddie.

Maddie continued to type on the keyboard. She was accessing the old videos from the last week in an attempt to find the kid clogging the toilet. "I got recruited on my second day of school this year."

"Second day?" I said. "How come not last year like Linus?"

Maddie shrugged her shoulders. "I don't know why they weren't interested last year."

"So what happened on your second day?" I asked.

"I stopped a bully named Gibson from pounding another kid into the dirt," Maddie replied. "I never stand for anything like that, and when I saw it, I got in the way."

I was confused. "You got in the way?"

"I didn't want to get into a fight with the kid," Maddie said. "And I didn't really know what else to do so I just sang the name of the bully over and over again, and really loudly. Like obnoxiously loud. Like, everyone stopped to see what the heck I was doing. After a few seconds, it was awkward enough that the turd just walked away. Should I have handled it differently? Probably, but it was a moment of panic when my brain just reacted without thinking. Oh well."

"I've had my own share of run-ins with Gibson," I said.

"Cob was so impressed with the unique way she resolved the situation that he recruited her there on the spot," Linus added.

"Walked right up to me and gave me my badge," Maddie said with a smile.

"You guys got a *badge?*" I asked.

Suddenly, Maddie's face became serious. She pointed at the screen. "There," she said.

On the monitor was a boy approaching the bathroom door. He was moving slowly and walking backwards while glancing both ways down the hall.

Linus leaned forward, getting his nose right up to one of the monitors. "Is it Christmas?"

"The screen is a little blurry," I said. "Is there any way you can clear it up?"

"Yup," Maddie answered, laughing. "*Enhance!*"

Sweet! A voice controlled computer system? How awesome!

I waited for the video to zoom in after Maddie gave her instruction, but it was taking longer than I thought.

Maddie giggled. "No, I'm kidding. You have to use the mouse if you want to zoom in on anything. Got ya though."

I snorted a laugh. "Pft! I *knew* you were joking."

"Right," Maddie replied, sliding the mouse and clicking it.

The camera zoomed in on the back of the boy's head.

"What for it," Linus whispered.

Onscreen, the boy pushed on the door to the restroom, looking over his shoulder one last time.

"Pause it!" Linus commanded.

Another click of the mouse and all the screens froze at the same time. Maddie had timed it perfectly so that the face of our suspect was looking toward the camera. His features were still blurry, but I could see he was wearing a white shirt and a white hat.

Maddie slid her finger up on the mouse, zooming the camera in. As it zoomed, the blurry image took a second to catch up with how quickly Maddie was working, but the paused video finally became crisp. In the boy's hand was a sheet of paper with a drawing of what looked like a horseshoe.

"*No way,*" Maddie said under her breath.

I was right. The boy on the screen was wearing a white hat, along with a button down shirt that had a fat bowtie. It was the same student that Cob had a picture of hanging behind his desk.

Maddie pushed herself away from the command center. "This is bad," she said. "This is *bad* bad! Brody, you need to get outta here now."

"What?" I asked, growing a little panicked. "Why? Who *is* he?"

"Nevermind who he is!" Maddie said, briskly walking to the door. She opened it and pointed out to the empty hallway. "Seriously. This is one you need to sit out."

A chill crawled up my spine.

"Now it's time for *you* to relax," Linus said to Maddie. "I'm sure it's not as bad as you—"

"Um, do you remember the first time we dealt with this kid?" Maddie said, slamming the door shut. "He's a basket case! A very *smart* basket case!"

I threw my arms up. "Who is he? I saw his picture on Cob's wall!"

Maddie and Linus stopped arguing and looked at me. And then they looked at each other only to return their eyes to me again.

Linus sighed. "He's known as the Soda Jerk—"

"Linus!" Maddie hissed.

"He's gonna learn these things sooner or later!" Linus scolded.

Folding her arms like a frustrated child, Maddie leaned against the door and pouted, but she didn't say anything else.

Turning his attention back to the screens, Linus pointed. "He's known as the Soda Jerk."

I imagined a title screen with this kid holding a root beer float.

Linus kept talking. "Nobody really knows *why* they call him that, but it's probably because he drinks soda like his life depended on it. Some say it's because he's a sugar addict, but I think it's 'cause of the caffeine. Most of the time, you can find him hanging out by the pop machines in the lower levels of the school. His real name is probably on his report card, but everyone just calls him Soda, even the teachers." Linus pointed at Soda's hat on the screen. "He even dresses like a real 1950's soda jerk."

"Wait," I said. "A real one? What does 'soda jerk' even mean?"

Maddie spoke from the edge of the room. "Back in the 1950's, diners served soda drinks that they'd have to make themselves. They'd put flavored syrup in a tall glass and then mix carbonated water in with it. The guys making those drinks were called 'soda jerks.'"

"And they wore that white shirt with a bow tie?" I asked. "Those guys dress like the ice cream man that drives down my street sometimes."

"Your ice cream man is dressing like _them_," Linus said.

"Okay," I said. "So what's the big deal with this kid?"

"He's a nut," Maddie grunted. "He plays with you psychologically, but worst of all his brain works ten steps ahead of where everyone else is at."

"He'd be good at chess," I said.

"Exactly, except he doesn't play fair," Maddie added. "He'll start by moving his pawn, but the game will end with him stepping foot off a private jet in Honolulu."

"Come on," I said, smirking. "You're making this up."

Maddie stared at me for a moment. "Of course, but the point is that this kid gets what he wants *whenever* he wants."

"What about that slip of paper he's holding?" I asked, looking back at the screens. "I think there's a horse shoe on it."

Linus glanced at Maddie again like they were keeping a secret. She shook her head at him.

"It's just a drawing," Linus said.

I wanted to press the issue, but decided not to. I was still trying to wrap my head around the fact that someone *chose* to wear a *bowtie* to school.

Linus took a seat at the command center. Pulling out his cell phone, he punched in a number and then switched the speaker on.

The line clicked. "Cob here," Cob's voice said.

"We got a problem, boss," Linus said, setting the cell phone on the desk. "Seems like the kid who's clogging the toilets is the Soda Jerk."

The phone fell silent for a second.

"Hello?" Linus asked, getting really close to the phone. "Did I lose you?"

The phone vibrated slightly from Cob's voice. "No, no. I'm still here. The Soda Jerk, you say? He's a bad *egg*. A *really* bad egg."

45

"And you know what they say about bad eggs, right?" I said, trying to involve myself in the conversation.

Maddie and Linus glanced at me, waiting for me to answer.

"Um, no. What do they say?" Cob's voice asked.

"Y'know," I said, holding my palms out. "That one bad egg ruins the bunch!"

Maddie put her face in her palm. "You're thinking of apples. One bad *apple* ruins the bunch."

Cob chuckled over the phone.

"Oh," I whispered, embarrassed.

Cob continued. "You're sure it was Soda? Is it possible that it might've been someone else wearing a white shirt or something?"

"It was definitely him, dude," Linus said. "And he looked super suspicious when he opened the door."

I heard Cob groan, and then he spoke again. "Maybe he's just messing around, huh?"

"Cob," Maddie said, walking closer to the phone. "That's not all…"

"No?"

"He had a slip of paper with him," Linus said, and then he stopped to look at me. "With a drawing of a horse shoe on it."

Cob hummed softly over the phone. It sounded like he was thinking of what to say next. "Hmmmmmm. Is he in the restroom right now?"

"No," Maddie said. "The video is from ten minutes before school started."

"And you're sure he doesn't have the Horseshoe with him?" Cob asked.

"He didn't look like he was carrying anything like

that," Maddie said.

Cob breathed heavily. "Good, good. I'll have someone make sure it's still in the nurse's office."

"What do you want us to do, capt'n?" Linus asked. "Get him from class?"

Again, Cob hummed. Finally, he said, "No. The bell's about to ring. Get him in the hallways before first period starts."

"Understood," Linus said as he took his cell phone in his hand. "We'll bring him back to Glitch once we have him."

"No!" Cob said, loudly enough that the speaker buzzed. "You can't bring him back here!"

"Why not?" Linus asked. "What're we supposed to do with him then?"

Cob mumbled something that I didn't understand. Then he cleared his throat. "Glitch is still under construction here. We got nowhere to put him so we can question him. Take him down to one of the art rooms on the first floor. There should be one without a first period class."

Maddie looked at Linus, confused, and then mouthed the words, "The art room?"

Linus shrugged. "You're the boss."

The phone blinked, ending the call.

"Why does he want us to take him to the art room?" Maddie asked. "Why not just take him right to Glitch?"

Linus shook his head. His jaw tensed up. "I'm sure Cob's got his reasons for it. Don't question it and just get the job done."

"We've only got a few minutes until the bell rings," Maddie said, cracking the door open an inch and peeking into the hallway. "How are we supposed to nab him?"

"If he sees either of us," Linus said to Maddie, "then he'll know something's up."

Both of the secret agents slowly turned their eyes to me.

"Of course," I sighed. "Get the noob to do the dirty work."

When homeroom ended, the bell rang. I was at the foot of the stairs back on the first floor. Students spilled out of their homeroom classes and into the hallway. I watched as the foot traffic grew thicker and thicker with kids I'd never said a word to.

I tapped my foot on the ground nervously, watching for Soda to show up. Good thing he would probably be wearing his bowtie and hat, otherwise there was no way I'd recognize him.

"All you gotta do is make conversation with him," is what Maddie and Linus told me. Apparently he's a "one-upper," so it would be easy to lure him in with just some casual talk. The trick, they said, was to keep one-upping *him* every time he did it to me, and to continue walking so he'd be forced to follow.

I stood on my tiptoes, looking for a white hat in the sea of different colored hair. Black, brown, blonde, red, and even some bright blues and pinks were in the mix. Mohawks were a little more common among the school body than I'd thought.

Leaning against the wall, I continued to act casual, but you know how that goes when you *force* yourself to look normal. I had my hand on my hip, with my butt sticking way out. My other arm was raised up so my head could lean into it, all the while bouncing my body up and down like I was listening to some "cool tunes" with some headphones.

I was also *pretending* to chew on gum. *Why* was I pretending to chew on gum? The funny thing was that I actually *had* gum in my pocket, even though gum wasn't allowed at Buchanan. Yup, I like to live life on the edge sometimes and just *chew* a piece of gum every now and again.

And then I saw him – the boy in the white hat and fat bowtie. The boy known as the Soda Jerk.

My brain flinched, trying to think of what I would say to spark up a conversation. Should I talk about his bowtie? Should I talk about soda? He was still about twenty feet away, but he was walking quickly.

Soda was by himself within the crowd of students. His backpack was slung over one shoulder as he stared at the floor, which was pretty much how everyone else looked too. His white hat leaned to the side of his head, and his white shirt was like a shining star against the dark colored clothing of the other students. He was easy to spot in a crowd.

I kept my head down as he passed. I don't know why, but I started bouncing my body a little harder, pretending the fake music I was listening to had hit the cool part.

Once Soda was a few feet in front of me, I pushed myself up and kept pace right behind him. The art rooms were down on the west end of the school, but we were headed to the east end. I'd have to turn him around if I wanted to get the job done, but how do you start a conversation with someone who's a one-upper?

"Cool shoes, man," I mumbled.

Soda didn't turn around. I must have spoken so quietly that he didn't even hear me.

I repeated myself, but louder. "Cool shoes, man!"

A kid next to me – *not* Soda – responded. "Hey, thanks! I saved up all summer to get them!"

"Oh," I said, surprised. Pointing at her shoes, I said, "Uh, neat! They're very… tennis… shoe-y,"

"Shoe-y?" the girl replied.

The bell to first period was going to ring in under four minutes! I had no time to discuss shoes with a girl!

"Yeah, shoe-y," I said. "Like, they're more *shoe* than… *other* shoes."

"Not more than *my* shoes," came a voice from in front of us.

When I turned my head, I saw that Soda was looking down at the girl's shoes as he continued to walk forward. Sweet! I had started the conversation without even trying! Now all I had to do was keep it going.

I pressed my lips together. "Your shoes are cool too, but I've seen cooler. My older cousin has some pretty expensive basketball shoes where you can pump air into the soles. They're pretty limited edition. Got 'em off some Australian website."

The girl rolled her eyes and sped up to get away from us. If I wasn't trying to get rid of her, I probably would've felt embarrassed.

"Oh yeah?" Soda said. "I got a cousin who has those shoes too, but his are directly from the factory, where they only made the prototype before the building burned down."

Seriously? Soda was really going to make up a lie that huge just to one-up me?

I smiled. This was going to be fun.

I stepped up my pace so that I was only a couple inches in front of the Soda Jerk. I was worried that if I got too far ahead too soon, that I'd lose his attention. "That's awesome that your cousin has the prototype of that tennis shoe. I wish I could get my hands on a basketball shoe like that, but I honestly think it would give me too much of an advantage on the basketball courts, y'know… during *basketball*… matches."

Soda had a hop in his step as he walked beside me. "I know, right? I'm actually not allowed to play basketball. The coach says I'm *too* good at it and that it's unfair for everyone else."

I shook my head. "Phew, I hear ya. I'm the same way when it comes to video games. I'm not even allowed to *watch* FPS tournaments because it intimidates the other players that I'm even *in* the room. It's probably best though because my doctor said that my thumbs are in pre-arthritic condition from playing so much."

Soda didn't skip a beat. "That's nothing! I broke *all* my fingers from playing so hard in a game tournament once. It was down to me and this other dude – everyone thought he was going to win, especially after my fingers broke. They were all like, *oh, there's no way Soda will beat him! Finally, someone else will take the trophy! It's about time too because Soda's won for the last three years in a row!* I just smiled, and kept on playing through the pain. I was barely even paying attention to the game, but I still won. They put up a statue of me after that."

"No way," I said, turning toward a water fountain while keeping ahead of Soda. "For real?"

"Yup," Soda said, nodding. "Everyone in the tournament *demanded* it. I said, *'no, don't do it,'* but they did it anyway."

At the water fountain, I leaned over and took a sip. When I was done, I said, "That's so cool. I bet you drive by that statue all the time. Where is it?"

Soda shrugged a shoulder and leaned his head to the side. "Oh, it's not anywhere here. It's where I used to live, back in Japan."

"Whoa! You used to live in Japan?" I said, beginning my path to the art rooms on the other side of the school. Soda didn't even notice we were now walking in the opposite direction. He was too into his own awesomeness.

"No," Soda said. "My family just went on vacation over there, so it was an even bigger surprise that I came out of nowhere and won the tournament."

"Nice," I said. "Reminds me of the time I blew out a bike tire right at the end of a race. I still won the race, but only because I was already at the finish line. Everyone thought I was tanked, but I kept going on my flat tire."

"Oh man, this one time I was in a bike race," Soda started, "comin' in last place because I wanted to give everyone else a shot at winning. *Actually* I let everyone get a two lap head start in a three lap race."

I nodded, trying my best not to laugh. We were already at the front lobby. Only two more halls to walk down and we'd be in the art rooms. The clock above the cafeteria showed that I only had two minutes before the bell rang again, I sped my pace slightly.

"So there I was, standing next to my bike," Soda continued, "while all these other bikers – *pro*-bikers too, I might add—"

"You gave the pros a head start?"

"I wanted to give them a fair race! So anyways, I was standing next to my bike as these other guys flew past me, pedaling as hard as their legs could. Everyone in the crowd was like, *Soda's never gonna pull himself out of this one! What's he done?* But I was cool as a cucumber, watching these guys pull the first lap around me, and then the second lap."

I turned down the first hallway. Most of the other students were in their classrooms so the halls were emptying out. If Soda would've noticed it, he might've caught on to my plan so I kept him talking. "Then what? You *couldn't* have pulled ahead while everyone was on their last lap, right? I mean, you were only on your *first* lap!"

"I know, right?" Soda cackled, staring ahead of us. I could tell his brain was working on the story because his eyes weren't focused on anything. "Well, I took off like a bat outta heck! I'm pretty sure my rims were glowing hot."

"That's crazy," I said, turning down the second hallway. The empty art room was just a few doors away. "And then?"

Soda stopped suddenly, looking at the lockers on the wall. "Wait…"

My brain froze and I didn't know what to say.

"Where are we?" Soda asked, narrowing his eyes.

I shut my eyes and spoke calmly. "Class is right down here. So, dude! *What happened in the race? There's no way you could've won!*"

Soda shook his head, and stared at me with intense eyes. This was it. I knew it. I totally botched the mission, and Soda was going to turn around and get to class.

"Heck yeah, I won!" Soda said loudly. He gripped the shoulder strap of his backpack and caught up to me.

I felt relief wash over me like I was standing under a waterfall.

"Anyway, after peeling out of the starting gate," Soda said, "I was able to catch up to the guy in first place, but at that time, the rubber on my tires caught fire because of all the friction from how fast I was going. It was crazy. I looked like that comic book guy who rides a motorcycle with flaming tires."

We approached the empty art room. I couldn't see anyone inside, but Maddie and Linus assured me that they'd be there.

Soda *continued* the outlandish story. "But when I

hit the last ramp, my bike flew into the air so I pulled back on the handlebars, performing a perfect backflip as my tires flew off the bike. I could *hear* people in the crowd saying things like, *Soda's gonna die! He'll never land the trick!* but, I kid you not, I landed perfectly on my feet with the melted frame of my bike still under me, only *one foot* away from the checkered finish line."

Finally, we were at the door to the art room! I stood back and held my hand out toward the room. "After you."

Soda was so absorbed in his story that he even *thanked* me for being so polite. "Oh, thank you," he said as he entered the empty art room. "So at that point, all I had to do was take one step forward, and I won the race. The whole crowd of people exploded with applause. I won a million bucks because of that race, but donated it to charity."

I stepped into the art room, looking for Maddie and Linus, but I didn't see them. At least not in front of us.

The door suddenly shut behind me at exactly the same moment that the first period bell went off. Saved by the bell, right? I think? I don't really understand what that expression means. I just know people say it if they barely make it somewhere on time.

When I spun around, I saw Maddie and Linus standing in front of the closed door.

"Cool story, dude," Linus laughed.

Soda turned around. The expression on his face morphed into anger. His eyes darted back and forth between Maddie and Linus until he finally looked at me. "Now that I know your face, I won't make the mistake of *thinking* you were a *friend*."

I'm not sure why, but his comment stung. "Sorry," I said.

"Don't apologize to him!" Maddie commanded. "That's his way of getting into your head! Don't let him turn this around on you."

Soda took a seat at one of the empty art desks. I was surprised that he wasn't trying to escape. "What can I do for you today, my darling?"

Maddie shook her head. "Do *not* call me darling."

Soda leaned back on his desk. "You got nothin' on me, guys. You're just a bunch of dogs chasin' cars."

"Why are you clogging the toilets?" Linus asked.

Soda's lip curled into a smile. "That's kind of a personal question, ain't it? How do you know it was even me?"

"Because we got you on video," Maddie said.

"Dude, *seriously?*" Soda asked, disgusted.

Maddie fumbled, a little embarrassed. "No, I mean, we got you on camera going *into* the bathroom. There're no cameras *in* the bathroom… that would just be messed up. But we *know* it was *you* and that you flushed a bunch of cotton swabs to make the toilet back up."

"So? It's a stupid prank. What's that gonna get me? An after-school-detention where they sit me in front of a computer and let me play games the whole time? Please! I'd be *happy* with that. I'll have you know, I'm able to get my entire family to Oregon without a single person dying of dysentery."

"We know you're looking for the Horseshoe," Maddie said softly, but sternly.

Soda's body language completely changed when she said it. He sat up in his chair and crossed his legs the way businessmen do when they're about to talk business. Pushing his hands into his front pockets, he shrugged his shoulders and replied. "You got no proof of that."

"We have you on video," Linus said. "With a picture of a horseshoe. Tell us why you're looking for it."

Soda stopped. His eye twitched.

"What do you want with it?" Linus asked.

Soda jerked his head in Linus's direction. "That's the million dollar question, ain't it?"

"So you don't have it?" Maddie asked.

"*Yet*," Soda said flatly.

"What do you want with it?" I asked, trying to sound tough.

"Nunya," Soda said, rolling his eyes.

"Nunya?" I asked, confused.

Soda chortled. "Nunya business."

Linus folded his arms. "Who are you working with, Soda? You *never* work alone, do you?"

Soda pressed his lips together. "I'm not saying another word until I get a can of your finest soda. No, scratch that. Until I get a whole *palette* of your finest *bottles* of soda!"

I could hear Linus grinding his teeth. It sounded like squeaky cheese, the fresh kind you get as curds in Wisconsin.

"Just go get some," Maddie said to Linus. She must've been playing the "good cop."

Linus walked to the door and opened it. Before he left, he turned back. "I'm getting Cob too. He'll want to be here for this."

Maddie nodded, and Linus stepped out of the

room. For at least a couple of minutes, we sat in awkward silence, avoiding eye contact with each other. Maddie walked to the entrance and leaned her head out. I think the room was too quiet for her comfort.

"New guy, huh?" Soda finally said. His eyebrows were lifted, and his mouth had one of those "sucks-to-be-you" smiles.

I glanced up, but didn't say anything. Maddie was still looking out the door.

"I can tell," Soda said softly. "For the record, that stint you pulled with me – where you got me to follow you without even knowing – was super impressive. Sorry about saying that stuff earlier, y'know, about not mistaking you as a friend. I was just a bit shocked. Now that I've cooled off, I can see you had some skill back there. Well done, friend."

I stretched out a smile, but it was genuine. It was hard to believe that Soda was a bad guy. He seemed so nice.

"No, really," the Soda Jerk continued. "What you did out there took talent. Not everyone can do what you did. It takes patience. I bet *Linus* couldn't even have pulled that off."

"Linus is the best though," I said, soft enough so Maddie couldn't hear me. "He probably could've talked circles around you."

Soda laughed, but the kind of laugh where air just puffed out of his nostrils. "That kid's overrated. Maddie is talented, yes, but Linus is just the *'popular'* guy." When Soda said "popular," he took his hands out of his pockets and used his fingers to make air quotes. After that, he stuffed his hands back into his front pockets. "Sorry. When I'm nervous, I put my hands in my pockets otherwise I'd get all fidgety."

"Trust me," I replied. "I get it. I'm nervous a lot."

"No way," Soda said with a smirk. "You? Nervous? You coulda fooled me with the way you got me down here. No, you *did* fool me."

I snickered, but quietly. Maddie was still standing at the door, watching for Linus and Cob to return.

Just then, a kid wearing a denim shirt with matching jeans stopped by the door. He was pushing a palette of bottled pop.

"What?" Maddie asked coldly.

The kid pointed at the palette. "Delivery," the boy said. "Some blond kid told me to wheel all this bubbly water down here. Didn't say why. Just that I was supposed to."

"Some blond kid?" Maddie repeated. "Linus?"

"Yeah, yeah, yeah" the boy replied, nodding quickly like a bobble-head toy. "*Linus* sent me."

Maddie stepped aside. "Go ahead. Don't talk to either of those two," she said, pointing back and forth at Soda and me.

"You got it," the kid said as he lowered his gaze. Pushing the cart through the door, he wheeled it closer to where I was sitting. When he stopped, he kicked out a latch that was under the palette, probably to lock the thing in place. I don't know, I'm not familiar with how palettes work.

"I've heard all about you, y'know," Soda said. "You're what everyone was talking about after Sebastian got busted in the candy scandal awhile back."

"Yeah?" I asked. I was actually surprised because life went on normally for me after that. Nobody ever made a big deal about it, but I thought that was because nobody even *knew* about it.

"And after that thing with Christmas?" Soda said in a high-pitched voice. "Whew! All the gossip in the schoolyard was that you were some type of *superhero!*"

"I wouldn't go *that* far," I said, trying to be modest.

"Look at you," Soda said. "You're even humble about it."

"Just gettin' the job done, right?"

Soda blinked. "Right."

The kid in the denim overalls walked back to the door and thanked Maddie. Then he disappeared from the entrance. Maddie kept her place at the entrance, watching like a vigilant hawk for Linus to return with Cob.

The palette next to us was filled with two liter bottles with the exact same flavor of soda in each one. There must've been twenty bottles of pop sitting there. When I looked closer, I saw that it was all the same brand of diet cola. I guess this was what Linus had ordered after Soda made his demand for "finest bottles of soda."

The Soda Jerk leaned back in his chair and started bouncing his leg up and down. "Your *first* day, and you get caught up in this whole 'Horseshoe' conspiracy. Tough luck, am I right?"

I glanced at Maddie. When I was sure she wasn't

looking, I switched seats to sit closer to Soda. I bet Maddie and Linus would've been proud to see that I was starting the interrogation myself. This spy stuff was easier than I thought.

"Tell me what the Horseshoe is," I said.

"Brother," Soda said as he shut his eyes. "You don't wanna know."

"But I do!" I said. "If it's such a big deal, then I think I should at least know *what* it is."

"The truth?" Soda asked.

I nodded at him.

"I don't know," Soda admitted. "Truly, I don't. All I know is that the Horseshoe is bad news, y'know? Like, *end-of-the-world* bad news."

"Yeah, right," I said, accidentally raising my voice.

Maddie didn't notice.

"If it was something that could *end* the world, then why would it be in a middle school?" I asked. "It's probably something completely harmless."

Soda shrugged, and then he put his hand on my shoulder. "I dunno. I'm willing to bet that you're right though. You're a smart cookie."

After the morning I had, it felt good to hear someone say that about me.

Soda continued. "For all we know, the Horseshoe is some kind of dumb object sitting in someone's locker somewhere, right? Probably just some kind of weak little baby toy."

And then I opened my foolish mouth without thinking. "Well, it's probably a *little* dangerous since it's locked away in the *nurse's* office."

The Soda Jerk fell silent, staring at me with his

piercing eyes.

I heard a buzzing come from his pocket – the obvious sound of a cellphone on vibrate. My heart dropped when I realized his hands were in his pockets because he had probably been sending text messages throughout our whole conversation…

…and I just told him where the Horseshoe was.

"Whoops," I whispered.

Soda jumped from his desk and stomped on the latch that the kid in denim had kicked out. I watched in slow motion as the palette of diet sodas sunk an inch, shaking each bottle just enough so a tiny mint that was hidden in each of the bottle caps dropped into the carbonated beverage.

Instantly, every bottle of diet soda burst open, spraying caramel colored pop all over the room. A few bottles tipped, which turned them into rockets that shot across the room.

Diving to the floor, I covered my head as the hurricane of pop rained down. I could hear Maddie screaming for me, but I couldn't see her.

And then as quickly as it started, it was over. The last drops of diet cola splattered on the floor, making gross *plop* sounds.

I tried to stand, but the ground was too slippery. Landing on my face in a puddle of pop, I rolled to my back. "The palette was rigged! That kid in denim must've been one of Soda's henchmen!"

Maddie didn't answer.

"Maddie?" I said, trying to stand on the wet floor. "*Maddie?*"

Her voice replied, cutting through the air like a ninja sword. "*Brody! Help me!*"

"Maddie!" I shouted, running to the door of the art room. I slid to a stop, and put both hands on the frame. "Maddie, where are you?"

"*Brody!*" Maddie's voice screamed from the down the hall.

I turned just in time to see Soda at the end of the hallway, stepping into another room that had several cardboard boxes stacked outside it. The kid in denim was holding the door open for him. Maddie was halfway between the Soda Jerk and me, sprinting down the hall.

"*Hurry up, Brody!*" Maddie shouted. "*He's getting away!*"

"Wait!" I shouted, running after her. I knew there

were other classes in the art rooms, but I didn't care if they heard me yell. "Maddie, wait!"

Soda was already gone. The wooden door he had escaped in was slowly shutting. I watched as Maddie dropped to her side like she was sliding to home plate. Her body barely made it through the small opening before the wooden door shut behind her, knocking the cardboard boxes to the floor. The "thunk" sound made my stomach turn. Maddie had a history of jumping into things head first and disappearing on me.

When I reached the door, I turned the handle and pushed my shoulder into it, but it was no use. The door had locked! Stepping back, I lifted my foot and kicked at the wood, but it didn't budge.

Slamming my shoulder into the door repeatedly, I did my best until my side was too bruised to keep going. Defeated, I set my forehead against the wood, and whispered. "Maddie. I'm sorry."

The sign on the door said it was the entrance to the drama club. The boxes next to me were filled with various costumes and set props – hats, sunglasses, mustaches, wigs, and tiny cups of makeup.

"Brody!" I heard Cob's voice shout from down the hall. "What happened here?"

Cob was standing outside the empty art room, along with about a dozen Glitch agents. I started walking toward them, listening to my shoes squeak with sticky pop.

"Where's Maddie?" Cob asked. "Where's Soda? Why's the room coated in a *sheen* of diet cola?"

"Soda got away," I admitted. "Maddie went after him, but... but I was too slow to catch up."

Cob took a step forward and motioned his agents

65

to follow. "It's alright, son. We're all here now. You can come back to Glitch and help us straighten this out."

I stopped and shook my head. "No," I said. "I *can't*."

Cob sped his pace down the hall, keeping his hands in front of him the whole time like he was trying his best not to spook a cat. "C'mon now. It'll all be fine. Just come back with us and tell us what happened. You can file a report when we're back at headquarters. Remember what I said about accepting responsibility?"

My thoughts ran wild in my head like a squirrel in a busy intersection. Soda had just *escaped*. Some kid in denim was also helping him. Maddie had *disappeared* behind the locked door. For all I knew, she had already been taken *prisoner*. The Horseshoe wasn't safe now that Soda knew *exactly* where to find it, thanks to me.

Cob wanted me to accept responsibility, but his way meant I'd have to go back to the Glitch headquarters and file a report like some sort of *adult*. I couldn't help but feel that truly accepting responsibility meant keeping the Horseshoe out of Soda's greedy little hands.

I think you know which path I chose.

The pop was beginning to dry on my forehead. I could tell because when I wiped it with my hand, my skin stuck together. It was nasty.

Cob continued toward me. "I know what you're thinkin' now—"

I twitched a grin. "Do you?"

Diving to my right, I slammed into one of the other classroom doors in the hall, flinging it open and stumbling into the classroom full of kids working on

66

crafting paper-mache wild animals. The students gasped as the teacher jumped back from his desk.

I heard everyone shout at me, but I ignored it the way my dad does when my mom yells at him.

From the door of the art room, I heard Cob's voice. "Valentine! What do you think you're doing? Get back here!"

If this were an action movie, I'd probably turn around with a clever one-liner, but it wasn't so I didn't. Instead of saying anything, my throat decided to wheeze out a high-pitched sound that kinda sounded like a giggle.

I ran to the door at the back of the room and pushed it open. Hopping through, I found myself in yet another art class that was in session, but the students weren't working on paper-mache animals. They were wearing tribal masks and running circles around the room.

I stopped in place, a little confused about what I was seeing until I remembered that the art teacher for this particular class was one of those stereotypical "artists." You know the type – dreadlocks, a self-given nickname like "Star" or "Moon," clothes that looked like they were made from 1970's couch fabric, and used a grading system based on *feelings* rather than letters. I'm still not sure whether *half-a-smiley-face-with-tears* equals an A or a B.

I snatched an unused mask and held it over my face, entering the weird circle of students.

Cob was the first to step into the room. His gang of Glitch agents poured in right after him.

I kept my eyes on Cob as I swirled around in circles among the rest of the kids in masks. It was only a matter of time before the teacher would stop what the class was doing and ask why Cob was there. All he had to do was say he was looking for someone who didn't belong in that class, and everyone would be forced to take off their masks. I had to act fast if I wanted to get away.

I crouched a bit until I couldn't see Cob and his agents, and then at the top of my lungs, I shouted, *"Oh sick! There's a rat in the room! It's as big as a potato!"*

Everyone in the art class, including Cob and the Glitch agents, freaked. Desks were turned over as students panicked, running wild in every direction. The muffled screams and shouts coming from behind the tribal art masks made things even crazier. It was like a mosh pit at a rock concert.

I stood tall in the middle of the chaos because I knew there wasn't really a rat in the room. It felt a bit like I was wearing some kind of invincibility shield from a video game. It was the only time in my life that I was completely calm in a roomful of crazies, which was the total opposite of how it normally would've been.

As I made my way to the exit, I let the tribal mask drop to the floor. Checking to see if Cob was following me wasn't even necessary. His voice was the loudest in the room, screaming something about "potato rats" being the grossest things ever.

Nearly ten minutes later, I was sitting behind the curtains of the stage in the cafeteria. Study hall was directly on the other side of the velvet drapery, but I was far enough away that being heard wasn't a concern.

At least I was safe from Cob and his men – not that Cob was going to punish me, but I knew that sitting around the Glitch headquarters was just wasting precious time – time I couldn't afford to lose.

I pulled my cellphone out of my pocket and flipped through my contacts list until I found Maddie. Pressing the "call" button, I held the phone up to my ear.

No answer.

When I scrolled through the other contacts, I remembered that I had also put Linus in there, which made me realize that Linus *wasn't* with Cob back at the classrooms, even though that's where Linus said he was going. *Why* wasn't he with Cob?

There was no answer when I called him either.

Sighing, I rested my back against the wall of the stage. Ten minutes was already too much time wasted. I still had no idea *what* the Horseshoe was, but that didn't matter. What mattered was that Soda knew exactly *where* it was, thanks to Brody "*Brainless*" Valentine.

Part of me wanted to try and find Maddie, but deep down, I knew she could take care of herself. So the only other option I had was to get to the Horseshoe before Soda did.

I slid my hand into my pocket and took out K-pop's business card. She said if I was ever in any trouble, I should feel free to call her. I couldn't imagine myself in more trouble than I was in at that moment, so I took her up on her offer.

But just like Maddie and Linus, she didn't answer my call.

Frustrated, I tossed the phone across the old wooden floor of the stage. I couldn't believe how *unreachable* these guys were! They were secret agents! If *anyone* should answer their stinkin' phones, it's them!

Suddenly, a vibrating sound pulsed three times. It was coming from my cellphone.

Crawling across the stage, I scooped my phone off the floor and looked at the screen. It said I had received a text message. The number was from K-pop.

"*Who is this?*" her message read.

I typed frantically, without caring if I had misspelled a word or two. "*brody valentine. in tribble, ned ur help.*"

After a moment, my phone vibrated again. "*Hey Brody! Never call me. Only text me, k? I prefer text.*"

"*Sry,*" I typed. "*Won't happen again.*"

"*So what's the haps? What kind of 'tribble' r u in? LOL.*"

I shook my head, and typed again, but slower. "*I botched a case. Maddie's gone. Soda's after the Horseshoe. Freakin out! Please help!*"

"*...um...*" K-pop texted.

I wasn't sure what she meant by the dots, but I assumed she was skeptical about helping. I continued typing. "*Pls! I rly messed up and told Soda where the Horseshoe was! If he gets it then it's my fault! I swear I'll owe you big time!*"

I started feeling lightheaded as I waited for her to text back. Staring at the screen of my phone, I watched the backlight dim, and then go black.

"C'mon," I whispered, staring at my phone. "*C'mon!*"

"*Sry,*" K-pop's text finally replied. "No can do."

I felt my shoulders sink into my body. I'm not the kind of kid who cries a lot, but I could feel tears working their way out of my ducts. I felt alone again, and it was awful. The whirlwind of emotion that I was going through would definitely lead to some painful ulcers when I got older.

The phone vibrated in my hand again as the backlight poured through my fingers casting shadows on the floor. I flipped the cellphone over and held my breath.

"*ROFL! JK! I'm down!*" was the follow-up text from K-pop.

I let out a sigh, slowly. This girl's sense of humor was going to be the death of me.

"*Where r u?*" she texted.

"*In the cafeteria. On the stage behind the curtains,*" I replied.

After a moment, she texted back. "*Cool cool cool. Be there in 10. Bringing friends.*"

I looked at her text, confused. Did she say friends? I typed, "*What? What friends?*"

K-pop didn't reply.

71

That feeling crept into my gut again – the one where it felt like I had just chugged a gallon of milk and it was all about to come back out, along with chunks of hot dog that I had eaten for breakfast. Please don't judge me for my breakfast choices.

Who was K-pop talking about? Was there anyone I could even trust at this point? Glitch probably had a "most-wanted" poster with my face hanging around the school already! As far as I knew, my picture was in every criminal database in the world, *plus* alien worlds and alternate dimensions! I had accidentally become a rogue agent! And not the cool kind of rogue, like the ones in movies where they go rogue and then end up saving the day! No, I was the kind of rogue agent that stupidly gave away a secret to a villain, *and then* let that villain escape, *and then* lost another agent in the field!

I punched myself in the forehead. "*Stupid! Stupid! Stupid!*"

"Easy, tiger," a girl's voice said from the shadows.

I spun around on the floor of the stage, peering into the darkness. I couldn't see anyone's face, but I could tell there was more than one kid hiding. "Who's there?"

K-pop stepped onto the stage, holding her cellphone toward me. Korean pop music was playing over the speakers in her headphones. "I told you. Ten minutes."

I clicked the button on top of my phone to wake it up. It had been exactly ten minutes since she sent her last text. I must've had a ten-minute nervous breakdown.

Go me.

"For a rock-star secret agent," K-pop said, "You're pretty insecure."

"He's not a rock-star agent!" a boy's voice said from behind her. Linus stepped out of the shadows, smiling at me. "S'up, noob."

"Where were you?" I asked immediately, getting right in Linus's face. "You said you were getting Cob, but when he came back to the art class, you *weren't* with him!"

Linus backed up with his palms out. "Dude, get off me," he replied. "I didn't even *find* Cob! I guess I missed him on the way to the Glitch headquarters!"

I was suspicious, so I gave him the evil eye. "Yeah, right. You would've passed him in the hallways if that were true."

"Really?" Linus asked, raising an eyebrow. "The new headquarters is upstairs. You know there's, like, a billion different ways to switch floors, right? No, wait, you don't because *this is your first day.*"

"Children, please," K-pop interrupted. "There's very little time, and we've got a lot of work to do."

I glared at Linus, but K-pop was right. I had to let it go if I wanted to get to the Horseshoe before the Soda Jerk did. "Fine," I said, turning back to K-pop. There were two other students standing beside her. "Who are *these* guys?"

The boy to K-pop's left stepped forward. He was huge compared to most of the other sixth graders at Buchanan. I recognized him from the yearbook photos of the football team. He was wearing a yellow t-shirt with a brightly colored design that looked like something from a Japanese anime. His long black hair matched the color of his black eyes. "The name's

Janky."

"Hello, uh... Janky," I said. Who names their kid *Janky?*

"Let's get one thing straight," Janky said. "I ain't a member of Glitch, got it? So if you feel like barkin' some kind of secret agent nonsense at me, think again."

"You're *not* an agent?" I asked.

K-pop smiled. "No, he's just one of my besties. I trust him with my life."

Janky stared into my eyes while pointing his thumb back at K-pop. "What she said. K-pop's been my friend since before we were in school, so if she says she needs my help, I help."

The boy on K-pop's right side waved his hand sheepishly. "And I'm Scooter. I'm normally a computer guy, but I've recently graduated to being a getaway guy."

Scooter looked like someone I'd probably try to sit with during lunch. He had huge circular glasses and tightly combed hair, but not the cool kind of combed hair. The kind of combed hair that said, *"I-have-no-idea-how-to-style-my-hair"*. He was wearing a vest and necktie combination, which was something sixth graders only wore if they were going to a dance.

"Getaway guy, huh?" I grunted. "I bet all this isn't even exciting to you anymore, is it?"

Scooter snorted, pushing his glasses up on the bridge of his nose. "Oh, no, this is *very* exciting! I'm normally stuck behind a desk during *any* kind of mission!"

My jaw dropped. I looked at K-pop, confused.

K-pop slapped her hand on Scooter's back, which made him wince in pain. "Scoot's a cool kid with skills that *sizzle* when ya drop 'em on a hot plate. No need to worry about him."

Linus pushed a section of the red velvet curtain aside and peeked out at the kids in study hall. As he scanned the room, he spoke. "Where's Maddie? K-pop said you texted her saying that Maddie was gone."

"She went after Soda when his trap went off," I said.

Linus turned around. "Whoa, what? He set a trap? And you just *watched* him do it?"

"Of course I didn't *watch* him do it!" I said defensively. "Some *other* kid walked into the room and set the trap!"

Linus groaned. "So you watched the *other* kid do it."

I shook my head, squeezing my eyes shut. "No, no, no! After you left, some dude came in with a palette of diet soda that was rigged with some small mints. Maddie let him in the room because he said *you* sent him to give Soda the 'finest bottles of pop.'"

Linus curled a lip. "Nope. I didn't send anyone."

"I know that *now*," I said. "Soda had his hands in his pockets, texting the whole time."

"What happened after that?" K-pop asked.

"That's when I accidentally told Soda where the Horseshoe was," I said slowly.

Scooter gasped.

K-pop made the exact same face my mom makes when she's disappointed. "Tsk, tsk, tsk."

Janky blinked slowly, and then burped. I'm pretty sure he wasn't listening.

"What the *spew* were you thinking?" Linus grunted.

"I don't know," I admitted. "Soda's a smooth talker, and he got me going. I didn't even realize I said it until *after* I did."

Linus rolled his eyes.

"Right after that, the bottled pop exploded, and in the chaos, Soda ran out of the room," I explained. "When I finally made sense of what was happening, Maddie was already down the hall, chasing after him. She managed to slide into the door he escaped through just before it locked shut. When I turned around, Cob was there with some other Glitch agents."

"Did Cob say anything to you?" Linus asked.

"He told me I had to fill out paperwork," I said.

"And then you ran away," Linus said, finishing my story.

"Soda knows the Horseshoe is in the nurse's office," I said. "I can fill out paperwork later. Right now, someone has to make sure that nutcase doesn't get what he wants."

Cracking half a smile, Linus nodded once. "Maybe you'll make a good agent after all. *Maybe.*"

K-pop slapped her hands together. "Alright then, boys," she smiled. "Time to grease up a plan, right?"

"We'll need to hurry," Linus said. "Because you *know* Soda's somewhere in the school doing the *exact* same thing we are right now. If we don't get to it first, then we're basically *handing* it over to him."

K-pop laughed. "Hold up. Do we even know if the Horseshoe is real? Are we *sure* it's not just some urban legend? There's a lot of talk about it, but no one I know has actually seen it with their own two eyeballs, or *one* eyeball if you're substitute gym teacher."

"Trust me, it's real, and it's dangerous," Linus

said as he stood up. "I'll be back in a minute. I gotta use the bathroom. I like to go on missions with an empty bladder."

K-pop stuck her tongue out, making a disgusted face. "TMI, dude. *Way* TMI."

Once I was sure that Linus was gone, I turned to K-pop. "Crazy stuff, right?"

She arched her brow while closing her eyes and nodding her head slowly, like she was an old wise woman. "Right," she whispered.

"This whole thing," I started, "is one big disaster, and it's all my fault."

"It happens," K-pop replied.

"But it shouldn't have," I said. "I might not be cut out for Glitch. I seem to make a mess of things."

K-pop shrugged, almost like she wasn't interested in what I was saying. "Yeeeah, but what're you gonna do?"

"Quit. If this is all that keeps—"

The half Korean, half Norwegian girl interrupted me. "No, you're right. If you can't do something well, then you oughta just give up. If you can't draw, then you should never pick up a sketchbook. If you can't make a free throw shot, you might as well walk away from the basketball court. If you can't run a mile, then you should just take off the tennis shoes."

"Fine," I snipped, a little annoyed. "I get it."

"You know what you *should* quit? Being a baby. Stop being so negative all the time. It's gross. Girls dig scars – not flawless, baby soft skin."

I chuckled. She was right. There was no point in being hard on myself. That wasn't going to help Maddie. If I wanted to get the Horseshoe, I was going to have to get out of my own way.

After a short time, I decided to come right out and ask. "What's the Horseshoe? Everyone's talking about it, but no one's telling me what it is!"

K-pop made a duck face with her lips and shrugged her shoulders in an overly exaggerated way, like a three-year-old child would. "No idea, but if it's in the nurse's office, it can't be good."

"That bad, huh?" I said.

"That bad," K-pop repeated.

"Like, end-of-the-word-bad?"

"Well, *no*, probably not like that," K-pop chuckled. "But maybe a few degrees *less* than that. Like, it won't *cause* the end of the world, but it might *cause* what *causes* the end of the world. Like, zombies or something."

"*Zombies?*" I gulped.

K-pop leaned her head to the side. "Awww," she said in an overly girly way. "It's cute how gullible you are!"

Janky chimed in. "I would face-punch every zombie if there were ever an invasion. Every single one of them would feel the flat end of my fist!"

"It wouldn't be an invasion," K-pop said. "It'd be more like a plague."

"Whatever," Janky said. "Face-punch. Every. Single. One."

Scooter cleared his throat from across the stage. "*Actually* that would prove to be most devastating because zombies infect their victims through their bites, so by 'face-punching' a zombie, you run a greater risk of getting infected by accidentally hitting their mouth, forcing a bite on you."

Janky sniffed hard, like he was getting snot out of the back of his throat. "Scooter, how would you like to help me perfect my face-punch technique? I could use a head model."

"Down, boy," K-pop said with a smirk. "Scooter's just being helpful."

Scooter pushed his glasses up again, but made a snide face at Janky.

Janky thrust his shoulders like he was going to punch Scooter. Even though Scooter was clear across the stage, he still flinched.

THE TEAM

LINUS K-POP

JANKY SCOOTER

This was the team I had to work with. These were agents of Glitch, along with a random student who was only there because he was "besties" with K-pop. It

79

wasn't exactly the awesome spy team I had hoped it was, but it would have to do.

Several minutes later, we were all gathered around a wooden box at the center of the stage, with a single lamp hanging above us, wavering slowly back and forth. Linus had brought a blueprint of the school along with him that he had spread out on the box. On it, he had chicken-scratched his plan for securing the Horseshoe.

"The Horseshoe is in a vial located in the back of the nurse's mini-fridge," Linus said.

"It's in a vial?" I asked. "It's not a *real* horseshoe?"

THE HORSESHOE*

LOT - 916
SAMPLE 419-427
PEDICULUS HUMANUS CAPITUS

* IS NOT ACTUALLY A HORSE SHOE.

Linus paused, staring at me long enough that I got uneasy. "After all this time, you really think we've been talking about a U-shaped piece of metal that they put under a horse's hoof?"

"Of course not," I said. Seriously, I *knew* it wasn't a real horseshoe everyone was talking about. I just blurted it out when I did. Sometimes I do that.

"Anyways," Linus said, still staring at me as if to warn me to keep my mouth shut. "It's in Nurse Duvall's mini fridge—"

I jumped, excited at having connected a few dots in my head. "*That's* why Mrs. Duvall looked upset this morning! I saw her talking to Principal Davis about something! It must've been this!"

Linus set his marker down and rested his head in his hands, with his fingers digging trenches through his hair. "Dude," he whispered. "If you wanna get the Horseshoe before Soda does, you're gonna have to stop interrupting me."

"Ever play the 'quiet-game?'" K-pop asked.

"Sorry," I said. Waving my open hand in smalls circles, I said, "You may proceed."

"Thanks," Linus said. "Anyways, the Horseshoe – it's in Nurse Duvall's mini-fridge, which is located behind a locked cage that's mounted to the back wall, behind her desk. *And* the nurse's station is the very *last* office out of all the offices at the front of the building."

"Cool," I said. "So we just slip in and grab it, right? Easy-peasy-pumpkin-pie."

K-pop's forehead wrinkled. "Linus only said *where* the Horseshoe is. He hasn't even gotten to the hard part yet."

"What's the hard part?" I asked.

Linus sucked in a gallon of air, and then spoke. "We'll need to dodge hall monitors just to make it into the front lobby, and there will be plenty, along with Glitch agents who are definitely looking for you, which means you'll have to wear a disguise, *just in case*."

"Nice," Janky said.

"Not you," Linus said to Janky, but pointing at me. "Brody."

"The last time I wore a suit," I said. "It was because my dog died."

K-pop giggled.

Too bad I wasn't kidding.

Linus continued. "Once you're inside the front offices, you'll have to slip by the staff working at their desks, which hopefully there won't be many since you'll go in around break time."

"So I'm the one going in," I said.

Everyone looked at me simultaneously as if they knew that was the plan the entire time.

I stuck my thumb up. "I'm okay with that."

"Once you're past the staff," Linus said, "You'll have to find your way back to the nurse's office. Have you been there before?"

"Once or twice," I said, trying to hide a smile.

"Such a *boy*," K-pop said.

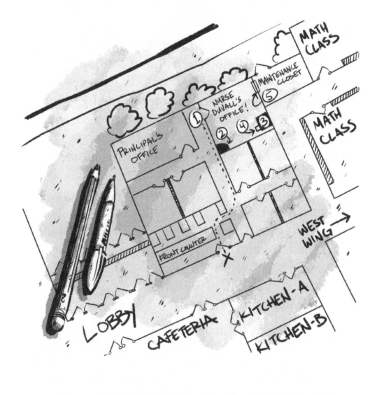

Linus drew a dotted line on the blueprint. "Mrs. Duvall always leaves her office at noon for lunch, so that's the best time to go in, but that also means her door will be locked. If it was a standard lock, we could give you a skeleton key, but it's not. It's a digital lock, which means it opens when you punch in a special code

83

or if you have a keycard."

"I assume we don't have her keycard," Scooter said, "but do we have the code?"

K-pop shook her head. "No, that would be too easy," she said as she set a dark gray tablet on top of the blueprint. Her eyes met mine. "You'll have to hook this computer tablet up so I can login from a different location and break the code."

I grinned like it was Christmas. "*Sweet.*"

"Once the door's opened," Linus said, snapping his fingers at me to get my attention. "You'll need to take out the motion sensor that controls the lights by shooting a chewed piece of gum onto the sensor in the corner of the room. It'll basically be the same as shooting spit wads from a straw, like when we were younger."

"Riiiiight," I sang. "When we were *younger.*" I'm pretty sure it had been less than 24 hours since I shot my last spit wad. "This is all beginning to sound a little more complicated than I originally thought. I thought it'd be easier than this!"

Linus sat up a bit. "It never is."

"Will the motion lights set off an alarm?" Janky asked.

Linus shook his head. "No, but the lights will switch on in a dark room that's supposed to be unoccupied. If they do that, and one of the staff checks the room, then *bam!* Brody's busted. Detention for *life.*"

Everyone fell silent, avoiding eye contact.

Linus went on. "Once the sensor is out, you'll be free to run to the back of the room, to the locked cage that houses the fridge with the Horseshoe. The lock on *that* is going to be normal, so you'll have to pick it. After that, you'll grab the Horseshoe and leave the room through the ventilation shaft behind the leather bench along the west wall. The shaft is literally only a foot and a half long and leads right into the janitor's closet on the other side, so you won't have to worry about crawling through dozens of feet of duct work like they do in action movies."

"Geez," I said. "And then?"

Linus let his shoulders fall as he exhaled. "And then that's it. You're done." He looked me in the eye and mocked what I said earlier. "Easy-peasy-pumpkin-pie."

K-pop snickered like she was excited for all the, uh… excitement. "Let's do this already! I'd like to get this case wrapped up before the concert this afternoon!"

Nearly an hour later, I was standing in the maintenance closet that was next to the front offices. K-pop was seated on an upside-down bucket, using the lid of a garbage can as a desk for her laptop. A white stick was hanging out of the side of her mouth from the lollipop she was sucking on.

Scooter was down the hall, dressed as a utility guy as he pretended to work on a water fountain in the lobby. To me, I could tell it was Scooter from how tall and gangly he was, but to everyone else, he just looked like another utility guy from behind.

The walkie-talkie next to K-pop's laptop chirped. "Scooter here," his voice cracked through the speaker. "The coast is clear in the lobby, over."

And then Janky's voice spoke over the walkie-talkie. "Yeah, this is Janky, checking in. Can you hear me? Am I coming in alright?"

The funny thing was that Janky was in the room *with* us.

"Uh, duh," K-pop said. "You're coming in nicely."

"Good good," Janky said, pushing the ear bud into his ear. "It's hard to hear you, but I think I'll just have to get used to it."

I laughed under my breath. "Get your finger outta your ear, maybe?"

K-pop punched the keys on her laptop, bringing up various windows. Finally, a box popped up that looked like footage from a security camera in the lobby. The image on the screen was of the door to the front offices.

The entrance to the closet we were inside of pulled open, and Linus slipped into the room, carrying a red duffle bag. "You ready?" he asked, aiming the duffle bag at me.

"No," I said, "But if we wait until I'm ready, then I'll never get out there."

"How about you?" Linus asked K-pop. "Are you jacked in?"

K-pop pushed the lollipop to the side of her mouth, making her cheek bubble way out. "Jacked and ready to attack, sir."

She handed me a seven-inch computer tablet, and a small USB drive that was in the shape of a pink cartoon kitten. On top of the kitten's head, K-pop had attached a set of wires that connected to a plastic card that looked a lot like a credit card.

"You'll stick this card into the lock," K-pop said. "There's a little slot above the doorknob – you'll know it when you see it. You ever stay at a hotel? It's basically the same style lock."

The butterflies in my stomach started to swarm at the thought of picking a lock.

K-pop noticed and smiled at me. "Don't worry about it. I promise it'll be super easy. Once you've got the card in the slot; that's when I can work my magic. I'll be able to crack the code from my laptop."

Linus glanced at his wristwatch. "Alright, people, the clock's ticking. Janky and Scooter are in place. K-pop, you're good to go?"

K-pop turned her back to us, pulling her headphones over her ears. She reached into her pocket and cranked the volume so loud that I could almost feel the bass in the floor. I guess that meant she was ready.

"That just leaves you, Brody," Linus said, pushing the duffle bag toward me with his foot.

"What's that?" I asked, suspicious.

Linus smiled. "Your disguise."

Another ten minutes passed, and I stepped out of the men's restroom, fully geared up in a black tuxedo complete with a killer bowtie, but not the same fat kind that the Soda Jerk wore.

If there was any moment where I could say I actually *felt* like a secret agent, it would be that one.

Linus said he was going to put his tux on in another bathroom down the hall, and that we were to meet back at the door to the front offices. He also said I wouldn't have to worry about any staff stopping me simply *because* I was wearing the fancy outfit, which was exactly the point of wearing a disguise. I didn't doubt it either because if I saw a kid wearing a tux, I'd do my best to stay out of their way because they were probably going somewhere important.

I glanced at my reflection in the glass of a trophy case nearby. I had to admit, I didn't look half bad. One tug on the lapels, and I was on my way back to meet Linus in the lobby of Buchanan School.

"Hey, kid!" shouted a voice from behind me.

My heart about stopped. I turned around and stared at the face of the boy who yelled for me.

It was a Glitch agent.

Wonderful.

In my best "grown-up" voice, I spoke. "Can I help you, good sir?"

The Glitch agent studied me as he stepped forward, saying nothing. He was chewing on a toothpick that hung from the corner of his mouth.

"Is there a problem?" I asked, hoping my voice didn't crack.

The agent walked until he was about two feet away from me, keeping his eyes glued to mine the whole way. Finally, he looked at the tux. "Nice suit, bro."

I let out a breath slowly, so it wasn't obvious that I had been holding it. "Thank you, thank you. I'm on my way to an important luncheon!"

Luncheon? Who says "luncheon" anymore?

"I bet it's a fancy one," the Glitch agent said, turning his attention to the empty hallway. "Better be careful out there though, alright? Lotta crazies today, y'know what I mean?"

"Duly noted, sir," I said. "Now if you don't mind, I best be on my way."

The agent wore a stone-cold expression as he chewed his toothpick. "Alright then, go on."

Without hesitating, I walked away, thankful that

the disguise had worked.

At that moment, my pocket started vibrating. For a second I was confused until I remembered that it was just my phone.

I pulled the cellphone out. The name on the screen said, "Maddie."

Maddie was calling me!

"Hello?" I said, answering the call.

Maddie's voice was hushed and spoke quickly. "I don't have much time, Brody."

"*Where* are you?"

"Don't worry about that. What you need to worry about is keeping the Horseshoe *out* of Soda's hands! This whole case stretches farther out than any of us thought – the *entire school* is in danger!"

"What're you talking about?" I whispered.

"Brody," Maddie's voice said, upset. "Soda *wanted* us to catch him! He's been playing us since the beginning! That was his plan *the whole time!* His plans... his *evil* plans! Brody... you're dealing with a monster. Soda... is a *monster!*"

That certainly didn't make me feel any better. "What do you mean? What's he planning on doing with it? Before you answer that, tell me what the Horseshoe is!"

"No time! I'll explain later!" Maddie's voice was quieter, as if she had taken her face away from the phone. "Someone's coming. Keep the Horseshoe *away* from Soda!"

The call ended.

My phone blinked at me as I stared at the screen. Maddie had just cranked the volume on this case all the way up to eleven.

Somehow, I made it to the lobby without running into a single other person. When I turned the corner, I saw Linus waiting at the doors.

"*Dude,*" I whispered, jogging to meet him. "I just got a phone call from Maddie."

Linus furrowed his brow. "What did she say?"

I was taken back. I thought Linus would've asked if she was okay or, at least, how she was. "She said this case is bigger than we thought."

"Always is."

"And that Soda *wanted* to get caught. That he was *playing* us from the start."

Linus put his hand on his chin, stroking a beard he

didn't have. "I'm not surprised – the kid's a master manipulator. He got what he wanted – the location of the Horseshoe. But we're in too deep now, and we have to get it before he does. Our current mission is still our priority."

"*Maddie* is our priority!"

"*Maddie* is a *pro*," Linus said. "She *knew* the risks when she joined Glitch. She can handle herself. She'll be fine. She'd also be mad if we went after her *before* securing the Horseshoe."

I knew Linus was right. It's not really like Maddie needed any help in the past. Besides, there were more pressing issues at hand, like retrieving the Horseshoe from the nurse's office.

That... and why the heck *wasn't* Linus wearing a tux?

"*Where's your disguise? Is everything alright?*" I whispered.

Linus turned his head away from me. It was hard to tell, but from the way his shoulders bounced, it looked like he was... crying?

"*Uh, dude?*" I repeated.

From the side of his face, I saw that Linus, in fact, *wasn't* crying, and that I had misinterpreted his body language. His fist was in front of his mouth as he tried to contain his *laughter*.

Linus's walkie-talkie chirped, and suddenly I heard K-pop's voice. "Uh, Brody? *What* are you wearing?"

The camera behind me buzzed when I looked at it. K-pop was watching me.

"A tux," I grumbled.

"*Why?*" K-pop asked.

Linus wiped a tear from his eye. I saw the utility guy down the hall turn his head and look at me, and then I remembered it was Scooter in his costume.

"It's a disguise," I said.

"You stick out like broccoli in someone's teeth!" K-pop giggled.

I huffed, putting my hands on my hips. "Well, it already worked *once* so I guess it was worth it."

"Whatever, Sir Valentine of Tuxedo-town," K-pop said.

"Where's *your* tux?" I asked Linus coldly.

"Are you crazy?" Linus laughed. "I wouldn't be caught *dead* wearing a tux!"

I remained silent.

"Welcome to Glitch," Linus said, patting my back.

"Thanks," I grumbled. "Can we get started now? Like, for real?"

"Of course," Linus said, opening the door to the front office about an inch. He pressed his face against the opening. "Good news. It looks like everyone's out for lunch."

K-pop's voice spoke over the walkie-talkie again. "You guys only have a few minutes until the lunch bell rings so you'd better hurry."

"If we didn't waste any time on a *prank*, then we'd be golden," I said sarcastically.

Linus didn't flinch. "A few minutes is more than enough time. You ready?"

"Nope," I said honestly.

"Too bad," Linus said, opening the door.

Most of the staff had left for the day, but there was still one woman left behind, facing away from the front counter, and typing at her desk. The counter was high enough that as long as Linus and I crouched, we were invisible. I mean, not really, but *she* couldn't see us.

But that didn't mean she didn't hear the door open.

"Hello?" the woman said.

Linus motioned for me to freeze by holding his fist in the air.

"Is someone there?" The woman asked, her voice slightly trembling.

I stared at the floor, listening for the sound of her feet walking on carpet in case she got up from her desk.

"Seriously," she said. "Is someone there? If this is a joke, it's not funny 'cause it's freakin' me out."

Her chair squeaked, which meant she had pushed it away from her workstation. From the noise she made, I could tell she was grabbing her coat and purse, and was trying to be quick about it.

"Yeah, right," she whispered to herself as she made her way to the front counter. "There's no way I'm staying in a haunted office by myself for another second! I'm outta here!"

Linus and I scampered to the end of the counter, just opposite of the woman. Another second later and we'd have been toast.

With his back to the counter, Linus listened for the front door to seal shut. When it finally did, he started gasping. I guess when he's stressed, he holds his breath too.

"This way," Linus said, taking the lead.

Keeping low, we cut a path down the long hallway. All the office doors were shut, and probably locked. The walls were made of a rough gray cloth to make it easier to push pins into it. Motivational posters and different goal charts ogled us as we looked for Mrs. Duvall's office.

Suddenly, the bell rang from the hallway, nearly making me jump out of my skin. It took me a moment to realize it was just the signal for the end of fourth period, which meant students were going to flood the lobby, waiting for lunch to start.

We stopped outside the last door in the narrow hallway. It was large and metallic. The numbered keypad was built under the handle along with the keycard slot at the top of the contraption, just as K-pop had told us.

"Go ahead," Linus said.

I took the plastic card that was connected to the tablet, and shoved it into the slot.

The tiny speaker in my glasses chirped. "Kay, gimme a second here," K-pop said, her fingers typing rapidly on her laptop.

Linus glanced over his shoulder to make sure we were good. I wondered how Scooter and Janky were holding up outside with a lobby full of students.

I swallowed hard, preparing myself for all the craziness that was about to go down. I memorized the entire plan Linus had worked hard to create. One slip up could mean disaster. No pressure, right? Especially since there were several tiny details to consider.

Once the door was opened, I'd have to shoot a piece of gum at the motion sensor, which should be in the corner of the room. From there, I'd have to pick the lock to the cage that housed the refrigerator behind Mrs. Olsen's desk. Then grab the Horseshoe and escape through the vent in the wall, which should lead us right back to K-pop in the maintenance closet.

"Here we go," K-pop's voice said. "Nine."

I repeated, pushing the correct key. "Nine."

BLIP.

"One."

"One."

BLIP.

"Six."

"Six."

BLIP.

"Zero."

"Zero."

BLIP.

"Aaaaand the last number is seven," K-pop said.

"Seven."

BLIP.

Linus looked at me with a face that said, "Here we go."

And then he turned the handle.

All of a sudden, the numbered keypad turned red.

"Uh-oh," Linus muttered.

At that instant, the lights in the hallway switched off and were replaced by a flashing red strobe light. Screaming from somewhere inside the walls was an alarm that I'm pretty sure everyone in the world could hear.

"Great!" Linus said as he pushed the nurse's office door open.

"What happened?" I shouted over the blaring alarm.

"I don't know!" Linus replied, running into the room.

Cupping my hands over my ears barely helped the sharp pain from the awful alarm. It sounded like a screaming baby was living *inside* my ear canals. Stumbling forward, I started to enter Mrs. Duvall's office, but Linus jumped from the door.

"*Go go go!*" he shouted.

"*What?*"

"*There's no vent! The blueprints were wrong!*"

"*What do we do?*"

"*Run!*"

"*What about the Horseshoe?*"

"*I got it right here!*" Linus shouted, showing me the small vial in his clenched first. "*Run!*"

Linus tore through the hallway, back to the front entrance. My calves burned from having to keep up. Through the glass windows, I could see students covering their ears, looking around, trying to figure out why there was an alarm going off.

At the exit, Linus pulled open the door, but stopped in place.

Two Glitch agents stood there, shocked to see us.

Linus pushed the Glitch agents aside and weaved through the students in the hall, leaving me behind. It wasn't like I was expecting him to hold my hand as we were getting chased, but an actual "escape plan" would've been nice.

As the two agents hobbled about, keeping themselves from falling, I slipped out the door, staying close to the brick wall.

"Get back here!" I heard one of the agents shout.

Ahead of me, I saw Linus jump in the air. His head popped up over everyone else. I pushed off the wall and walked into the crowd of students.

Everything was a blur of activity. Colors blended together as I crouched to keep from being seen. Every few seconds I glanced over my shoulder, I saw the Glitch agents filtering through students, trying to find Linus and me.

Just then, Linus gripped my elbow and yanked me to the other side of the hall. "This way!" he hissed.

We moved through the rest of the students. The alarm we had set off abruptly stopped, confusing everyone for a second time. Kids looked at each other, puzzled as to what the alarm even meant. Once Linus and I were past the thickest part of students, I saw Scooter, holding the boy's restroom door open.

Scooter kept his head down, but didn't say anything as Linus and I stepped into the bathroom. Right before the door shut, I saw Scooter tape off the entrance with a sign that said, "OUT OF ORDER."

"What happened back there?" I asked. "You had the whole plan laid out!"

"It's all just part of the game," Linus answered, making sure the stalls were empty. "Half the time, our plans never work out the way we hope! We're lucky we made it as far as the nurse's office door before everything went haywire."

Turning the metal handle on the sink, I started rinsing my hands with warm water. Whenever I'm around a sink with soap, I always wash them, probably because I'm a little crazy.

Linus set the vial from the nurse's office down on

the shelf under the mirror. And then he smeared his hands down the front of his face, pulling the skin so he looked like a zombie.

"So now what?" I asked, panting.

As if the universe was answering my question, my cell phone vibrated in my front pocket. I pulled it out and looked at the screen. The call was from a number I didn't recognize. I answered it, switching on the speaker so Linus could hear the conversation too.

"Yeah?" I said, holding the phone under my chin.

"Very impressive, Valentine," the voice on the other side said. I knew it was the Soda Jerk as soon as he spoke.

"What do you want?" I asked, upset.

"Uh, really?" Soda said. "I want the *Horseshoe*. Duh."

I wasn't sure how to respond. "Well, ya can't have it. We got it first just to keep it out of your gooey hands!"

Soda chuckled over the speaker. "I *know* you did. I *planned* for that."

I took a pause so I could wrap my head around what Soda just said. "Um, what?"

"I got you to tell me where the Horseshoe was," Soda explained. "Which was all I needed to do. I *knew* you'd be scared that I would go after it – so scared that *you'd* get it yourself *just* to know it was safe. I'm just a kid at Buchanan – a kid *without* a team of secret agents or gear that I could even use to get the Horseshoe." Soda stopped for a minute, slurping a drink on the other end of the line. After sighing, he said, "All I had to do was pour myself a glass of root beer, and watch as your team of bumbling fools did the work *for* me."

Linus dropped his head forward, shaking it as he let out a laugh.

"He played me again," I whispered.

"I told you this kid was dangerous," Linus said. "He plays the game twenty steps ahead of everyone."

Soda continued. "And now that you have it, you're going to willingly hand it over."

That time, I laughed. "What makes you think I'm gonna do that?"

The phone made noise as if Soda were rubbing the microphone on a piece of cloth. And then the it fell silent, like the calm before the storm.

"Hello?" I asked, making sure the connection was still there.

A girl's voice answered. "Brody…"

I felt like the air had gotten knocked out of me. It was Maddie's voice. Soda had found Maddie.

Linus clenched his fists as he paced back and forth, staring at my cell phone.

"Are you okay?" I asked. "Where are you?"

"I… I don't know," Maddie said. "I don't recognize anything here."

"Are you hurt?"

It sounded like Maddie giggled. "No way. Soda knows better than to hit a girl."

The phone cackled again. Soda's voice returned. "Bring the Horseshoe to the spot behind the bumper cars, where the porta-potties are. Come *alone*, which means Linus has to sit this one out. Be there in twenty minutes, or else."

"Or else what?" I sneered.

"Or else we cut Maddie's hair," Soda said.

Maddie's voice spoke in the background. "Don't listen to him, Brody! Don't let him get the Horse—"

My phone blinked. Soda ended the call.

Linus's jaw muscles twitched as he stared into space. His fists were still clenched at his sides. I wasn't sure what he was thinking, but I knew he was angry.

"What do we—"

"This is *your* fault," Linus growled. "If you weren't such a dolt when talking to Soda earlier, *none* of this would've happened."

Linus was right. I said nothing.

"Are you working with him?" Linus snipped. "Is this why his plan's working so perfectly for him? That would make a lot of sense right now if *that's* what was happening."

"No!" I said defensively, my voice cracking. "I would *never*—"

"Then *why* is he *winning?*"

I wanted to keep arguing, but it was hard after Linus said that.

Linus shook his head at me disapprovingly.

"I messed up, alright?" I said. "I get it, but I'm *not* working with him. This – *all* of this was an accident, and it was my fault, okay? I'm the one who screwed up, so *I'll* be the one to take responsibility!"

Cob's words returned, cutting me like a knife.

Linus pushed me against the bathroom wall and pointed his finger at my face. "If Maddie gets hurt at all, I promise I'll make sure you spend the rest of your life in *The Shanty* – a place reserved for the *lowest* of the low. Kids who have gotten into twenty fights, and kids who cut in line on pizza day."

Linus was talking about a place worse than detention called The Shanty. Nobody really knew whether the Shanty existed or not, but everybody had a friend of a friend who was never seen again after serving time there. I've heard stories of kids going to The Shanty, but I also thought they were just that – *stories*.

"Seriously," Linus said. "Even one hair on her head gets cut, and I swear—"

"I get it, okay?" I replied, annoyed. "You think you're the only one who *doesn't* want her to get hurt?"

"It just seems like she's always getting in trouble when she hangs out with you," Linus said. "Her parents would probably tell her not to hang out with you anymore!"

"Whatever, man," I said. "After this is over, and

103

she's alright, I'll stay out of Glitch. Would that make you happy?"

"Very," Linus said flatly. He walked to back of the restroom.

"Where are you going?" I asked, still angry. "There's only one door in here."

Linus approached the second hand dryer on the wall, the one that nobody ever used because it was installed too low and made you look awkward if you used it. With the butt of his fist, he pounded on the huge circular button three times really fast, and then waited, bobbing his head like he was counting. The fifth time his head bobbed, he punched the button three more times at the same speed.

The dryer clicked. The wall around it split open an inch. Linus placed his hand on the cold tiles and pushed forward, revealing a secret door.

I stared, in awe of the new opening.

Linus didn't wait or motion for me to follow when he walked through the opening, but I did.

Inside the compartment, he pulled a handle on the wall. The secret door slowly shut, sealing itself with a "*fshhhhhh*" sound.

I expected the corridor to be cold and wet, the way an underground cave was, but it was just the opposite. It was dry, and felt warm. There wasn't an ancient musty smell either. It was odorless and felt really clean.

"How long has this been here?" I asked, studying the walls.

"Forever," Linus said. "This was created when the school was built in case there was ever a fire. These passages connect to every major hallway in the school, and lead outside. Weren't you in here when Christmas was chasing you around a few weeks ago?"

The first time I had met Christmas, he chased me into these hallways. I managed to escape because the whole thing gets twisted and confusing if you're sprinting at full speed. "Yeah, but the part I was in wasn't kept up like this."

"Principal Davis just had them repainted," Linus explained. "There was inspection last week. The report said these corridors felt like a 'nightmare' and like something out of a horror movie. If they weren't brought up to code, the school was gonna get fined."

I slid my hands on the smooth coat of dry paint on the walls. "But what about the secret door in the bathroom? You can't tell me *that* was part of the school's original building plan..."

Linus continued walking, glancing over his shoulder at me. "Cob *might've* had something to do with that one."

A low thumping sound started creeping up on me. It was quiet enough that I couldn't place exactly where it was coming from, but just that it was coming from somewhere back there.

"What's that sound?" I asked.

Linus didn't stop. "It's nothing."

The thumps grew a little louder, and sounded like someone was playing bass music farther down the corridor.

"No, seriously," I said, feeling more paranoid. "Is something going on back here? It sounds like a bunch of *gymnasts* are jumping around."

Linus turned around and glared at me. "There's so much about this school that you have no idea about, alright? Just assume it's nothing and keep walking."

"Are we in danger?"

Linus took a moment to answer. I could tell by the way his eyes darted back and forth that he was thinking of how to answer my question. After a second, he said, "The sounds you're hearing are from kids who are mostly harmless... *most* of them anyway."

"Anything to do with all the ninja rumors?" I joked. Of course there weren't any ninjas at the school, but I wanted to try and smooth things over with Linus.

"It's nothing to be concerned about today," Linus said. "And since you're dropping out of Glitch after we save Maddie, then it's nothing you'll *ever* need to be concerned with."

So much for smoothing things over.

When we passed one of the doors to the courtyard outside, Linus ignored it, continuing down the hall. From behind the door came the sounds of a fully functioning carnival, complete with the bells and whistles of rides that probably hadn't passed any safety checks in the last twenty years.

"Hold on," I said, pointing at the door. "The carnival's this way."

Linus stopped. "I know, but we're not going there yet."

"We have, like, *zero* time," I reminded. "Soda's going to be waiting for me behind the bumper cars within the next few minutes, if he's not *already* there."

"You can't go out there alone," Linus said. "We have to grab a couple things first."

"From where? *Glitch?* Won't that be like turning ourselves in?"

Linus shook his head at me. "No, not from Glitch. I have some junk stored back here in case anything goes wrong, just like it did today."

"Oh," I said.

"It's just around the corner," Linus said, continuing his march down the corridor.

When I turned at the fork in the hallway, I saw Linus step into one of the side closets that was filled with cleaning supplies. Apparently the workers who painted the corridors had left all their buckets of paint back there also.

Linus walked across the room, to a rusty toolbox that was laying on its side on the floor. He flipped it over with his foot, and took a knee next to it. When it opened, I could see a collection of supplies – wigs, mustaches, wristwatches that were probably communicators, sunglasses that would let you see what was going on behind you, stacks of dollar bills, and a bunch of fake student I.D. cards taped to the top of the toolbox. All the I.D. cards had Linus's face on them. Wow, right?

"You didn't even lock that thing," I said, surprised as I stood over Linus.

"Don't need to," Linus said, moving some of the items around as he looked for something. "Sometimes it's best to hide things in plain sight. Nobody would take a look in this rusty old box. Would you have?"

"No, I wouldn't have wasted my time with it," I said.

"Exactly," Linus said as he wrapped his fingers around a set of glasses inside the box. "*There* you are."

I watched as Linus brought a pair of glasses closer to his face. They were black with thick rims, very similar to the glasses K-pop was wearing. Actually, they were *exactly* the same kind that K-pop wore. He blew the dust off the top of the frames. With his fingernail, he flicked a tiny button on the side of one of the hinges.

"Are those for me?" I asked.

Linus nodded as he handed me the glasses. "Put them on."

I slipped them over my face. They were heavier than I expected.

Linus returned to the rusty toolbox once more out and pulled out a portable television, the kind with a two-inch screen and an antenna that pulled out from the side. It was also the same kind my dad took to church on Sunday mornings so he could watch the game during the church lunch. Smearing his hand across the face of the small TV, Linus cleaned the grime off. And then he flipped the switch on the side of the unit.

The two-inch screen flickered, and slowly grew brighter. A black and white image of the small TV was *on* the screen. When I looked at Linus, the screen switched and showed Linus's face.

The TV was connected to the glasses I was wearing! There was a camera built into them!

"Sick!" I exclaimed.

Linus tried not to, but I saw a smile carve across his face. "With those glasses, I'll be able to see everything you're seeing, and I'll also be able to hear everything you hear."

"Nice," I said with a stupid grin. "It's also a two way radio?"

"The transmission is weak at times, but it still gets the job done. Say something."

"Um, something," I said, hearing nothing from the unit.

"Piece of junk radio!" Linus tapped the side of the small TV in his hands. "Oh wait, I forgot to flip the volume switch. There, that should do it. Say something again."

I thought I'd try to be funny. "Something again."

My voice came out way louder than I expected, but then I realized it wasn't from the small TV that I heard it from. My voice had come from the school's speaker system that was mounted on the wall. I slapped my hand over my mouth. Everyone at Buchanan had just heard me say, "Something again," over the PA system. *Why* couldn't I have said something funnier?

"Uh, hehe," Linus laughed, a little embarrassed. "This thing's pretty outdated. Remind me that I'll have to replace it when this is all over."

I nodded, keeping my hand in place.

"I switched the mic off," Linus said. "You're okay."

Moving my hand away from my mouth, I spoke, but quietly. "Sweet."

Linus accompanied me back to the exit that led to the carnival in the schoolyard. The ringing bells from carnival games were powerful enough that we had to speak loudly.

Linus handed me the small vial we took from the nurse's office. The one that everyone was calling the Horseshoe. The one that had given me so much trouble the whole day. The one I was supposed to hand over to Soda.

"Awesome," I said sarcastically.

"School's out for the day," Linus said, pushing the door open a crack. "Which means *everyone* is going to be out here, including the school staff, Cob, and *all* the Glitch agents."

"Suckerpunch too," I said.

"You're right," Linus said. "Christmas and his goons will be out there as well." He pointed at my tuxedo. "Good thing you're all dressed up, right?" he joked.

I smirked. "Right. If things go south, at least I'll have something nice to wear at my funeral."

Linus laughed. He held up the portable TV again. "Remember, I'll be with you the entire time, alright?"

"Where are you gonna be?" I asked, watching all

the students outside the door.

"Close," Linus said. He stopped and looked me dead in the eye. "Doing this takes guts, Brody."

I understood what Linus was saying, but didn't want to press it. "Maddie needs help."

Linus pushed the door open, and I stepped out from the corridors.

There was barely a cloud in the sky as the sun burned brightly overhead. Since the temperature was around fifty degrees, my tuxedo felt nice and cozy.

The door slammed shut behind me, but because of all the carnival noises, I almost didn't hear it.

I turned around, hoping to see Linus, but he wasn't there. It didn't matter. I knew he was seeing everything that I was seeing, and hearing everything I was hearing.

The place where I was standing was behind most of the carnival. You know the spot. I'm sure you've been in a similar place before at a carnival – the wet and stinky spots behind all the games and rides. To my left was a huge metal trashcan, already overflowing with lemonade and half eaten funnel cakes. To my right were bundles of cable, snaking their way through the grass.

Too bad I was in the middle of a terrifying mission, otherwise I would've been in danger of having some fun.

As I stepped in the swampy grass, I kept my eyes on all the kids who were walking through the carnival. A huge banner hung from the tallest pole at the other end of the track. The text on it read, "HAPPY 100TH BIRTHDAY, BUCHANAN SCHOOL!"

You'd think walking inconspicuously through a

carnival would be a piece of cake because of all the laughter and rides, but it wasn't. All the commotion just made me more paranoid that I'd get caught.

My eyes were drying out from how intensely I was watching my surroundings. It was like that moment in a video game, where there's so much to worry about that you become aware of everything that's happening around you.

Nearby, there were kids sharing a ball of cotton candy. Behind them, a few students were standing next to one of the carnival games where you pop small balloons with darts.

Next to them was a line for a pirate boat ride that sent kids hundreds of feet into the air while swinging upside-down.

Bells started ringing. Someone had won a prize nearby, but I couldn't tell where it was because there were so many games.

A small crowd of girls sat at a picnic bench, stuffing funnel cakes into their mouths. I think they were all on the cheerleading squad, but I'm not positive since I've never been to a game.

About twenty steps in, the carnival opened up, circling all the way around the track. A line of games and rides curved all the way down and around the field. Several of the larger rides were at the outside of the circle.

The concert stage was at the far end of the track, opposite of where I was standing. There were drums and several guitars waiting to be played as roadies moved back and forth, making sure the instruments were set up properly and in tune.

I stole a glance behind me, hoping I was in the

clear, but as usual, I wasn't. Three Glitch agents had already noticed me. Two of the agents were already making their way out. They were going to circle around me. The agent that remained in place raised his wrist and started speaking into his watch.

"Of course," I said to myself.

The Horseshoe was sitting in the palm of my closed hand. Time was running out, and I couldn't afford to play a game of *cat-and-mouse* with the agents.

Even in the thick crowd of students, if I took off running, everyone would notice it. The good thing was that the agents weren't about to make any sudden movements either. The problem was that I had no idea what to do.

Linus spoke over the speaker in my glasses. "Walk straight and keep it casual."

I spun around, looking for my teammate, but he wasn't anywhere I could see.

"Don't worry about where I am," Linus said. "I can see you, and that's all that matters. Now walk straight. Those agents are closing in on you from the outside."

Through the faces of students, I saw the two agents that were circling around me. Without wasting another second, I did as Linus instructed. "Nice! Where are you?"

"Keep quiet!" Linus snapped. "Your voice is still coming through over the speaker system!"

"Sorry!" I replied, immediately slapping my hand over my mouth.

"Good," Linus said. "In about ten feet, I want you to cut a hard left turn."

I counted two feet with each normal step I took. There wasn't anything special about the spot Linus had ordered me to turn at, but I did it anyway. I rotated left, and continued walking.

"Keep going, keep going, keep going," Linus whispered. "Stop! Bend down and act like you're tying your shoe!"

I halted, instantly dropping to my knee. As I played with my shoestrings, I saw the legs of one of the agents only a meter away. I kept my head down, watching his feet stumble back and forth, trying to figure out where I disappeared to. After a moment, he continued moving forward, searching for me.

"Wait for it," Linus said. "Alright, you're good. Keep going straight. You're almost to the bumper cars, but there are still two agents you need to worry about."

I obeyed, feeling a rush of excitement surge through my body. When I searched the crowd for the faces of the last two agents, my excitement quickly drained. They had their eyes set on me and were quickly catching up to my spot.

"Speed up a little," Linus said.

So I did.

"Faster," Linus said. "Those guys are gaining on you!"

Without meaning to, I started jogging.

"Faster!" Linus yelled. "Another twenty feet!"

My jog turned into an all out sprint. It was like a nightmare, where I knew I was getting chased by someone, but had no idea how close they were. I wanted to look behind me, but if I did, I knew I'd end up tripping.

"Keep going straight, but be ready to turn left in *three…*" Linus started.

My legs burned.

"*Two…*"

My hand still clenched the Horseshoe.

"*One…*"

My vision was starting to blur.

"*Turn left! Now!*" Linus shouted.

I dug my right foot into the soft earth and switched directions, without even looking to see what was in front of me, which happened to be a small crowd of students. I smashed into some of the kids, causing a chain reaction that knocked the whole group to the ground.

"What's your deal?" shouted one of the boys I tackled.

I started apologizing, but stopped when I saw his face. He was painted white with black circles on his cheeks. Two black lines were drawn down each eye starting at his brow and ending above his lips, which were painted red. The students behind him were painted the exact same way, and they were all wearing black tuxedos.

I had just blitzed a herd of mimes.

Linus spoke again through my headset. "Don't waste time," he said. "Get up and disappear in the crowd. Those agents are only a few feet away!"

"Sorry, guys!" I said, leaving the group of fallen clowns. Right as I slipped into student bystanders, the Glitch agents appeared, confused at the pile of kids in tuxedos.

"Sift through them!" one of the agents said. "One of these guys has got to be him!"

"Nice work," Linus said.

I looked at the vial in my hand. It was unharmed and safe. But my glasses weren't. In the scuffle, I had cracked one of the lenses and the other was completely missing.

Whoopsies.

Another whistle blew in front of me. I looked up to see a whole line of students waiting patiently for their turn at the bumper cars. The huge oval shaped track was before me. Mini cars were driving in wonky circles, ramming each other as students laughed like maniacs.

I rushed over to the other side of the track, to where a line of porta-potties stood like majestic buildings, basking in the light of—nah, I'm kidding—they were *giant nasty poop boxes on wheels*. I was just thankful it was cold out. Those things are like massive baking ovens when the temperature is over eighty degrees.

Massive.

Poop.

Baking.

Ovens.

Ew.

Just… ew.

That's when a high-pitched horn honked once at me. A golf cart slid to a stop right next to the line of porta-potties. Sitting behind the steering wheel was a sixth grader dressed as a clown – not like one of the mimes I ran into, but a full fledged, oversized necktie wearing, weird haired, *clown*. Sitting shotgun was the scruffy looking kid who set off the bottled soda trap earlier.

"Get in," the clown snarled.

"Where's Soda?" I asked.

The clown's eyes narrowed. "*Get in. No questions.*"

I crawled into the back of the golf cart.

The clown kept his eyes forward. "The blindfold back there. Put it on."

Next to my legs was a long piece of black cloth. "I'm kind of claustrophobic, so I think—"

"*Put it on!*" the clown commanded.

I took a deep breath, and did as the clown had told me. Removing my broken glasses, I slipped them into my front pocket, and then tied the blindfold around my head.

The golf cart jerked forward, and we were on our

way. The sound of the carnival grew quieter as we drove. The cold air was biting my cheeks from how fast the clown was driving. I had to keep my body upright by leaning over the entire time, which meant we were driving in a large circle. At least we weren't going too far from the school.

Finally, the golf cart stopped. A hand grabbed my elbow and yanked me out. I said nothing as I was escorted to a secret location where Soda was probably going to meet with me. Either that, or I was about to die. At least I was already wearing the tux, right?

My foot caught the lip of a step. I stumbled forward, feeling the soft grass turn into a solid floor. The hand gripping my elbow never let go.

The sounds of the carnival were drowned out wherever I had been taken. I could still hear the bells and whistles of games and rides, but it sounded like I was hearing everything under water.

"Sit," the clown growled. At least I think it was still the clown. I did a really good job of tying the blindfold around my eyes so I couldn't see a thing. A smarter agent would've kept it loose so they could sneak a peek at their surroundings. Actually, a smarter agent probably wouldn't have put it on in the first place.

I took a seat.

"The Horseshoe?" the clown asked.

Holding my palm up, I presented the small vial. I felt cold fingers snatch it from me.

Footsteps clomped until a door slammed shut, and I was alone.

Panic set in. I was beginning to feel claustrophobic, which is a *terrible* feeling. I could still

119

hear everything outside the blindfold, but since I was in an area with very little noise, my brain started freaking out.

My lungs took shorter breaths of air until I finally started gasping. Leaning forward in my seat, I did my best to calm myself, but it was worthless.

Beneath the blindfold, I felt my eyes swell with tears, and I finally couldn't take it anymore.

I ripped the piece of cloth off my face and gasped loudly, feeling the air cool my sweaty forehead. I was still freaked, but at least my pulse was slowing down.

After catching my breath, I took in my surroundings. I was sitting on a rickety wooden chair that looked like it was from some antique shop. The floor beneath me looked like dirt, but only because it was covered in dust. Under the blanket of filth was a solid concrete floor.

On both sides of me were long pillars of bamboo trees looming over my head. I thought I heard a door slam only a moment ago, but I couldn't see one anywhere.

A monkey howled in the distance.

"Where the *heck* am I?" I whispered as I stood from the creaky old chair.

A quiet little *clink* sound hit the ground. When I looked down, I saw that it was the broken pair of glasses I had placed in my front pocket when I put the blindfold on.

I picked up the broken glasses and inspected them. They were pretty badly damaged from my run-in with the mimes, but I hoped they still worked. Opening the glasses carefully, I pulled them over my face.

"Linus?" I whispered, stepping away from the

rickety chair. "Linus, can you hear me?"

He didn't respond. The speaker built into the glasses was silent.

The sound of shuffling feet came from behind the trees.

"*Linus?*" I asked again, whispering a little louder. Please, glasses! Work!

Just then, Maddie stumbled through the bamboo trees. She looked disheveled and stressed out. Her hair was tied into a frizzy ponytail on top of her head, and her cheeks were covered in dirt. She stopped at the edge of the forest and struggled to keep herself upright.

Immediately, two goons stepped out from behind the trees. They both had rubber bands pulled back tightly on their thumbs, aimed right at me.

"Where's the Horseshoe, Brody?" came a thin and menacing voice from behind Maddie.

I didn't answer.

A third kid stepped out from the forest. He was taller than his two minions and better dressed. It was The Soda Jerk. He stopped when he was standing next to my friend. "*Where's* the Horseshoe, Brody?"

I shook my head. "No clue what you're talkin' about."

Soda lost it and shouted like a maniac. "*Don't play games with me, Valentine! You think I look like someone who likes playing games? I know* you know where it is, so you'd better give it up 'fore I do somethin' *crazy!*"

I swallowed hard and took a seat on the antique chair again. I thought for a moment, feeling lost and confused. "*You* have it," I said. "I already *gave* it to you!"

Soda raised his eyebrows and sighed, pulling a pair of scissors from his back pocket. With his other hand, he took Maddie's frizzy ponytail and started rubbing it between his fingers. And then he spoke, softer than before, as if he didn't hear what I just said. "I'm going to ask you one more time. The Horseshoe... *where* is it?"

Maddie's gaze met mine, and we stared at each other for a moment.

A glint from the scissors distracted me, and I looked back at the psycho holding Maddie's ponytail.

What was Soda talking about? I gave that clown the Horseshoe already! Why would he keep asking me where it was? Did I give it to the wrong person?

"Don't," I said, surprised by the crack in my voice. "Please... don't..."

The scissors flinched slightly. I heard the metal squeak against itself.

"Wait!" I cried out.

The Soda Jerk opened the scissors. The scraping metal made my stomach turn.

I was at least fifteen feet away from Maddie. Even if I was the fastest kid in school, I wouldn't be able to reach her before she got her hair cut.

I spoke again, my voice cracking the same as before. I felt defeated and helpless, but I couldn't just give up, so instead, I begged. "Please, I'll get it for you, okay? I'll *find* the Horseshoe, and I'll hand it to you personally. Just please... *don't* do this this."

Soda stared at me with his cold black eyes.

And then I heard the scissors snip.

I want to say that it was Maddie who screamed, but I knew it was me because I nearly passed out from it. Falling off the chair, my cheek hit the cold floor.

Everything was a blur as I stared at Maddie. She was on her knees, cupping her hands over her face. Soda and his two goons disappeared behind the trees. I heard the door slam shut again, leaving Maddie and me alone.

My heart was broken. I had completely and utterly failed. Soda had the Horseshoe, and Maddie's hair had been chopped off. I was probably the *worst* secret agent in the history of secret agents *ever*.

I laid on the floor, feeling sorry for myself.

The blur of colors that was Maddie's body, sat straight up instantly. "Brody!" she whispered.

All I could do was groan. "Guhhhhh... I'm so sorry 'bout your hair... your beautiful *beautiful* hair..."

"Brody!" Maddie said again. "Get up!"

Ignoring her, I continued grumbling. "…if I could've just *saved* you… saved the *school* from that, that, that… *jerk*… then maybe I could be a *real* agent like you… maybe you'd even say *yes* if I asked you to go *out* with me… but I *killed* that dream, didn't I?"

Maddie stopped, and then giggled. "Go *out* with you?"

I whimpered as a response.

"Brody, get up!" Maddie said, sliding across the floor. She put her hand around my arm and pulled me to a sitting position.

My bones felt like they had all disappeared at the same time, like I was just a mushy pile of muscles and blood vessels "Sorry 'bout your hair," I said again.

Maddie laughed loudly. She took her hand and gripped the choppy hair at the top of her scalp, and then she did the most horrifying thing I'd ever seen in my life – *she ripped her hair off of her head.*

I squealed again, but shut my mouth as I watched her full head of blonde hair, still attached to her, fall from a bundle that was hiding underneath the thing in her hand.

She was wearing a wig! Soda had cut the ponytail off of a *wig!*

"The cardboard box outside the drama club's room!" I said. "The one with all the costumes! You took one of the wigs!"

"The room was *filled* with those ugly wigs," Maddie said, running her fingers through her real hair.

"How did you know Soda would try to cut your hair?"

"I didn't," Maddie answered honestly. "I just

grabbed one so I could follow him in a disguise."

I was confused. "So… you used a blonde wig to disguise your *actual* blonde hair?"

"It was the heat of the moment!" Maddie said. "Besides, ponytails are enough of a disguise!"

"But why didn't you just put your *real* hair in a ponytail?"

Maddie glared at me. "What were you saying about wanting to go out with me?"

Nervously laughing, I put my hands behind my neck. "Hehe, uh, nothing. I was just… uh… heat of the moment, y'know!"

I chewed my lip as I stared at the chopped up wig in Maddie's hand. "But why did he cut your hair? I got the Horseshoe for him! I gave it to his freaky clown friend! *Why* did he keep asking where it was!"

"He was probably making sure you gave him the real deal," Maddie said. "He was putting pressure on you to see if you'd cave and tell him the truth."

I pushed my lips to the side, making a "*huh*" sound.

Maddie smiled softly at me. "Nice poker face by the way. It takes a lot of talent to pull off a bluff like that."

"Right?" I asked, and then stopped. "What kind of bluff?"

Maddie patted at her blue jeans, dusting them off. "The decoy Horseshoe. You did a great job keeping a straight face when he asked you where the Horseshoe was. It'll be a little while before Soda realizes you gave him a *decoy* Horseshoe."

"Ummmmm," I hummed until Maddie understood why I was stalling.

"That *wasn't* a decoy?" Maddie shouted. "*You seriously gave him the real thing?*"

"In my defense, Linus was with me the entire time! He never said anything about a fake Horseshoe either!"

"Never get a *boy* to do a *girl's* job," Maddie grumbled. She spun around and ran to the edge of the bamboo forest.

I jumped from my chair and caught up to her. "Wait, where are we? Where's there even a bamboo forest close to the school?"

"What?" Maddie asked, confused and angry. "This isn't a *real* forest."

As she said it, I realized the bamboo trees weren't

126

real trees, but long sheets of canvas draped from the ceiling that had been camouflaged with plastic leaves. "This is all fake?" I whispered.

Pushing one of the canvas paintings aside, Maddie revealed a ladder that connected to a catwalk twenty feet above us. "This is a funhouse. We're in the jungle themed room."

"Right, I knew that," I said, lying through my teeth.

"Sure ya did," Maddie said, climbing the ladder.

I followed behind her and crawled onto the catwalk that was looking over the rest of the funhouse. Other students were running through rooms with different themes, completely clueless that we were watching them from above.

Gripping the handrail, Maddie sped down the catwalk. "I can't believe you gave him the real Horseshoe."

I struggled to catch up, feeling my knees shake from being up so high. "What was I supposed to do?"

"*Give him a fake one!*" Maddie replied, annoyed. "Do you realize what you've done?"

"No!" I shouted. The sound effects from the funhouse masked my voice so I wasn't worried about anyone hearing me. "Because nobody will tell me what the Horseshoe even is!"

Maddie stopped in place and turned around, which made me bump into her. With the most serious face I've ever seen on a kid, she said, "Lice. The Horseshoe is a vial of head lice."

I stared, waiting for Maddie to laugh and tell me she was joking, but she never did. "Are you serious?"

"Do I *look* like I'm kidding?"

"I've been carrying a small vial of head lice in my hands for half the day?"

"Gross," Maddie said, glancing at my hands.

"Why would Mrs. Duvall even have a vial of head lice in her fridge in the first place?"

Maddie turned and continued walking down the metal walkway. "Someone was doing their science fair project on head lice," she explained. "They were storing it away in Mrs. Duvall's fridge. It was the safest place for it since it was locked. After the science fair was over, I guess they never threw it out."

"That's…" I paused for effect. "…*disgusting!*"

"You're tellin' me," Maddie said. "And now Soda is moving it around the school."

"What's he want with it?"

"He's going to open it at the concert at the end of the day."

"But that's… *madness*," I said. "He'll infect kids with head lice!"

"That's the point," Maddie said. "I don't know *why* he's doing it. Only that he is."

"That vial was so small though. How's he going to spread it to everyone?" I asked, but before Maddie could respond, I knew the answer. "The hats that they're planning on tossing out to the students."

Maddie nodded. "All he has to do is tap the vial on each hat. He doesn't even have to infect everyone in the school! All it takes is for a good chunk of the student body to get it, and *everyone* will freak out. Lice isn't dangerous, but it *is* gross, contagious, and annoying."

"You were right," I said. "Soda *is* a monster."

Suddenly, Maddie started running along the shaky

catwalk. "There! It's Soda and one of his goons!"

Three rooms away, I saw Soda standing next to the exit of the funhouse. Another kid was by his side, laughing with him, but it wasn't any of the previous goons who had helped him earlier.

The other kid was dressed sharply, wearing a vest and tie combo. His hair was perfectly combed into place, like he was some sort of model. When I saw his face, I recognized it immediately. It was Christopher Moss, or as I've come to know him, Christmas, leader of Suckerpunch, and the most dangerous kid in the school.

"OMG!" Maddie whispered, gripping the handrail of the catwalk.

"Christmas!" I hissed.

Maddie sprinted to the end of the catwalk and slid until her foot stopped her against the ladder that led to the room Soda was standing in. She gripped the metal sides of the ladder, using it to slide all the way down to the floor of the funhouse.

Soda and Christmas jumped back, surprised by Maddie's sudden appearance, but they didn't stay in place long. They both ran out the front door of the funhouse, to the carnival outside.

I wasn't as graceful as Maddie, and used the metal rungs to climb down safely. When I reached the exit, I stepped out, feeling the cool breeze splash against me.

It surprised me to see that the bumper cars were only a few yards away. The spot where I had boarded the golf cart was literally closer than the bumper car track. The grass showed several circles carved out by the golf cart's tires. It felt like the clown had driven in a large circle because that's exactly what he did.

"Do you see them?" I asked.

Maddie was scanning the carnival like a robot. "There's too many people out here!"

"*That's* not something I can fix!" I said.

"Maddie!" Linus shouted as he ran up to us. K-pop, Janky, and Scooter trailed behind him.

"Where were you?" I asked Linus.

"Out here," Linus said. "After that clown took you into the funhouse, I had to switch your glasses off because of all the feedback it was generating. I really have to get that piece of junk fixed."

"Or get a new one," I suggested.

"Or get a new one," Linus repeated, agreeing.

"You're alright!" K-pop said to Maddie, her face

beaming.

"Not yet, I'm not," Maddie said, running to the side of the bumper car track. She pointed her finger toward the middle of the racecourse. "There! It's Soda!"

K-pop stepped forward, fists clenched. "Janky! Sick 'im!"

Without saying a word, Janky thundered across the grass, clearing the side gate of the bumper car track in a single bound.

Soda didn't know what hit him when Janky tackled him to the ground. The vial of head lice flipped from his hand, sailing through the air, until bouncing on the hard concrete track.

Maddie and K-pop gasped, afraid the vial had cracked open. Luckily, it didn't.

I sprinted across the grass and leapt over the gate. The mini cars were still driving wildly, smashing into each other as I slid across the ground. Snatching the vial, I rolled to my side, barely getting run over by one of the cars.

"Give it back!" Soda shrieked from the side of the track.

Janky was picking himself off the ground, holding his head. He must've hurt himself when he tackled Soda.

Jumping into one of the empty bumper cars, I slammed on the gas, speeding away from the Soda Jerk. Cranking on the wheel, my car skidded across the track, crashing into someone else's ride.

"Sorry," I shouted as I spun the wheel.

The girl in the other bumper car shook her fist. "Where are you going? We have to exchange insurance information!"

I pushed the accelerator, circling my car away from the weirdo kid that took bumper cars too seriously.

"You're dead meat, Valentine!" came Soda's voice from behind me.

I looked over my shoulder, checking my blind spot. Soda was in a red bumper car that was barreling toward me. I don't know how he got his car to go faster than mine, but he did, rear ending the car I was in.

My head whipped backward as my car jumped forward.

Again, Soda rammed his car into mine.

The cluster of cars cleared out of the way in front of me, and I pushed down on the gas, swerving left and right, dodging other careless drivers. Sparks rained down from the metal poles of bumper cars as they scraped the roof of the track. That's how they were powered.

Suddenly, my car got bashed on the right side. "Pull your vehicle over!" shouted the kid in the other car. A Glitch agent was behind the wheel, another was in the passenger seat frantically trying to get his seat belt on.

At the same moment, another car smashed into my left side. "Give it back to me!" hollered Soda's voice. Like things couldn't get any worse, right?

"This is the craziest thing to ever happen to me!" I shouted, spinning my steering wheel around.

My bumper car bobbed forward, but suddenly switched to reverse. I fell against the dashboard, watching as Soda and the Glitch agents collided. If this were a movie, their cars would've exploded and I'd have walked away in slow motion without looking back, but since this was real life, Soda and the agents just shouted insults at each other.

Pressing the brakes, I spun the wheel, whipping

my bumper car in the opposite direction. The track before me was jammed with other cars, but I had no other way to go.

"Gangway!" I shouted, stomping my foot on the gas. "I'm comin' through!"

The wind blasted my face as my car sped forward. Kids spun their wheels, kicking at their gas pedals, trying to get their vehicle out of the way before I tore a path through them.

But nobody moved, and my car bumped into the rest of the group. Not even violently either. Like, my head bobbed forward, but that was it. Everyone in the group laughed. I might've chuckled, myself.

"Brody!" Soda shouted from behind me.

Why do villains always announce they're coming after you when you're not paying attention? If he hadn't shouted my name, he probably would've taken me by surprise.

I crawled out of the car and hopped the gate on the other side of the track. The students in line cheered me on, even though they had no idea what was happening.

Soda dashed through the line of students, sprinting toward me at full speed. The kid was fast, I'll give him that.

I clutched the vial of lice in my fist. Where could I even take it? The nurse's office was back in the school, too far for me to make it without getting creamed by Soda or even the Glitch agents.

Spinning in all directions, I tried to find a teacher, but *not* to my surprise, there wasn't one around. But when you *don't* need them, they're *everywhere*, right?

I looked across the track, past the games and the

carnival rides, at the stage where the concert was to take place, and saw a glimmer of hope. Principal Davis was standing next to the microphone, reading from a sheet of paper, probably practicing his "happy birthday" speech before the show started. A huge banner hung behind him with the words "Annee Mu," painted across the front of it.

And to the left of the stage was a police car. There were *police* somewhere at the carnival! All I had to do was get to the stage before Soda or Glitch got ahold of me!

Stomping across the grass, I weaved in and out of student cliques as Soda gained on me.

The stage was clear across the field. There was no way I was going to make it if I didn't do something different soon.

Diving over the countertop of one of the carnival games, I rolled along the ground until the sidewall stopped me. A cardboard box filled with baseballs for the game stared at me from the counter I had cleared.

"*What're ya doin', kid?*" the bald man in charge of the game shouted. "*Are you nuts? You could've really hurt yourself!*"

Soda slammed into the counter.

He popped his knee up, and then pulled his whole body over. "Give it back!" he growled as he started sliding over the edge.

Before Soda's feet were on the floor, I kicked at the box of baseballs, spilling them across the ground.

Soda panicked, which only made things worse. His feet tried to find the floor, but instead, rolled across the tops of all the balls. His legs kicked out in front of him and his back hit the ground.

I didn't wait for the Soda Jerk to get up. Jumping the sidewall, I started running through the other carnival games. The adults managing the games scolded me the entire way as I dodged water guns, darts, and baseballs.

Ironically, there weren't any carnival games that involved throwing horseshoes.

I glanced over my shoulder. Soda was still there, catching up to me. Then I looked out the front windows of the games I was cutting through. Yup. A handful of Glitch agents were following me out there too. I was beginning to think it was hopeless. If I got away from

Soda, the Glitch agents would get me. If I got away from the Glitch agents, then Soda would get me.

I started screaming at myself in my head.

Gaaaaaaaaaaaaaah! Just run! You can do this! Stop thinking you can't! The school needs you right now, and failure is not *an option!*

Crunching down on my teeth, I gave it all I had, blasting through the last carnival ride. Raising my leg, I slid it along the counter, barely losing any speed. On the other side, I slammed my foot down and kept running.

I heard Soda slam into the wall behind me. The crash was so strong that the canvas roof of the game caved in, making a "*whoomph!*" sound. I managed to look back once. Soda was stuck inside the carnival game. I was safe from him!

But not the Glitch agents.

"Stop!" shouted the agent in front.

Obviously, I didn't. The concert stage was straight ahead of me. A bunch of roadies were sitting on giant black crates, taking their fifteen-minute break.

"Guys!" I shouted. "I'm supposed to make an announcement on the mic! It's super important! Where do I go?"

The roadies glanced at each other, mumbling something about how I was probably legit since I was wearing a tuxedo. Then the tallest, dirtiest of the group of adults pointed at a staircase behind them.

"Up there, dude," he murmured.

"Great, thanks!" I said, running up to the stairs. I pointed at the Glitch agents as they slowed down in the front of the roadies. "And by the way, those kids *really* wanted to see all your piercings!"

"Righteous!" the lead roadie said. He spun around and pulled his shirt off, clean over his head. It was a bit much, and not what I expected at all, but it managed to shock the Glitch agents enough that was able to get away from them.

The principal was still over by the mic at the front of the stage. I was totally in the clear as I dragged my feet across the floor, gasping loudly to catch my breath. The vial of lice was still in my hand, completely unharmed. Goosebumps ran down my arms at the thought of finally ending this terrible case.

At that moment, Cob stepped out from behind one of the guitar amps on the stage.

I stopped instantly. "Cob!"

He presented his open palm to me. "Gimme the Horseshoe, Brody."

"But Principal Davis is right there," I said. "I'm about to give it to him and tell him all about Soda."

Cob took one step forward. "I know," he said. "Gimme the Horseshoe, and *I'll* do it."

"But..." I was confused. "What?"

Clenching his fist, Cob snarled. "*Gimme* the Horseshoe, Brody! I'll take it from here, alright?"

Now it was weird. Cob's anger was a red flag. I gripped the vial tighter and put my hand behind my back.

Through his glasses, Cob stared at me, but started speaking softly. "I'm sorry," he said. "Please, that vial is dangerous, and the principal would rather it come from *me* than you. He doesn't even know you're an agent with us yet."

I wasn't sure why Cob was being so demanding, but there was already too much time that had been wasted. I started walking around the leader of Glitch, toward Principal Davis to give him the vial myself.

Cob's eyes flashed with anger. He grabbed my collar and violently pushed me back until I slammed against some speaker cabinets. I tried to push back, but my body was too shaky from all the running I had just done.

With his other hand, Cob grabbed my vest at my shoulder and threw me down to the ground. He started swinging his foot to kick me, but I moved fast enough that he missed. Scooting back, I kept the vial sealed in my hand.

"*What's your deal?*" I shouted.

Cob lifted his foot again. I tried to move away, but found myself completely cornered against a stack of crates. He stomped on my ankle.

I howled in pain as I pulled my leg away from him. I hoped that maybe the principal heard me, but we were far enough backstage that I highly doubted it. Besides, a massive purple curtain was blocking Principal Davis from my view.

Cob's eyes squinted. He held his hand out, palm up. "The vial, please."

"*What the heck is your problem?*" I asked sharply.

Cob kept his eyes on mine. "The vial. *Now!*"

I studied my boss's intense face. He looked insane. "You were just going to let Soda do it, weren't you? You're somehow a part of this, *aren't* you?"

"You have no idea what you're dealing with, noob," Cob hissed. "Now hand over the vial!"

I tightened my grip around the Horseshoe. "You're no better than Soda or Christmas."

Punching the crate behind my head, Cob screamed. "Don't you *dare* compare me to those middle school bullies! I'm working for the good of the school!"

"*By helping Soda?*"

"Glitch is going to get shut down, but *I* can prevent it!" Cob said. "If Soda gets away with this then the '*powers that be*' will *see* that Glitch *can't* shut down! That Buchanan School *needs* Glitch to keep the students safe from terrible pranks like Soda's!"

That was the *second* time Cob had mentioned the "powers that be."

"Who are the 'powers that be?'" I asked.

"They're the ones who control everything!" Cob said. "They're the real guys in charge!"

"You mean Glitch *isn't* at the top of the chain?"

Cob pressed his lips together and shook his head.
"You have no idea how high all of this goes. And you
never will because my little scheme is still going to
work!"

"You... *you* planned this?" I whispered. "This is
all *your* doing?"

"Of course it is!" Cob snarled. "You think *Soda*
could come up with this on his own?"

"But why the clogged toilets? Why go through all
the trouble of getting Soda to take the Horseshoe?
You're the *leader* of Glitch! You could've gotten the
vial yourself!"

Cob shook his head. "And *risk* getting caught? No
way! I couldn't be connected in any way! Soda was the
perfect man for the job. All I had to do was plant the
seed to get Maddie and Linus to go after him."

"*The clogged toilets were a lie?*" I asked.

Cob's smile looked vicious. "And from there, Soda managed to get all you guys to do the dirty work *for* him. If I had caught you outside the art classes, Linus still would've gotten the Horseshoe himself. That's how that kid rolls."

"What does Soda get out of this?" I asked.

"Christmas promised him the key to the pop machines in the basement," Cob said. "An unlimited supply of soda for the Soda Jerk for the rest of his years at Buchanan."

"*That's* how Christmas is involved," I said. "Of course he'd be part of this. It involves creating *chaos*."

"That's not the *only* reason," Cob sneered. "He specifically requested that I put *you* on the case so that *you'd* be the one to get busted in the end."

"Me? But why?"

"I dunno," Cob replied. "Maybe 'cause you embarrassed him in front of a cafeteria full of students?"

I heard a crack in the speaker system.

Cob continued. "*So what* if I'm responsible for giving a few kids lice? It's a necessary sacrifice that I can live with."

"And here I thought *Soda* was the monster," I said. "But it was *you* all along."

"Please," Cob said. "I'm a stinkin' genius! *I'm* the one who orchestrated this whole thing! You think Soda's smart just because he got you to do his dirty work? Who do you think *gave* him the idea to steal the vial? Who do you think told him *exactly* how to work you guys, huh? Me! It was me! It was *all* me!"

The speaker system cracked again.

142

"And you're gonna pin it on the noob, right?" I asked.

"Right. Nobody cares about the new kid. Now… if you're not going to give me the vial, then I'll just have to *take* it from you!" Cob said, raising his foot in the air again.

"I'll take that!" a man's voice said from behind Cob.

Cob spun around, only to see that Principal Davis was standing with his hand outstretched toward me. A small group of policemen were standing a few feet behind the principal. Soda was at the back of the huddle with his eyes fixed on the ground.

"But I…" Cob whispered. He cleared his throat. "I caught Brody with the vial of head lice from Mrs. Duvall's office! He was planning on—"

"Enough, Jacob!" Principal Davis shouted, using Cob's real name. "The entire school heard *everything* you said! Your voice is coming through the speaker system!"

"But… *how?*" Cob asked, his voice trembling. He looked back at my eyes, but then I noticed he wasn't looking at my *eyes*. He was looking at my *glasses*.

The hair on my neck stood on end as I took the broken spyglasses off my face. Linus must have switched the mic back on – the broken one that played my voice through the speakers that were nearby! *That's* why the speakers cracked during our conversation! And with an entire stage full of gigantic speakers, I bet the whole *town* heard Cob's confession!

Funny how often bad guys get in their own way. Last time, it was Christmas who ended up saying too much, and I'm pretty sure President Sebastian wasn't a stranger to it either.

"Wait!" I said.

Cob turned to look at me.

"Any criminal *daft* enough to explain their whole plan *deserves* to get busted, right?" I said, reminding Cob of his own words from earlier that morning.

The daggers that came at me out of Cob's eyes made me regret saying what I did. I probably should've just kept quiet.

Cob and Soda were escorted off the stage by the policemen. Neither of them said a word as they walked down the short staircase. Christmas was still somewhere in the carnival, but it didn't matter. Their plan was shot, and the rest of Buchanan School's 100th birthday was no longer in danger.

"Brody," Principal Davis said as he took a seat on the crate next to me. "May I have the vial, please?"

I had almost forgotten the vial was still in my hand. I gave it to the principal. "Absolutely. Get that stinkin' thing away from me."

144

Principal Davis laughed as he put it in his front pocket.

"You'd think Mrs. Duvall would've gotten rid of that thing after the science fair," I said. "Why would she keep it?"

Just then, Mrs. Duvall herself stepped onto the stage. "Because I'm working on finding a *better* treatment for lice. You don't think I'd keep a specimen like that around for fun, do you?"

"Working on a better treatment?" I asked. "You mean you're, like, a scientist?"

"A little bit, yes," Mrs. Duvall answered. "Lice have a waxy covering on their surface that makes it difficult to simply wash them out of your hair. I'm working on a way to remove the wax first. My hope is that by removing the wax, the treatment will be faster *and* easier."

"A *secret* scientist," I whispered. "Working undercover as a nurse. Wow."

Mrs. Duvall cocked an eyebrow and looked at Principal Davis.

The principal sighed. "Brody's got quite an imagination."

"Well, thank you, Brody," the nurse said. "You really saved the day, didn't you? And in such a handsome tux."

I shrugged my shoulders, a little embarrassed because the beautiful nurse was paying me a compliment.

Principal Davis escorted Mrs. Duvall off the stage. I brushed the dust off my tuxedo sleeves and stepped over to the ladder. The roadies were still showing off their piercings to the group of Glitch agents, who actually seemed interested in seeing them.

Linus, Maddie, and the rest of the gang were waiting for me at the side of the stage.

"Nice work," Linus said. "You cracked *another* case."

I took my glasses off and tossed them to him. "I couldn't have done it if you hadn't turned the mic back on."

Catching the spyglasses, Linus laughed. "Okay, *we* cracked another case. It's all part of being a *team*."

"So everyone heard everything?" I asked. "Cob and I said a bunch of stuff about Glitch – stuff that should probably be secret."

"Not everything," Linus said. "I guess I switched the microphone on at exactly the right time so that just the end of the conversation came through."

"Nice," I said.

"I'd *love* to say it was intentional, but it was just pure luck," Linus said. "So Glitch is still a secret."

"But that still means everyone knows what kind of danger they were in," I said. "I botched that part. Cob said that our jobs are to keep everything on a straight path so it's like nothing ever happened – that the kids of Buchanan should never know what's going on behind the scenes."

"Don't worry about Cob," K-pop said. "I'm pretty sure he won't be part of the agency anymore after this."

Scooter chimed in, pushing his glasses higher on the bridge of his nose. "Pretty sure? I certainly think there's no way he'll be with Glitch after this."

"*Sarcasm*," K-pop sighed. "Look it up."

Scooter still didn't get it. "I have no need to research the definition of 'sarcasm,' as I already know what it means."

K-pop threw her hands in the air. She continued to egg Scooter on as they walked away. Janky hobbled behind them, still acting like an ape, scratching at his head and armpits – he was a weird kid, but that's what made him cool.

Another voice came from behind my friends. "Hey, man…"

Maddie and Linus stepped aside to let the boy through. It was Gibson, and he looked nervous.

"Look, dude," I said with my hands up. "I'm not in the mood for any of your stuff right now."

Maddie took a step toward him. "*None* of us are."

Gibson put his palms out, surrendering. "No, no," he said, avoiding eye contact. "I just wanted to say... thanks. What you did was super cool."

We all looked at one another, as if to say, "Did he really say that?"

"I had lice when I was younger," Gibson said. "It's a terrible experience."

I nodded.

"That's all," Gibson said, kicking at the ground. He was obviously out of his comfort zone. "Oh wait, uh, sorry for being kind of a jerk to you too."

"Why the change of heart?"

Gibson looked me in the eye. "You just did something awesome. People will remember you for that. When people remember me, they'll think of the kid that pushed others around. And y'know, I don't want to be remembered like that. Buchanan would be a better place if we all tried to be a little more awesome – if we tried to be a little more like you."

I wasn't sure what to say, so as usual I said something dumb. "Cool, man."

"Nice," Maddie said.

"If you ever want to ride bikes or whatever," Gibson said. "Go ahead and give me a call."

"Will do," I replied, bumping Gibson's fist.

The band members of Annee Mu took their spots on the stage. They had finished tuning their guitars and making sure the microphones all worked. Beefy riffs tore through their half-stacks as they checked their levels.

Linus, Maddie, and I walked toward the front of the stage, but not where everyone could see us.

"Without a leader, will Glitch still exist?" I asked.

"What do you mean, 'without a leader?'" Linus replied. "Glitch will find a new leader, and be better than ever."

"Aren't you next in line after Cob?" Maddie asked Linus.

Linus smiled. "Maybe."

"Does that mean I'm still in?" I said. "Can I officially say I'm a secret agent now?"

"Not *officially*," Linus started, "since you can't tell anyone anyways. But yes, I'd say you were officially part of the club. That is, *after* you pass the physical fitness test."

"Oh great," I whined. "What's *that* consist of?"

"Typical stuff," Maddie said. "It's easy though. I think the hardest part was, like, doing ten push-ups or something, which is super easy."

"*Ten* push-ups? Like, in a *row?* One after another?" I asked. "Man, I don't know about *that.*"

"I hope you're joking," Linus said.

"Of course I am!" I replied.

Maddie and Linus looked at each other, laughing nervously.

"*Seriously*, guys," I said. "I can do ten push-ups."

The guitars crunched on stage as the lead singer took to the mic. "I'd like to welcome everyone to the one hundredth birthday bash of Buchanan Schooooool!"

The crowd cheered.

The singer grabbed the microphone and pulled it closer to his mouth. "But first, I'd like to give a shout out to *Brandy Valentine!*"

Principal Davis ran onto the stage and handed the singer a sheet of paper.

"*Sorry!*" The singer screamed into the mic as he read the note from the principal. "*Brody* Valentine! This first song is dedicated to him for *saving* the school from… *lice?* Is that right?" The lead singer glanced at the principal, confused.

The principal threw out a thumbs-up from the side of the stage.

"Uhhhh, alright then," the singer said. "*Let's rock and roll!*"

Altogether, the band hit the same chord as the drummer slammed on his cymbals. The speakers were so loud that the earth shook under my feet. Kids at the front of the stage were jumping up and down in time with the music as the singer started wailing away on a guitar solo.

I took my bowtie off and tossed it on the steps next to the stage. Maddie and Linus had joined K-pop, Scooter, and Janky near the back of the stage, so they'd be safe from any crowd surfers.

For the first time all day, I let myself relax, watching the students bounce around in front of the stage.

Buchanan was safe again. Cob's plan had been spoiled and Glitch was going to remain a secret agency within the walls of Buchanan School.

Cob had mentioned the 'powers that be,' and while I still didn't know what he meant by it, I had a feeling it wasn't going to be the last time I heard of them.

The lead singer pointed at me, and made a gesture that said, "Come up on stage."

I looked over at the best group of friends I've ever had. Maddie and Linus were nodding their heads with huge smiles. K-pop had both her thumbs up, punching the air in my direction. Scooter fist pumped like he was honking a horn on a semi, and Janky stood stone-faced, giving me the nod of approval.

Stepping onto the stage, I was blinded by the bright spotlights that had focused on me. The crowd of students roared from the field.

The lead singer of Annee Mu stepped up to the mic and started chanting my name. By the third time he said it, the entire school was shouting it with him. He put his hand on my back, and mouthed the words, "*Do it, man!*"

I took one look at the sea of students at the front of the stage, holding their hands out to me.

And then… letting go of everything, I fell

151

backwards into the sea, and crowd surfed.

It was an awesome end to an otherwise terrible day.

Stories – what an incredible way to open one's mind to a fantastic world of adventure. It's my hope that this story has inspired you in some way, lighting a fire that maybe you didn't know you had. Keep that flame burning no matter what. It represents your sense of adventure and creativity, and that's something nobody can take from you. Thanks for reading! If you enjoyed this book, I ask that you help spread the word by sharing it or leaving an honest review!

- Marcus
m@MarcusEmerson.com

AND DON'T FORGET TO CHECK OUT THE
6TH GRADE NINJA SERIES
BY MARCUS EMERSON!

Marcus Emerson is the author of several highly imaginative children's books including Diary of a 6th Grade Ninja, The Super Life of Ben Braver, and Recess Warriors. His goal is to create children's books that are engaging, funny, and inspirational for kids of all ages - even the adults who secretly never grew up.